DREAM OF THE
BLUE ROOM

A NOVEL BY

MICHELLE RICHMOND

F
Ric

MacAdam/Cage Publishing
155 Sansome Street, Suite 550
San Francisco, CA 94104
www.macadamcage.com
Copyright © 2002 by Michelle Richmond
ALL RIGHTS RESERVED

Library of Congress Cataloging-in-Publication Data

Richmond, Michelle, 1970—
Dream of the Blue Room / by Michelle Richmond.
p. cm.
ISBN 1-931561-24-9 (Hardcover : alk. paper)
1. Yangtze River (China)—Fiction. 2. Married women—Fiction.
3. Young women—Fiction. 4. Friendship—Fiction. 5. Death—
Fiction. I. Title.
PS3618.I35 D74 2003
813'.6—dc21

                                                    2002153552

Manufactured in the United States of America
10 9 8 7 6 5 4 3 2 1

Book design by Dorothy Carico Smith.

DREAM OF THE
BLUE ROOM

A NOVEL BY
MICHELLE RICHMOND

MacAdam/Cage

In the dream Amanda Ruth is not dead, she is only sleeping. We are lying under a sycamore tree beside a rugged mountain path. The grass around us is littered with the pits of fruits we have eaten: peaches and figs, plums and nectarines. Her fingers are still wet from our feast. In the cool mountain light, they glisten. So elegantly she sleeps, one leg bent slightly beneath her, one arm flung wide on the grass.

I slide the strap of her sundress off her smooth brown shoulder. She does not stir. All down the front of her dress are small blue buttons. I undo them one by one, careful not to wake her. A fine rain begins to fall. I feel her fingers in my hair and discover that she is awake, smiling, watching me.

"You look different," I say. "Older."

"Yes. Thirty-two, now."

"But I thought you had died."

"Died?" she says. "What do you mean?"

I tell her never-mind. I tell her it was only a dream. She asks me to describe it. I say, "You were dead. You'd been dead for a long time. I missed you terribly. I went to China to find you."

"No," she says. "You went to China to lose me."

"That's right. To let go of you. But now it doesn't matter."

The wind rustles the tree above us; raindrops are

slapping the leaves, the sound getting increasingly louder. Soon, the drops will work their way down through the branches and begin to fall on us.

"You went to China?"

"Yes."

"And what did you see?"

"Well," I close my eyes, trying to remember, trying to come up with some answer, some truth that will satisfy her.

"Was it wonderful?"

"Yes," I want to say. I want to tell her that China is everything she dreamt it would be, a strange but familiar place. I want to tell her that I finally lived up to my promise, and we have been to the center of the earth together. But then the rain stops, the mountains disappear, and Amanda Ruth is gone.

TWO

The shellac is smooth beneath my fingers, rising slightly over the photos, a random Braille I know by heart. Amanda Ruth would have laughed at it, her mother's lack of good taste, the collage of photographs she carefully cut and arranged on the round cookie tin: Amanda Ruth as a baby, wrapped in her proud father's arms; Amanda Ruth in her majorette's costume with gold piping at the shoulders; Amanda Ruth sitting on the narrow bed in her dorm room at Montevallo. I hold the tin in my lap and recline on a deck chair. Its metal seat is wet from the spray.

My husband, Dave, is down in our cabin sleeping. He does the sleeping for both of us. I do the staying awake. I am an insomniac of the old order. I spend long nights waiting for my mind to snap shut, mornings bent over the coffee pot, hands shaking from exhaustion and caffeine. I haven't slept since we left New York two days ago.

It is five past midnight. Muddled voices drift up from the lounge. Lights glimmer along the riverbank. There is the cool dark drift of the Yangtze, the smell of something not quite clean. I feel a welcome heaviness approaching, a soft weight pushing against my eyes. I dream of water, a white body drifting naked upon it. I extend my arm and bring the body toward me, look into the round wet face of Amanda Ruth. She opens her eyes, takes my hand and stands; we are on land now, walking, the jagged pebbles of the riverbank cutting into our bare feet. Amanda Ruth is eager to show me something. We walk for many hours, coming at last upon the mouth of a cave. The entrance to the cave is thick with growing things.

When I wake, it feels as though I have slept for a long time. I lift my watch to catch the moonlight, scan its small silver face.

"Twelve forty-five," a voice says. Startled, I turn to see a man sitting a couple of feet away. He is long and slim and gray-headed, with a broad, handsome face and thick eyebrows. He looks to be in his early fifties, although he could probably go several years in either direction. He wears a white oxford with the sleeves rolled up to his elbows, loose linen pants and brown sandals. His toes curl inward, oddly out of tune with the lean symmetry of his body. He holds a glass of white wine in each hand.

"Here," he says.

I accept, taking the glass by its stem. "Thank you. Now, I suppose your plan would be to get me drunk and then toss me into world's longest river."

"Third, actually." His accent is Australian. "After the Congo and the Nile. Don't worry, it's too risky. There'd be a search of the ship come morning, when your husband reports you missing." His speech is slow, as if he has difficulty forming words, but in his eyes there is none of the dullness of a drunk.

"Australia?"

"Perth."

"Maybe they'd think I tossed myself over. I'm sure it's been done." I taste the wine, which is too sweet. Within moments I feel a pleasant light-headedness coming on. "What makes you so sure I'm married?"

"I saw the two of you this afternoon in Shanghai. You bought a scarf before boarding the ship. It was dark green. The woman who sold it to you thought it went well with your eyes."

"You speak Mandarin?"

"I try," he laughs, "but I wouldn't trust my own translation." He scans the river. I study his face in profile—the long line of his jaw, the thick tendons of his neck, a tiny mole riding high on his cheekbone. He turns suddenly, locks eyes with me in that way men do when they know you've been staring.

I look away, clear my throat. "Are you here on business?"

"Pleasure. Sort of."

"Traveling alone?"

"Who's asking?"

"It couldn't be me—I'm a married woman." He is staring at me, his eyes focused somewhere near my mouth. I can't remember the last time I flirted with anyone. It feels good.

"Yes," he says, "I'm on my own." He raises his glass in my direction. "To you, Jenny, and your first trip to China."

I hesitate. "I never told you my name."

"Sorry. This afternoon I heard your husband calling

you. He was trying to catch up. You were in the market on Huaihai Road, remember? He shouted your name several times, and finally you stopped and waited for him."

"You were spying on us?"

"You make it sound so sinister. I was just observing. Look, I'll tell you about myself, and then we'll be even. My name is Graham. I'm fifty-three years old. I have no children, no wife, no siblings, no family at all to speak of. I was in the crane safety business for twenty years. I don't eat carrots or squash, and I'm a big fan of sweets of any kind, particularly Key lime pie. I'm rotten at poker but good at backgammon." He takes a long sip of wine. "Now you know more about me than I know about you, which means you've established a power position in our relationship."

I can't help but laugh at Graham's rushed monologue. "You win."

"What do you have there?" he says, eying the tin.

I lie. "Just some postcards."

"You'll have plenty of time for writing. They're predicting rain. Of course, Xinhua is always coming out with exaggerated reports of flooding to drum up support for that awful dam."

The ship jerks, tilting us starboard. I reach out and clutch Graham's arm. The ship rights itself. Embarrassed, I let go, noting the tiny pink marks my fingernails leave on his skin. "How did you know it's my first trip to China?"

"In Shanghai you looked nervous, like you'd just

landed on another planet. Let me guess. You're from the Midwest. One of those wheat and corn places."

"Not quite. A small island near New Jersey. You may have heard of it."

"New York City?"

I nod.

"I've always wanted to go." He pours me another glass of wine.

The air smells like rain, mixed with a hint of vinegar. I feel myself relaxing for the first time since Dave and I set out for China. On the plane from JFK to Hong Kong we argued. From Hong Kong to Shanghai we hardly spoke. When I reached over the armrest on the last leg of the flight, hoping for a truce, he pulled his hand away as if he'd been stung. I can't help but wonder if Graham has me pegged. Does he look at me and see a woman trying to piece her marriage back together? Do I give off some vague scent of desperation and neglect that makes me an easy target for men on the prowl? If this were Animal Planet, I'd already be dead or pregnant.

"Earlier," Graham says, "I saw your husband with the captain."

"I'm not surprised. By tomorrow Dave will know everyone on the ship." I picture him standing with his hands in his pockets, chatting up the captain. He would ask about celestial navigation, slowly draw out the story of the captain's maritime career, inquire about the wife and kids. It's one of the things I've always admired about my husband; he can convert strangers to friends within minutes.

Graham settles into his chair as if he plans on staying for a long time. In the sky there are no stars, and only the dimmest suggestion of a moon, the round warmth of it emerging periodically from a mass of slowly moving mist. Low hills make soft silhouettes against the sky. In the darkness, the river looks black and endless.

Graham glances over at my empty glass. "Impressive." He lifts the bottle to pour me another.

My head feels warm and slightly off-center. "I better not. I drink when I'm nervous."

"Do I make you nervous?"

"It's not often I discover a strange man watching me sleep."

"It's a habit, I confess. Most people seem so much friendlier when they're sleeping."

"Did I?"

"Yes. When you woke up you started asking me all sorts of questions, demanding that I account for myself. But when you were sleeping I was free to observe without hassle."

"Spoken like a true voyeur."

"You were completely yourself, because you didn't know to erect a defense against me. Like today in the market. You and Dave were among strangers, and you thought you would never see any of these people again, so you didn't bother to be discreet. I even saw you arguing."

I think back to the afternoon's small battles. There

were several, but I can't focus on a single one. Graham stares at me, expectant, as if he's waiting to hear the source of my marital troubles.

"These days, we're always arguing about some silly thing or another. Dave didn't really want to come to China in the first place."

What I don't tell Graham is that Dave and I have been separated for two months, living disconnected lives on opposite sides of Central Park. We'd planned and paid for this trip months before the separation. To his credit, Dave understood how much I needed to make it, to fulfill some unspoken obligation to Amanda Ruth, and I think that's why he agreed, in the end, to come along. As we rode together in the taxi from his place to the airport, two duffle bags squeezed between us on the seat, I secretly hoped that this trip might somehow save our marriage. I thought that if I got him away from New York City, away from our routine, we might stand a chance. I imagined us discovering each another anew in this exotic place, where none of the old rules would apply.

Suddenly Graham stands, moves his chair a few inches closer to mine, and sits down again. "What do you think of me?"

I consider my words carefully. We are two grown adults who know, at least vaguely, the rules. Two adults on a ship in the dark while my husband, who has fallen out of love with me, is sleeping. Everything I say to Graham from this point on is a negotiation. Each word defines the boundaries between us. "I'm not sure yet."

We sit for a while in silence, and I pretend to sleep. At some point, a glass shatters. I open my eyes to find Graham's wine glass lying in pieces by his feet.

"It's my hands," he says, all his cool composure gone. His hands are in his lap, palms up, and he's looking at them as if they belong to someone else. "You probably think I'm drunk." He sweeps the glass shards under his chair with his sandal. "You come out for a quiet evening and here I go breaking things. Do you want to be left alone?"

"It's all right. You're pretty good company."

"What about Dave?"

"Won't even know I'm gone."

"We'll sit here all night, then?"

"It's a deal."

"Good. I don't get much sleep these days anyway."

"We have something in common. I'm an insomniac too."

"Not true. I caught you sleeping."

"Only napping."

"Your eyes were moving," he says. "What were you dreaming about?"

"I can't remember. It was nothing, just a dream."

"Let us learn to dream, gentlemen, and then we shall perhaps find the truth."

"What?"

"Friedrich Kekulé, the German chemist."

In college, I knew a guy who never read entire books, only first chapters. From these he gleaned quotes that he kept in a big red notebook under various headings: nature, romance, fear of death, etc. Once, in a Lower East Side apartment after three martinis, he confessed to me that he memorized these quotes as a way of attracting women. He'd drop them into conversations at parties, in bars, on first dates. His tactic seemed to work; he was rarely without a date. Ever since, whenever a man reels off an interesting quote, I find myself testing him.

"Kekulé?" I ask. "Wasn't he the one who said politics is just applied biology?"

"No, you're thinking of Ernst Haeckel. Kekulé found the molecular structure of benzene. It came to him in a dream." He talks on about Kekulé for a couple of minutes, then, perhaps noting my lack of interest, stops midsentence. "I've become a bit of a nerd," he says, blushing.

We fall into an easy silence. Beneath us, the grumble of the engine, and in my bones a dull vibration. Every now and then the ship passes a cluster of lights along the riverbank, or changes course to overtake a barge laden with large, rectangular boxes. The lights of passing sampans blink in the dark. One heads straight toward us, and I'm certain the *Red Victoria* will slice right through it, but at the last minute the tottering boat swerves out of our way.

"What are they doing?"

"Shedding their demons," Graham explains. "In the old days, the Chinese believed that demons attached themselves to boats with an invisible cord. By crossing the bow of our ship so closely, they severed the line. According to their superstition, the demons have now tied themselves to this ship."

"So right now we're dragging scores of demons?"

"Yep."

I feel no need to end the conversation, or to move it to the next level. Every once in a while Graham slaps at a mosquito, or I shift in my chair to get more comfortable. I doze periodically through the night, never falling into a complete slumber. Whenever I open my eyes, unsure of my surroundings, I hear Graham's voice nudging gently at the edges of sleep, reporting the time. "2:15," he says. "We should be about seventy kilometers from Yangzhou." And then, in case I've forgotten, "It's me, Graham. We're on the Yangtze. Your husband is below deck sleeping. You have succumbed to the charms of a strange man."

At 3:30, I stir and realize that my head rests on his shoulder. He has pulled his chair so close to mine, the metal frames are touching. His arm is propped on the shared armrest, and his hand dangles about an inch from my leg. My sarong has slipped up over my knee, exposing a length of thigh; if I were to lift my leg by a fraction, our skin would touch.

"Are you awake?"

"Yes." He lets his hand drop, and for a second his fingers brush my thigh, sending goosebumps down my leg. It has been months since Dave has touched me in an even vaguely sexual way. I let my own fingers meet Graham's, just briefly. I tell myself it means nothing, that the touch was accidental, but I can't help but feel that I've crossed some invisible line.

I think of Dave and the woman he rescued two years ago from a burning car on the Palisades. I think of their monthly meetings at a coffee shop in Chelsea, the way Dave always checks himself carefully in the mirror before going to see her. These meetings are no secret. Dave has always sworn there is nothing to them, that he just feels some duty to be there for a lonely and grateful woman. I imagine them together, their knees touching under a small round table. I think of her sipping a glass of iced lemonade, watching him from that burned face, scarred and shiny from the accident. Though he has never told me, I believe that she loves him desperately. I believe she looks at my husband and sees the man who saved her life, the man who saves her once more each month by taking the C train down to Chelsea to meet her. I know she was beautiful once, before the accident, because Dave showed me a picture she had given him. I can't help but wonder how many times the woman's hand has touched Dave's thigh in the intimate way that Graham's just touched my own, how many times Dave has imagined what it would be like to do something more with this woman, to kiss her, or even take her to bed. But for all he may have thought of it, envisioned it, desired it, I know he has not done so.

"It's not postcards," I say, feeling suddenly intimate, ready to confess.

"Pardon?"

"In the tin. Not postcards."

"I figured as much. You've been holding on to that

thing like it's filled with diamonds."

"Kind of a long story."

"We've got two weeks."

So I begin to tell him about Amanda Ruth. I tell him about the ashes, how her mother came to me with the tin a few days after the funeral and said, "Amanda Ruth always wanted to see China. You're the only person I know who might actually go there." Amanda Ruth never knew the name of the village where her father was born, only that it was somewhere along the Yangtze.

"I plan to scatter her ashes at the Three Gorges," I explain. "I think that's where she'd want to be."

I wait for Graham's face to betray some mild amusement, some hint of disdain at this sentimental plan, but he just nods and says, "Makes sense to me." Encouraged, I tell him things I've told no one but Dave, things I haven't spoken of in years. I tell him about those long days on Demopolis River in Alabama, the way Amanda Ruth would steam big pots of rice and we'd eat with chopsticks out of small porcelain bowls we found at the flea market. How we stashed five-pound bags of rice in the closet of Amanda Ruth's bedroom, because Mr. Lee threw away any he found in the pantry. Peasant food, he called it.

I tell him about the photograph in the newspaper fourteen years ago. Alone in my old bedroom, home for Christmas vacation from Hunter College, I studied the photo with a magnifying glass, searching for answers. She was wearing jeans and a white T-shirt, and her neck was wrapped in a long pale scarf. Were it not for the strange angle of her leg, the stiffness of her pose, and the impossible tangle of her hair across the asphalt, one might even have surmised that it was just a photograph of a sleeping girl. College Girl Slain, the headline read. The town's first murder mystery.

When I'm finished with my story, I feel emptied out, slightly cheapened. "I haven't talked about her this much in years. I didn't do her justice."

"Try," Graham says. "What did she look like?"

"Long dark hair. Slender, but curvy. I wonder what she'd look like now." I try to picture her, aged by many years, with little lines starting to form around her eyes; but in my mind Amanda Ruth is always seventeen, diving into Demopolis River, her bathing suit startlingly blue against the earthy brown of the river. Or she is a newspaper photo in black and white, laid out like a sleeping mannequin behind the skating rink. In the close-ups the police showed me during the interrogation, Amanda Ruth's lips were parted, as if she had something to say but never got around to it.

Suddenly the moon disappears. For a moment there are no other boats in sight, and I feel as if we're alone in the dark dead center of the universe. Moments later a barge comes into view, the Red Victoria bellows out a warning, and the moon reappears, a faint orange hole in the black sky.

"Your turn," I say. "Tell me something."

"How about a poem?"

"By whom?"

"The twentieth-century Chinese poet Ping Hsin:
　　Bright moon—
　　All grief, sorrow, loneliness completed—
　　Fields of silver light—
　　Who, on the other side of the brook
　　Blows a surging flute?"

"That's nice."

We're still sitting on deck at five in the morning when the sky begins to lighten. Low hills have given way to mountains whose jagged peaks zigzag across the sky. Graham is dozing finally, his legs stretched out in front of him, his arms dangling over the side of the chair. His shirt is askew, his face marked by sleep.

I could so easily lean over and touch him, and yet I'm entirely unprepared for whatever might come next. I would like to bring him into the conscious world with a kiss, like the prince in the fairy tale about the girl who sleeps through wars and centuries and famines. Instead, I touch his hand; he doesn't stir. I leave quietly. A small group of passengers is awkwardly practicing tai chi by the pool, led by the cruise director, a twenty-something Chinese university student named Elvis Paris.

I walk through the well-lit hallways. There is the rush of water through pipes, the hum of showers. I think of childhood vacations with my family in Alabama, rising while it was still dark out, backing down the driveway with headlights off, engine dead. Escaping, my father called it: his idea of adventure. On those mornings before the neighbors rose, the air damp and cool, the shapes of jasmine and azaleas barely visible in the dark, our small town in Alabama seemed as exotic and lush as China could ever be, a country newly discovered.

Sometimes we would drive to Amanda Ruth's, and she would be waiting on the front porch with her mother, her small red suitcase propped on the bottom step. My father would get out of the car, load Amanda Ruth's luggage into the trunk, and open the door for her like a chauffeur. We rode with our thighs touching, made a tent with picnic blankets suspended over our heads, and in our secret cave Amanda Ruth told me long, made-up stories about her ancestors in China.

In the cabin, Dave is sprawled across the bed. I undress and lie down. The full-sized bed feels oddly intimate. At home in New York City we have a king-sized mattress that takes up the entire bedroom; our bodies don't touch all night. *Didn't* touch, I correct myself. After twelve years of marriage, it's difficult to think in past tense. I keep imagining the separation is some joke that Dave will grow tired of, keep hoping that one morning I'll wake in our apartment at 85th and Columbus to find him sleeping heavily beside me, the way he is now. A few hairs around his ears have gone gray. I put my face to his neck and breathe in; his smell is sweet and clean. He doesn't wear cologne and has always smelled better to me than any other man. I haven't washed his pillowcase since he moved out. Each night I go to bed with his pillow positioned neatly on the left side of the bed, but in the morning I wake with my arms around it, like a grieving widow. Each morning, still, I smell him, though the scent grows fainter by the day.

At 6:15, a female voice booms from the loud-speakers mounted at regular intervals along the hall-ways: "Please come to Yangtze Room for delicious Chinese breakfast. Today for your pleasure we have many exciting activity." Dave rolls over and lays an arm across my stomach. His arm is heavy, warm against my skin. I stroke it, feeling the fine hairs beneath my fingers, watching his face, wanting to hold him but not daring to. He opens his eyes, looks confused for a moment. Then recognition crosses his face; he is orienting himself to this ship, this cabin, this bed. He is orienting himself to me.

"China," he says, smiling. He raises his arms toward the ceiling, palms up, fingers interlaced, stretching until his knuckles crack. Love kicks in my gut. I know these motions completely, have visualized them every morning during the two months of his absence. It's like a fingerprint, this waking ritual; no two people wake up in exactly the same way. It is so familiar that I feel, for a moment, as if we have returned to our life, our marriage, as if everything is in its right and proper place, as if my night on deck with Graham was a small infidelity I must carefully hide from a husband who still loves me.

"What time is it?"

"Early."

"When did you come to bed?"

Because he does not know the difference, because he sleeps with the conviction of a dead man, because I could disappear for weeks at a time without attracting his attention, I tell him I came to bed at midnight.

"Long day ahead," he says, yawning.

THREE

There was more for Amanda Ruth on our warm river in Alabama than there will ever be for her here. In Shanghai, I walked through the crowds of people in button-down shirts and plastic sandals, the women in tan mini-stockings that circled their slender ankles; I peered beneath their broad hats, searching for Amanda Ruth's face. But there was no one like her. Her mother made sure of that, with her wavy hair and narrow nose, her rounded hips swinging side to side in the smooth, close skirts that Amanda Ruth's father followed all the way to Alabama, before he knew what an unkind place that could be for a Chinese man who had charmed a Callahan.

"One of our own," they said, "with one of them." They said it loudly. They wanted him to hear.

Several times in that glittering city hunched up to the banks of the Yangtze, I saw men who reminded me of Mr. Lee, the man whose face went from confusion to fury the day he found us in the boathouse—Amanda Ruth's back arched above the floor, her long hair trailing the wooden planks as I covered her stomach and legs with kisses. Mr. Lee shouted his daughter's name once, then toppled the grill, covering us with ashes. The smell of burnt shrimp lingered in our hair that afternoon as we sat stunned on the floor where he had left us, afraid to move, afraid not to move. There was no smile in his catalogue of smiles for that moment, no upturned mouth to hide the fury of finding a daughter gone to the devil, a devil his wife taught him to believe in.

"How could he resist her?" Amanda Ruth said every time she told me the story of her parents' courtship. "She must have been the most glamorous missionary ever shipped out to San Francisco to save the sinners." The pastor never considered that she would return with her own sin, the man whom she always introduced as "John Lee, American citizen," though they had other names for him: Chinaman, Yellow Boy, Chink. For his wife he had given up every bit of his honor; he had none left to give up for his daughter.

What would Amanda Ruth have given up? Nothing, or anything, depending on the time of day. She was as flighty as any American girl in the eighties, with her Reagan-era ego, her promise of eternal riches. Pizza Hut, Esprit, Madonna—the language belonged as much to her as to me. She taught me how to say thank you and hello, the only Mandarin words she knew, though they came out of my mouth as well as hers sounding ragtag and borrowed. "Shay-shay," we said every time the clerk gave us change at the K&B, where we bought little teacups painted with Chinese scenes, cheap earrings in bright cloisonné colors. When we met by her locker at school, locker eight (a number for good fortune, she said), we greeted one another with "Ni hao!" She said it loudly, mockingly, as if to atone for the slight and lovely difference in her eyes.

I listen to the river churning beneath me, and I think of the pair we were before that awful moment of discovery. Before my Dave and all the boys who came before him. Before Amanda Ruth became our town's first murder mystery, her face a smeared collage of ink dots that made the front page for weeks.

How could I forget those mornings beneath the pier—her skin shimmering silver like the silken belly of a fish, her hair river-sweet and sticky, our toes sliding together in the slick warmth of river water, schools of fish passing like quick feathers between our calves? Before she tried to prove she was the daughter her parents wanted.

Saturday afternoons, she'd rinse her pantyhose carefully in the bathroom sink, then fling them over the shower rod so they'd be fresh for Sunday. They swallowed her up, those Sundays, those deacons who said to love God's children but couldn't love her father, those Bible studies where Jesus was nowhere to be found because the Jesus her parents had told her about could never stand to listen to all that gossip, all those crazy questions. "Amanda Ruth, is it true your daddy's Oriental? Do you eat monkeys? Do you pray to Buddha?"

"Boo-duh," she mimicked, whispering on the phone with me. I imagined Amanda Ruth locked in her bedroom, which I knew as well as my own, except for the changes Mr. Lee had made after the incident in the boathouse. "He replaced all my Madonna posters with

Andy Gibb!" she whispered, and even I had to laugh at that, her father's idea of a normal American adolescence. More than anything, he wanted her to be a typical American girl.

FOUR

It is winter in New York City, and Dave and I are heading north on the Palisades for our tenth anniversary. We have reservations at a bed and breakfast in the Poconos, a place that promises a heart-shaped bed and satin sheets. Our marriage is going to pieces.

Dave is driving slowly because there is ice on the road. We have been behind the same red car for several miles. Terri Gross is interviewing a famous composer on the radio, and they're talking about the role of the symphony in the twenty-first century. Dave and I haven't spoken since the George Washington Bridge. I've tried to think of conversations we might have, topics I might broach, something impersonal that poses no potential for disaster. These days, there is so little we can discuss that doesn't lead to discord. More and more, we avoid conversation altogether. As our four-wheel-drive skirts over the icy road, I'm trying to pinpoint in my mind the moment when our marriage went wrong. But there is no set point, no big issue, no great infidelity that led us to our current state of disharmony. Instead, it has been a gradual slipping. Whatever cord connected us slowly and imperceptibly weakened.

Despite this, I have hope. I still love my husband. In my suitcase, there is a stash of fine silk underwear. Our room at the bed and breakfast has a private hot tub. I already spoke with the proprietor, who recommended a quiet place for our anniversary dinner—candlelight, champagne, chocolate—all the accoutrements of rekindled passion. I refuse to simply bow out of this marriage.

Up ahead, something flashes, a spot of sunlight on metal. The car in front of us shimmies left, right, loses control. "Hang on," Dave says. He swerves into the next lane to avoid the car, which spins twice before skidding over the embankment. In a second, maybe two, it is over. Dave eases into the right lane and pulls onto the narrow shoulder. "Could be bad," he says, backing in the direction of the accident. Cars fly past us at seventy miles per hour. Dave stops, gets out, peers over the embankment, down the cliff, where the car rests on its side, smoking, the driver-side door facing the sky. The cliff is steep, the car positioned about fifty yards down. Inside, someone is moving. "Call 911," he says to me, then shouts down to the driver, "Stay calm. I'm coming to get you."

He goes around to the back of our Jeep, opens the hatch, retrieves a rope, carabineer, knife, and climbing belt. I watch as he pulls these things out as if from a magic hat. After four rings the operator answers. I report the necessary details. "My husband's an EMT," I add. "He knows what he's doing."

Dave puts on his belt, attaches it to the rope. We secure the other end to the Jeep's tow bar. As he begins backing down the cliff, the hood of the overturned car bursts into flames. "Hold tight!" he yells down to the driver, then, to me, "Find some water! Take out the first-aid kit!" My heart races as he plunges toward the fire. I reach into the back seat and pull out a six-pack of bottled water, grab the first-aid kit from under the seat. Another car has pulled over. Three guys of college age get out and stand on the shoulder beside me, looking down, clearly uncertain what they should do. One of the young men begins to scrabble down the cliff, but it is steep and icy and he doesn't have a rope; his friend reaches down and pulls him back up. Meanwhile, Dave is dangling a few inches above the flaming car, perched precariously on a rock. Seized with terror, I find myself praying out loud.

He manages somehow to open the driver-side door, cut the seatbelt, and pull the driver out. Her head is moving, and I can see that he's saying something to her. With the burning car so close, there's no time to properly strap her in. He puts one arm beneath her knees, the other under her back, bride style. "Pull us up," he shouts, and the three guys swing into action. They grab the rope and start tugging. He holds her, his legs working over the rocky ground. Moments later, he is standing on the shoulder, panting, the burned woman in his arms.

"It's okay," he is saying to her. "You're going to be okay." He looks up at me, at the stunned spectators. "Third-degree," he says quietly. "Make me a cool compress."

While I moisten bandages with water, Dave lays the woman on the ground, checks her pulse. He gently applies the compress to the whitened skin of her face, speaking to her softly. *Can you hear me? Can you feel this? How many fingers am I holding up?* Her breaths come in little jerks. She is babbling, naming things that have no clear connection. "Bicycle," she says. "Lamp. Purse. Billy." Dave watches over her while we wait for the ambulance to arrive.

I look back toward the city, that angular oasis shimmering silver in the cold afternoon light. The clean lines of the George Washington appear magical from this distance. I am thinking that I belong there in that city I understand, with its numbered streets and sensible subways, its orderly blocks, its parallel avenues running north to south. Dave, on the other hand, belongs right here—on an icy roadside cliff, rescuing a dying woman.

Seeing him in action, I love him more than ever. While he ministers to the victim, I stand above them, helpless, watching this intimate communion between the savior and the saved. And I understand, for the first time, what, for him, must be lacking in me: I am not burned or broken. I am not clinging to life.

FIVE

"Is it just me or are we sleeping in a discotheque?" Dave says, sitting up in bed and eyeing the room. The décor is late-seventies Euro-chic: shiny black plastic headboard and matching dresser, faded red satin sheets and black velour coverlet. On the wall above the bed, a faded print of Big Ben hangs in a scratched plastic frame.

"Back in the seventies this ship belonged to a British cruise line," I explain, reciting the information I received from the travel agent in New York. "In the eighties, they sold the ship to China, and the *Victoria* then became the *Red Victoria*."

"God save the Queen," Dave says, shaking the covers off. He runs his hands through his hair. I want to tell him to stop. I want to tell him that it isn't fair for him to do these ordinary things that pull me limb from limb. I can't stop staring at his hands. I remember sitting with him at John's Pizza on 65th Street in New York City, not long after we met. We had just ordered a large pepperoni and two Cokes. His hands were on top of the table, one folded inside the other, as if he were readying himself for prayer. There was something disconcertingly feminine about his hands, some gentleness that seemed at odds with his exceptional height and deep voice. Months later, he lay breathing heavily in my bed. He slept on his back, hands resting on his stomach; they seemed to be perfectly alert and precisely posed, while the rest of his body sighed and shifted in his masculine and ungraceful sleep. Sometimes, even now, I will catch a glimpse of his hands—which at times are so alive as to seem disembodied from him—and I will feel as undone as if we had just met, and we'd yet to share intimacies.

He gets out of bed. "How'd you sleep?"

"I didn't."

"Why don't you take those pills I gave you?" He heads for the shower, not waiting for an answer. His stomach looks firmer than it did when he moved out, almost too firm, like one of those guys who sell exercise equipment on Sunday morning infomercials.

"You look different," I say.

"Do I?" He shuts the door behind him. The shower begins to hum.

For the next half hour we maneuver around each other in the small cabin. I emerge from the shower, wrapped in a towel, and am looking through my suitcase when I feel Dave watching me. "What's that?" he says, eyeing a red scratch that stretches from thigh to knee.

"Roller-blading accident in the park."

"Since when do you roller-blade?"

"Since you left." I almost wish he'd ask who I was skating with. If he did, I wouldn't let on that I'd been alone. Instead, I'd try to make up some story about a guy I met at a dinner party, someone athletic, witty, and well-paid.

"Hey," he says, reaching out and touching the upper tip of the scratch. My heart lifts.

"Yes?"

"You should put some iodine on that." It's all I can do to hold my mouth in some semblance of a smile, hoping I look lighthearted and unconcerned. Dave sits on the edge of the bed and begins lacing his boots.

"It almost feels normal," I say.

"What does?"

"This. The routine. Getting up. Dressing. Like we used to."

"Hmmn."

"It's nice," I say. Dave looks away, feigning great interest in his bootlaces, and I immediately feel stupid for opening myself up to him.

He stands, tucks in his shirt, straightens his collar. "What's it been? Two months?"

"And four days."

He turns on the television and finds the English-language news. I know what that means: end of subject. "Look at that," he says. "An earthquake in Japan. Big one. Massive damage. What I'd give."

He doesn't finish his sentence, but I know what he means: what he'd give to be there, aiding in the rescue, saving people. Not here, with me. "They say there's flooding upriver," I offer. "Could get bad."

"Yeah?" He brightens, but only for a moment. "I'll believe it when I see it."

***

At 6:45 we go down to breakfast. The tables have been set with white china and gleaming silverware, linen napkins in bright blues and greens. "Table seven," the hostess says when Dave shows her our room key. She leads us to our table, where a thin girl in red-framed eyeglasses is sipping Diet Coke from a can. "Very pleasant company," the hostess says. "I trust you all have happy together."

Our pleasant company wears a white blouse that slouches off her bony shoulders. She is young, pale, and unhealthy looking, with dark circles under her eyes and fake blonde streaks in her hair. "Morning," she says, grinning. Before we can introduce ourselves, a waiter appears with menus and two large cups of steaming coffee. There's no sign of anything Chinese in the restaurant: no chopsticks or steaming noodles, no pots of green tea. All of the crew members have adopted western names. Our server's name tag says Matt Dillon in bright yellow letters.

Pleasant company points to the name tag. "Like the actor?"

Matt Dillon beams. "Yes! I like very much *The Flamingo Kid*. Also *Rumblefish*." He takes our orders, promising to be back soon. The girl turns to us. "I'm Stacy. Just graduated from Michigan State with an art degree. My parents sent me here to paint landscapes. What's your story?"

Dave reaches out to shake her hand. "I'm Dave. This is Jenny. We're on vacation from New York."

"What do you two do?"

"Right now I manage a clothing boutique in Manhattan," I say, unfolding my napkin and placing it in my lap, trying to avoid further conversation on the subject.

"That's nice," Stacy says. "You must meet a lot of interesting people."

I want to tell her that I once had ambitions. I want to tell her that I too am an artist at heart, although I don't know what kind. It never ceases to amaze me that I ended up in retail, considering how much I hate to shop. "It's just temporary," I say, then add, laughing, "if you can call eight years temporary."

Stacy turns to Dave. "And you?"

"I'm an EMT."

"EMT?" Stacy adjusts her glasses. They look slightly off, as if they're a fashion statement rather than a necessity.

"Emergency medical technician."

"That's fascinating. Must be something, to actually go out there and make a difference."

Soon after we married, Dave left his lucrative position as a bond trader to pursue his dream job, and eleven years later he still loves it—the danger and adrenaline, the possibility, each shift, of going out into the world and saving someone's life. My own work offers no such excitement. The women who shop at the boutique on 74th and Columbus rarely surprise. They are the sort who somehow manage to stay cool and fragrant in their silk suits when the rest of New York is sweating. They treat me with a snobbish politeness, as if to say that they admire my taste in clothes but would never invite me to their dinner parties. Dave, on the other hand, plays the hero to junkies and heart attack victims. His is the last hand some people cling to before they die, the first face others see as they reenter the world of the living. Though he would never say it, I know that he was always a little disappointed, upon coming home after a shift, to enter the safe and mundane world of our Upper West Side apartment, to find the dishes clean and the sofa cushions straight, his wife cheerful and in good health.

Matt Dillon returns with three orders of World Famous Yangtze River Flapjacks. Stacy douses her plate with syrup and says, "What a relief. I was afraid they'd be serving monkeys or something."

Throughout breakfast I watch the door. We've almost finished our meal when Graham appears alone in the doorway of the dining room. He spots me and comes over to our table. "Morning." His face and voice betray no sign of the intimacy we shared, and I wonder if the bond I felt with him was one-sided. Perhaps I've been married so long that I'm no longer capable of judging a man's intentions.

"You two know each other?" Dave asks.

"I imposed myself on your wife last night while you were in your cabin counting sheep. I'm Graham."

"Dave." Dave has his palm up and is gripping Graham's hand lightly. He has always shaken hands this way—quick to assert the fact that he is not prone to combat, not interested in one-upmanship. That's one of the things that attracted me to him when we first began dating. He was so unlike the boys I knew from home, the macho types with their big voices and firm hand-shakes, their need to always be in control.

"We're stopping in Nanjing this evening," Graham says. "I know a great spot for dinner. Why don't you two join me?"

Dave puts an arm around my shoulder, as if we're best buddies, as if this whole trip was his idea. "Sounds great."

***

Dave and I have been assigned to the green group, which is led by Elvis Paris. Stacy, a sketch pad and pencil box in hand, sidles up to us. "Mind a third wheel?"

We disembark at Yangzhou in an oppressive drizzle. As we step off the gangplank onto the floating dock, Elvis Paris distributes parkas. "Follow me!" he shouts, waving the green flag over his head. We pass through narrow streets crowded with commerce. Everything is for sale: glass medicine bottles, plastic sandals, colorful shirts, porcelain bowls, combs, teacups, cameras, jade trinkets, fake leather purses, batteries, chopsticks, jewelry, toothpaste, lamps, socks, radios, pencils, post cards.

An elderly woman gives haircuts on the sidewalk. Her salon consists of a rusted metal chair, a yellow comb, a bowl of water, a pair of scissors, a hand-held mirror, and a tin can in which she collects payment. Nearby, a young boy in red shorts squats on the ground, selling ears of corn from a plastic bucket wedged between his legs. Every few yards, another group of old men crouch around a table beneath an awning, the slap of mahjong tiles echoing through the street. A toddler in split-crotch pants stops and pees on the sidewalk while his mother holds him by the underarms; the child chatters at us as we pass. A wheelbarrow loaded with watermelons stands right next to a modern ice cream freezer, which is decorated with pictures of Popsicles, drumsticks, and a smiling Chairman Mao. A young woman in a blue dress passes out freshly pressed white linens from a steaming basket. A legless man sells incense sticks from the back of a rickshaw.

Traipsing behind Elvis Paris, handbags and heavy cameras clutched beneath our rain gear, we resemble a herd of dumb and graceless cattle. Locals stare and point. Shouts of "Hal-loooh!" come at us from every direction. A woman in an old-style Mao suit tugs at my sleeve and tries to sell me a pack of postcards. "Twenty yuan," she says, "twenty yuan." When I shake my head she brings the price down to fifteen, and when I refuse again she goes on to Dave, then works her way through the group.

Roadside snack stalls and restaurants fill the air with fragrance: steamed buns, bowls of rice and beef, spicy soups, green vegetables, pork wrapped in shining banana leaves. We pay two yuan each to enter a park filled with elderly people practicing tai chi in orderly groups. The air is hot despite the rain, alive with the sound of music playing on portable cassette decks—Chinese opera and a few rousing songs of patriotism. There is other music, too, the chatter of birds. A man walks past holding a small bamboo cage; inside, a tiny nightingale pecks the bars. The limbs of the trees are draped with hundreds of similar cages. Each cage holds two tiny porcelain dishes, intricately painted, and a single captive bird, singing for its master.

Outside the park, Elvis Paris takes us to a string of brightly decorated stalls and urges us to shop. Dave buys a linen tablecloth for his mother. I choose a hand-painted barrette for my niece. "May I borrow Dave for a minute?" Stacy asks. "He's the same size as my brother." Dave models for her, arms held out to the side, while she holds up one shirt after another. She looks at me. "What do you think?"

"I like the yellow one."

"Me too." She pays for the shirt, an oxford with tiny dolphins printed on the fabric.

Half an hour later, Elvis Paris waves the green flag over his head and herds us back to the ship for lunch. My mouth is still watering from the rich smells of food in the city, but on the ship we are served a decidedly un-Chinese meal: salad with heavy dressing, creamed corn, and rubbery chicken drenched in salt.

Stacy swishes her fork around in the corn. "Just like Luby's Cafeteria," she says.

Dave laughs. "You could drink it through a straw."

"So, how'd you decide to be an EMT?" she asks.

"By accident. I was a bond trader with an amateur interest in photography. One weekend I went out with an ambulance to shoot a day-in-the-life piece for a free weekly. The first call we took was a crash scene on the

West Side Highway. Blood everywhere, smoke, people screaming. There was this one kid, couldn't have been older than six or seven, and his legs had been crushed below the knee. I bent down to take his picture, and through the lens I could see that his face was totally blank. He didn't look scared, or like he was in pain, just blank. I took a few shots, and then I heard the kid say, 'Hey mister.' I was so surprised I almost dropped the camera. 'Hey,' he said. 'Can I have some water?' I gave him some. Right then, I was hooked. Suddenly, bond trading seemed like a huge sham."

Dave came home that afternoon with his shirt and pants covered in blood. He couldn't stop talking about the crash site, and about the attempted suicide on Amsterdam the ambulance had been called to after that, the heart attack victim at Lincoln Plaza. "I'm quitting my job," he said over dinner. I congratulated him. I thought he was finally going to pursue his dream of being a photographer. When he told me he'd decided to be an EMT, I laughed. I thought he was kidding. You marry someone with certain expectations, certain beliefs about the kind of person he'll turn out to be. Of course, you never know for sure; it's always something of a gamble. Usually though, you have a good sense of all the possibilities. With Dave, it seemed like an easier bet than most: he loved photography, he took photos constantly, the walls of his apartment were filled with beautiful black-and-white scenes, each a completely different story.

Above our bed, there remains a photo he took one

summer in the Bronx, of three children playing on a jungle gym. Two of them are upside down, arms dangling. The other child, a girl, stands in the foreground, one hand on her hip; she looks straight into the camera, smiling. After Dave left, I spent hours looking at the photo, trying to imagine how the girl must have perceived the strange man behind the camera, what my husband looked like in her eyes. Now, watching Stacy, I'm struck by the same question: what does she see? Someone a few years older, experienced? Does she look at his ring finger, bare, and realize that he is a man who has lost faith in his marriage? At one point her eyes linger on a faint scar that stretches over the bridge of his nose, and I find myself wondering if, like me, she finds this imperfection attractive, disconcertingly sexy.

Dave and Stacy spend the meal in private conversation, laughing every now and then at some shared joke while our table companions, a middle aged couple from London named Winifred and Mack, regale me with long meandering stories about their annual vacations to Alaska and Hawaii. "We went ice-fishing through a hole," Winifred says, "just like real Eskimos!" Mack nods and says enthusiastically, "On Molokai, we met an actual leper!"

After dessert, Dave stretches and yawns. "Can't seem to shake this jet lag. I think I'll go take a nap."

"I'll come with you," I say, imagining an afternoon seduction—twisted sheets, sweaty limbs, cries so loud that people passing in the hallways pause briefly to envy our passion.

"Suit yourself," he says. I feel something at the core of me shrinking. As he's leaving, he turns to Stacy. "Why don't you join us for dinner in Nanjing?"

She looks at me. "You don't mind?"

"The more the merrier."

"Then it's a date."

After lunch I wander the ship searching for Graham, feeling foolish. What will I say if I see him? I find him standing at the rail in the same place we met last night. He grins. "You found me."

Something tells me to walk away, to make some excuse, to stop this thing before it starts, but then I think of Dave and Stacy at lunch, leaning close and laughing. I think of the ease with which he talked to her, while every conversation he has with me seems to be an effort. I think of the woman he meets each month at the café in Chelsea, I remember him carrying her up the cliff from her burning car that afternoon on the Palisades, how she lay limp in his arms like a bride, how he stood on the side of the highway, panting from the climb, looking down at the burned and bleeding woman with something akin to love. I think of how easy it is for him to be unfaithful to me in a million innocent ways, and I take my place beside Graham at the rail.

The sun has emerged from behind a dark layer of clouds, and the river slides swiftly beneath us. Hills slope away from the river, every inch cultivated, the bright green rows interspersed with stripes of burnt orange earth. We pass two boys playing on the banks. Beside them is a bamboo raft, neatly constructed, tied together with rope. One boy is naked, the other is wearing white underwear. When they see us they jump into the river and swim toward us, shouting. Graham translates: "I am a big fish. I am swimming to your boat. I am going to eat you up. Fear me, small boat, for I am the big fish of the rushing river."

"They'll grow up to be poets," I say.

Graham waves to them. "Or criminals."

A little farther down the river, a girl is standing in a tree. She wears a brown dress that skims her skinny knees. Carefully she turns her back to us. The limb upon which she is standing shakes, it is very thin, I am sure it will collapse beneath her. She shouts something into the weeping willows, which seem to sway at the sound of her voice. An elderly woman emerges from the green. She smiles and waves at the boat, shouts, and then the girl begins waving too.

"What are they saying?"

"The woman wants us to come to shore," Graham says. "She wants to sell us tortoise wine."

Oxen bathe near the muddy banks of the river, their corpulent bodies rolling in the brown water. Here and there a single ox is led along by its owner, its neck encircled in a tattered piece of rope. When wet, the oxen are slick and black, their broad backs shining. When dry, their skin is gray and dusty, and they all have an ancient, worn-out look. The sight of them becomes so familiar that, when I spot a bloated lump drifting downstream toward our ship, I think it must be a dead ox. But it is much too small for that.

I point toward the floating object. "Look."

Graham has already seen it and is leaning over the rail to get a closer look. "Is it?" he asks, obviously thinking the same thing I'm thinking.

"Hard to tell."

Finally we come within a few yards of it. The body lies face down; the gray shirt and pants balloon with water. The only visible flesh is the grotesque back of a neck, and a pallid foot puffed to twice its normal size. "Oh my God."

"Better get used to it," Graham says. "You're going to see a lot of them. During the rainy season, people working on the dikes get washed into the river and drown. On the rougher parts of the river it's not uncommon for someone to fall out of a sampan and simply disappear. Then, of course, there are the suicides."

"Doesn't someone go looking for them?"

"Rarely. The Chinese are rather fatalistic about this river. The families mourn, of course, but seldom does anyone try to find the body."

"Why not?"

"It would be near to impossible. British travel logs from the early part of this century are filled with accounts of people going overboard or being swept from the riverbank. Even in those cases when it would've been easy to reach in and rescue the drowning person, the Chinese invariably steered their boats away. In those days, anyone who rescued someone from the river was responsible for that person for the rest of his life. No one could afford another mouth to feed."

A wave catches the body, rolling it over like a big floating toy. The other foot comes into view, clad in a red cloth shoe. I look into the face of a young man, puffed and pale and strangely lifelike despite the stillness of the features. The eyes are closed, the skin slick.

"What should we do?" I say.

"There's nothing we can do."

"Shouldn't we inform the crew?"

As if on cue, Elvis Paris appears beside us. "Very inviting scenery, yes?"

"We just saw a dead body."

Elvis Paris doesn't even pause to consider the possibility. "I think there are no bodies here."

"Look." I point to the corpse, which is drifting away from us, moving slowly downstream. Anyone can tell from the red shoe, the clothes, the hands that have just come into view and look as if they are waving, that the figure is human.

"This is not body." He smiles patronizingly, like an adult trying to convince a child that there are no monsters under the bed.

"Look here," Graham says. "If it's not a body, then what is it?"

Elvis glances again, feigning curiosity. "Ah, is a dog!"

Graham smiles. "Isn't it a bit large for that?"

"Is a very big dog!" Elvis Paris says, quite serious.

Graham laughs. "Do dogs wear shoes?"

Elvis thinks for a moment. His eyebrows arch.

"Maybe it is a very wealthy dog! Maybe this dog is capitalist roader!" He turns on his heels and walks away, laughing at his own joke. Graham and I stand side by side, watching the body become smaller, disappear.

"I suppose corpses are bad for tourism."

After a few minutes, I've already forgotten the facial features of the dead man. I try to re-create him in my mind, but only the red shoe and the waving hands form a clear picture. The massive river fills my vision. It is wide here, home to hundreds of boats whose collective rumble reminds me of Saturday mornings in Alabama, dozens of lawnmowers kicking to life. Along the riverbank women are doing laundry and bathing their children. The sun blazes red. I scan the river for fish, but don't see any. The air is strangely absent of birds. Graham has become quiet. He leans on the rail, his hands shaking violently.

"Are you all right?"

He remains quiet for a moment, as if he's deciding whether or not to tell me something. "How much do you want to know about me?"

I look away from him, scan the unfamiliar landscape, and say exactly what I feel: "Everything."

His shirt smells faintly of starch. His hands, clenched and shaking, strike me as beautiful. I imagine his hands beneath my skirt, moving up the backs of my thighs. I imagine them on my breasts, the slight pressure of them against my neck.

"Very well," he says. "I have ALS."

"ALS?"

"Amyotrophic lateral sclerosis. A mouthful, huh? You'd know it as Lou Gehrig's disease."

I'm caught off guard, unable to think of the appropriate words. Late-night telethons flash through my mind, some sitcom actor pleading for donations in front of a bank of phone volunteers. In the background phones ring, while numbers blink urgently on the screen. *With just a dollar a day, the price of a cup of coffee, you can help us in the race to the cure.* I say the only thing I can think of. "How long have you known?"

"Eleven months."

I try to think of anyone I know who has ALS, some acquaintance or friend of my parents, but no one comes to mind. I've heard of the disease, of course, but I don't know its causes and effects, whether or not it is deadly, what kind of toll it takes on its victims. "Are you in pain?"

"It comes and goes. At this moment, my hands hurt. An hour from now they may not. But then there are pressure sores, muscle cramps. Sometimes my eyes burn. My feet swell up. I have difficulty speaking. There's a long list. I won't bore you with it."

"Is there a cure?"

"No. Just painkillers, and a drug called Rilutek that slows the progression but doesn't stop it. It's degenerative. You get worse and worse, and then you die. Half of us are gone within 18 months of diagnosis. I'm one of the fortunate ones. The doctors say I may have another year in me."

I reach over and hold his hands, feeling their

tremor. "God. I don't know what to say. I'm sorry." Another year, a death sentence. It occurs to me that no one can save him. This is not a burning car, an earthquake, an overdose. This is not an emergency that can be contained.

He moves toward me, so close I can feel heat on my bare arm, the pressure of his leg against mine. We're standing side by side, saying nothing, when the sky opens up. The rain does not ease in like the rain in New York City, which is laughable. The rain here is like Alabama in the summer: it starts with drops as big as my fingertips. It ends in exactly the same manner.

SIX

Too often I find myself thinking of Amanda Ruth, summers by Demopolis River, her parents' cabin in Greenbrook with the path that led down to the water. In the afternoons Amanda Ruth and I would walk out to the pier, which swayed so wide beneath us I thought it might collapse, plunging us into the murky water, where thin snakes curled their slick, harmless bodies around the barnacled stilts. At the end of the pier was the boathouse with its sun-bleached door. She would slide her finger under the rusty latch, coax it out of the hook, and swing the door open. When the light flooded in, dozens of roaches scurried into the corners.

The boathouse had only two rooms. The blue room was the one farthest from the door. It had no floor, just the water rising against three wooden walls and, on the far side, a blue canvas curtain. When the tide was out you could see the film left on the walls, a slimy green line marking where the water had been. The blue room housed the boat, which bobbed on the surface like an immense fiberglass toy. Amanda Ruth would climb in first, then hold my hands as I stepped carefully over the rail. We would descend into the hull and lie on the narrow vinyl seats. We closed our eyes and listened to the boat knocking against the wooden walls, the stilts of the boathouse creaking beneath us, the occasional hum of passing jet skis, the voices of kids as they float downstream on inflatable rafts. There in our secret room, Amanda Ruth told me stories of her grandparents' lives in China, and of her father's immigration to San Francisco when he was a boy. The stories were her own invention, a rich history to substitute for the one her father refused to reveal. "That makes me first generation," she would say.

"First generation what?"

"American, doofus. My dad says he'll take me to China, to my ancestral village."

This was only wishful thinking. Both of us knew that Mr. Lee would never take her there. China was Amanda Ruth's romance, not her father's.

The door from the pier opened onto the barbecue room, which had a small metal table, two wooden chairs, and a grill on wheels, the lid always raised to reveal a dusty pile of charcoal. In one corner there was an old mattress and, beside it, an Igloo chest. A small window faced out to the river. It was in the barbecue room during our sophomore year of high school that Mr. Lee came upon us, Amanda Ruth lying on her back, her short summer skirt hiked high above her knees, her bare stomach glistening with sweat. We had the boom box on, some heart-shattering Ella Fitzgerald tune, so we didn't hear the rubber soles of his deck shoes padding down the pier. I remember how, when he opened the door, a shaft of light shot through and set Amanda Ruth's legs aglow, and how, for the split second before I saw him, I believed something otherworldly had happened, that my touch had set in motion some miraculous transformation. Amanda Ruth gasped and shot upright, tugging at her skirt, and then Mr. Lee's shadow intersected the sunlight, and I knew we'd been caught. His hand came down hard against the boom box, the music shut off, and without a word he toppled the grill, which struck Amanda Ruth on the shoulder. Coal dust filled the air, blinding us, and in an instant he was gone. Ashes and bits of charred shrimp settled in our hair, on our tongues.

Amanda Ruth was crying, her shoulder cut and bleeding. "We should leave," I said. "We can go to my house." But Mobile was half an hour away, and besides, we were too young to drive.

After a few minutes Amanda Ruth combed her hair with her fingers, wiped her eyes, and became very businesslike. "We'll wait until he leaves and then we can go up to the house. Mom will talk to him, calm him down."

"What if he comes back?"

"He won't."

"Do you think he'll call my parents?"

"No. He'd be too embarrassed."

We huddled there in the room where he had left us, not talking, suddenly unsure how to be with each other, how to act. The sun beat down on the boathouse. We were thirsty, but we didn't dare go up to the house for water. For the rest of the day we listened for his steps, which didn't come. In the evening, when it began to cool and a slight wind rippled the water, we slept as much from boredom as exhaustion. In the middle of the night, we finally heard his car kicking to life in the driveway.

The next day, Mr. Lee took away all of Amanda Ruth's privileges—television, music, weekend outings with friends—and forbade her to socialize with me. We saw one another at school and ate lunch with the same group of kids under the oak tree beside the science building. But she was required to come straight home after seventh period, and the only activities he allowed her to take part in were those involving the youth group at their church. For two summers he sent her to an expensive camp in the Blue Ridge Mountains of North Carolina, where she sang religious songs around a campfire, rode horses, and attended mandatory weekly mixers with the boys from the neighboring camp. At the mixers they were not allowed to dance. Instead they played Scrabble and swung baseball bats at unbreakable piñatas, stuffed themselves with chips and miniature pretzels, Coca-Cola that came not in cans, but in bottles. "It's like something out of the fifties," she wrote in one of her letters from camp. "Any minute you expect Richie Cunningham to walk in and fire up the juke box."

The summer after our senior year, things changed. Mr. Lee was having problems with his printing business. He couldn't afford to send Amanda Ruth to camp and had no time to keep watch over her, a task he entrusted to Mrs. Lee, who refused privately to enforce her husband's rules. That summer, I spent long weeks with Amanda Ruth at Demopolis River. Her father spent weeknights at their house in Mobile and only came to the river on weekends. Friday mornings we would search the cabin for any evidence I had been there: a pair of my size 6 sandals, articles of clothing left in the laundry, strands of my hair captured in the prongs of her hairbrush. Amanda Ruth's mother became our ally, participating in those weekly searches to rid the house of me.

In the woods a couple of hundred yards from the river house, there was a pond beneath the willows where Amanda Ruth and I lounged when the pier became too hot. Tadpoles clustered in the shallows, their tiny bodies shining blue in pools of sunlight. From a distance the disturbances they made on the surface of the water would fool us into thinking it had just begun to rain. Dragonflies dipped and soared on the edges of the pond, sometimes racing by within an inch of our heads, their buzz louder than a bee or yellow jacket, like a zipper being pulled right beside our ears. The dragonflies always played in pairs. They had green bodies with maroon or black wings that lost their color at the outer tip. Sometimes one would light on our towel and lie there so long we thought it must be dying.

Amanda Ruth was enthralled by the minutia of insect life: the high, tittering racket of the crickets, the lethargy of yellow jackets who fumbled across the window screens; they seemed to always be stumbling, unsure of their direction, yet somehow more dangerous than the bees who plunged their furry heads into the petals of the wildflowers. Once, a yellow jacket lit on the tank top she wore with the bikini bottom of her bathing suit. By the time we got the shirt off her, the yellow jacket had made its way inside and stung her in the small of her back. I made her lie flat on her stomach on a towel while I extracted the tiny stinger with my fingernails. It was the beginning of summer, and we had already spent hours on inflatable rafts, drifting, eyes closed as we talked and planned, falling into the easy friendship we'd shared throughout childhood and into adolescence. Our skin, pale from days indoors, had quickly blistered and her shoulders had begun to peel. After pulling the stinger I rubbed her back with lotion, then sat in the shade beside her, braiding a length of pine straw.

"No fair," she said. "You're wearing your top."

"So?"

"So take it off."

"Dare me?"

"I double dog dare you."

I untied the bow behind my neck, then the other between my shoulder blades, and tossed the bikini top onto the grass. I lay on top of her, feeling the cool stickiness of her skin, the curve of her back beneath my stomach.

I hadn't touched another girl since that day we'd been caught, both of us reduced to frightened tears and shame. The boys at school liked me and were insistent; on many occasions I had found myself stripped bare in the bedrooms of those whose parents were out of town. More often than not I enjoyed it, although it seemed that only my body was involved, while my emotions and intellect remained detached. The boys all seemed so young, either too confident or too shy. Hair grew in unusual patterns on their bodies. Too often there was the smell of sweat on them, or worse, the overbearing scent of cologne. They talked about things that did not interest me: soccer and beer and TV, loud high school bands with meaningless names like Fruit and Not the Senate whose music did not move me.

As I lay on top of Amanda Ruth, I felt a nervousness rattling in my stomach, and along with it a feeling of being in exactly the right place and with the right person, a wholeness I had not felt since we'd last been together. Her body felt as familiar as my own, although she had changed since that day in the boathouse, gained a softness and a stillness that wasn't there before. She was more narrow than the boys I knew, her waist so small that I imagined if I were a man of considerable size I could put my hands around the whole of it, fingertips touching.

After a while she moved, repositioning herself so that she was lying on her side on the towel, facing me, her head propped on her hand. We lay there for a minute or more, looking at one another, and I did not know what to do. I sensed that she was different now, experienced.

"Have there been other girls for you?" she asked, picking up the pine straw I had begun to braid and dragging the tip of it along my skin, slowly, from navel to sternum.

"No. For you?"

"There was a girl at camp. We write letters. Her name is Celine."

"What about boys?"

"None," she said. "You?"

"A few."

"I could have guessed."

"What's that supposed to mean?"

"For me it's only girls." She had her hand on my hip and was looking in my eyes, so serious. I felt strange lying there topless, having a serious conversation. Her bathing suit bottom had green leaves on a black background. There was an imprint of grass on her thigh. "You, on the other hand, aren't sure what to make of anything," she said.

"Do I have to be sure?"

"It would just be easier if you knew."

"Easier for whom?"

She didn't answer. She was kissing me. And I was thinking that this was easy. This was how it was supposed to be. She kissed me so softly, her hand lightly touching my breast, and when she came closer I could feel her hair brushing against my shoulders. Her hair was long and soft and it got in my eyes when she kissed me, strands of it fell into my mouth. She was warm all over. She laid me back, put her mouth to my neck and then she was kissing me there, then my collarbone, my belly. I could feel her fingers so close, the pressure of her hand against me, an opening up, a gentleness I'd not known before. She took her hand away and lay on top of me, pressing her thigh gently between my legs. The rhythm came easily, I felt myself rocking against her. She was speaking softly into my ear, not a whisper but a sound so low it was almost not sound at all, a thing no boy had ever said to me. "Come, Jen. Please come." There was no fear in this, no shame, not the ugliness her father made us feel that other time, years ago. I felt the warmth pressing out of me, the deep, final push, the letting go. And after that the pulsing, and the softness of Amanda Ruth now motionless on top of me, her breathing as heavy as my own, her heart so fast I could not count it, could not number the beats of it, though I wanted to assign a number or a name to the thing that we had done, wanted to add it up and mark it down.

All summer we lived like that. Gradually we ceased to fear her father, making love in the secluded shade beside the pond or in the boathouse. She insisted on doing it in the barbecue room where we had spent one long terrified afternoon, and in that room she was more passionate than anywhere else, as if by her boldness she could erase history, undo the thing that had been done.

By midsummer, it was as if Mr. Lee had disappeared. He no longer came to the river on Friday evenings. He had fired two of his employees at the print shop and had to work weekends. Mrs. Lee stayed in her room until late afternoon, when we made burgers or shrimp on the grill, thick hush puppies fried to a golden brown, crunchy and slightly sweet, drizzled with lemon juice. We ate on the deck behind the house in the good light of summer, listening to the slow wash of the river, the bark of dogs in the distance, the voices of mothers calling children home to supper. We drank lemonade over crushed ice, and Mrs. Lee seemed happy to have us there.

"It's so much better with just us girls," she'd say, and then act as if she felt guilty for having said it. Sometimes I would catch on her a sweet tangy whiff of alcohol, and once we found three wine coolers hidden beneath a paper sack in the pantry. "Not that I don't love your father," she'd say to Amanda Ruth. "It's just more relaxed this way."

The week before Amanda Ruth left for college, we had the place to ourselves. It rained for six days straight. We played house in the near-to-flooding boathouse that rocked on its spindly stilts, only venturing up to the cabin for food and showers. Nights during the rains we thought it might wash away. The river had risen dramatically, flooding several of the low-lying houses. It stopped within inches of the floorboards of the boathouse.

On our last night, we sat at the end of the pier with our legs hanging over, submerged halfway to our calves. The river was cold from the rain, murky from mud and silt that had floated downstream. Although the rain had stopped the grayness had not lifted; it would hang on for a couple of days, that stultifying softness that seems appropriate only for sleeping. We'd done our share of that, and now my whole body felt heavy, my brain soggy, my senses blurred.

"I have a surprise for you," Amanda Ruth said.

"What kind?"

"A trip."

"Where to?"

"The University of Montevallo has an exchange program with China, a sister city called Yibin on the upper reaches of the Yangtze. I'm going next summer. I want you to come with me."

"That would cost a fortune."

"I've done the calculations. If we both work part-time and take out student loans, we can do it."

"It's the other side of the world. We don't speak Chinese."

She laughed. "You can get a language partner at Hunter, and I'll get one at Montevallo. Just watch. By May I'm going to win you over." I didn't tell her that going to China sounded about as plausible as going to the moon.

Amanda Ruth became serious. "What about us?" she asked. "Are we going to see other people?"

The question struck me as odd, forced me to think about us in a way I had not before. She was my best friend, the person I trusted most, the person I most desired to spend time with. But I had never thought of our relationship as one that could last in the way boyfriends and girlfriends could last, something that could be permanent. I assumed I would go away to college, have boyfriends, fall in love in the proper manner. The men I met in New York would be different from the clumsy and brutish boys I had known thus far; they would be sensitive and intelligent, they would have a softness to them, they would know how to please me physically. I didn't think of myself as a girl who liked other girls. I loved Amanda Ruth; that was all.

Several minutes passed. A bullfrog called from across the river, its deep, awkward croak echoing in the stillness. The moon was low and full, the trees cast their shadows onto the river. Amanda Ruth moved slightly away from me on the pier, so that our thighs no longer touched. "You didn't answer me."

"I haven't given it much thought."

"I've hardly thought of anything else."

"What about dating?" I said. "Don't you think we should date in college?"

"Isn't that what we're doing now?"

"This is different."

"How?"

I couldn't look her in the eyes, couldn't think of any answer that wouldn't sound all wrong. Amanda Ruth was crying. "I get it," she said.

"There's nothing to get." I put my arm around her shoulders. She resisted, but only for a minute. "We're best friends," I said. "We've had a whole summer together. Isn't that enough?"

That night the rain returned, heavier now, as if the sky was emptying itself of every last drop of water. We brought fresh sheets down from the cabin and curled up on the old mattress in the boathouse. I felt the humid weight of the air bearing down on us as we lay there, holding on like sisters or cousins, listening to the deluge, awed by the lightning that flashed across the darkened sky. At some point I drifted off to sleep and dreamt that we were moving, swirling down the river in our own muddy version of the flying house in *The Wizard of Oz*. When I woke I realized that the little boathouse was shaking.

"Wake up," I whispered.

"What is it?"

"I think we should go up to the house."

I looked out the window and saw logs rushing past, big limbs ripped from trees, the white flash of a lawn chair, a mattress with its silver coils exposed.

"We're probably under a tornado watch," I said, reaching for the radio, but Amanda Ruth pulled me to her. She kissed my neck, slid her hand underneath my shirt. She rolled me onto my back and lay on top of me. Her hair covered my face. Thunder pounded the roof, the power of it reverberating in the flimsy walls. I listened for the shrill whistle of a distant locomotive. Growing up on the Gulf Coast, it was the sound I feared most. I knew how a tornado could fool you, how it sounded like a train but was really a dark funnel hurtling unchecked across the land. There were stories of bizarre deaths and miraculous survivals, such as a woman who was lifted from her bed while she slept, the sheets stripped from beneath her, before the tornado returned her to the mattress, unharmed. Small fishing boats were found miles from the owners' houses, suspended in the air after the storm, the bow driven through the trunk of a massive oak tree. A baby was discovered alive in a bed of pine straw three days after a tornado snatched him from his mother's arms.

Amanda Ruth shook her hair so that it tickled my face. She held my wrists down with her hands. "I'll visit you at Christmas," she said. "I've always wanted to see them light the tree at Rockefeller Center."

"And we'll go ice skating in Central Park, and walk down Fifth Avenue wearing big hats."

"And buy smelly cheese at Zabar's?"

"Of course. And see a Broadway show."

We kissed to seal the pact.

SEVEN

By late afternoon the river is deep yellow, and the air smells of something newly decayed. For miles the river-bank has been deserted, just bamboo huts and groves of orange trees. The sun is already low in the sky when Nanjing flares up ahead, a city of gigantic candles, dozens of refinery towers breathing flames into the dusky light. It smells as if the whole city is burning. The voice on the loudspeaker announces our arrival: "We are approaching beautiful Nanjing. Please find your leader for exciting tourism promenade into famous city of industry and culture."

Slowly, people begin emerging on deck. Their pale, bloated faces show signs of an afternoon of drink, sleep, and Bingo. There is a great deal of blinking and yawning as the passengers adjust to the gloomy light of the rain-soaked afternoon. Elvis Paris appears at our side, green flag in one hand, clipboard in the other. "Nanjing is number one beautiful city of China!" he says, pointing to an imposing row of towers rising on the hill. "Nanjing makes all modern things for the good of the people. Petroleum, lead, zinc, iron."

We pass under a huge, monstrously ugly bridge, which is lined with clusters of egg-shaped lanterns and supported by four concrete towers. The Voice calls out the landmark: "Yangtze First Bridge, amazing feat of Chinese engineering and work ethic of the people." A huge red banner hangs from the bridge, the characters written large in white. All of the guides, including Elvis Paris, point to the sign in unison, as if on cue, and The Voice translates: "Love the Four Modernizations. Work Hard for the People."

"What are the Four Modernizations?" Dave asks.

"Every Chinese child knows the Four Modernizations!" Elvis Paris says proudly. "Industry, Agriculture, Defense, Science."

Elvis Paris must have seen the bridge dozens of times in his endless travels along this familiar route; nonetheless, he gazes up in undisguised awe. "This bridge is true symbol of modern China. Twenty thousand feet long. This bridge is very great, but the Three Gorges Dam will be greater."

We find Graham, then wait for Stacy, who arrives several minutes after our appointed meeting time, wearing a blue denim mini-dress and loafers. "We almost left you," Dave says, teasing.

"You wouldn't have." She's looking at him the way I've seen so many women look at him over the years—that mixture of attraction and curiosity, amusement and, perhaps, hope. Dave's not the kind of guy you notice immediately. His handsomeness is of a more subtle quality. I can't count the times I've been sitting with him in a restaurant, halfway through the meal, when one woman, then another, and another, glances over and *sees* him. I know these women are seeing him because something crosses their faces—something quick and instinctual—before they look away. Then they'll keep glancing back, trying not to be obvious, perhaps hoping to catch his eye. He's not the kind of man who causes a stir when he walks into a room. Instead, women notice his presence slowly, like a vapor or a faint scent, like the music in the background that you don't even know is there until a single odd note rises above the ambient noise. I've tried to analyze this quality in him, tried to figure out exactly what it is about the composition of his face, the measured gestures of his hands, that draws women slowly and inevitably toward him. Twelve years, and I've yet to pinpoint it. Even as I love him for his mystery, his ability to keep me guessing year after year after year, I know that I've lost any such mystery for him.

We hang back until the other passengers have departed, then make our way over the slippery gangplank. Graham leads us up a muddy stairway, then through a group of rumpled soldiers half-heartedly stacking sandbags. We pass beneath a canopy of sycamores, fragrant in the rain, and find ourselves beside a little stream that cascades toward the river.

"The Chin-huai," Graham explains. "Mooring place of the legendary flower boats."

"Flower boats?" Stacy says, digging in the soft sand with the toe of her shoe.

"When I first traveled to China twenty years ago, you could still see them here. A paper lantern glowed on every boat, and a girl in a bright silk dress stood at the stern. The girls held paper fans printed with the names of songs you could have them sing."

"Sounds romantic."

"Sure, but it was business. Each singsong girl had a couple of old men who accompanied her song with handmade string instruments, and when she was finished you had the option of spending the night with her on the boat. If you both agreed, the old men would disembark, the girl would put out the lamp, and you'd be left alone with her."

"You talk as if you'd been with one of the singsong girls yourself," I say.

Graham winks at me. "Maybe I have."

I imagine Graham floating down the silver river, lulled by the sound of the singsong girl's voice, the flicker of lights. I imagine him shuddering under her touch. There are no flower boats now, and the voices of the singsong girls, were there any here today, would be drowned out by the din of harbor traffic and the train rumbling over the bridge. The stream is almost clear though, and the occasional gum wrappers, Baiji Juice bottles, and tattered shoes that float downstream seem benign in comparison to the immense volume of garbage that litters the great river for which the Chinhuai is destined.

Graham leads us through a series of narrow lanes to a small storefront with a ceramic Buddha hanging in the doorway. A young couple sits at one of the tables, talking quietly. Two teenaged boys are smoking cigarettes by the window. They all turn to stare when we walk in. The owner greets us with laughter. She stands on her tiptoes and slaps Graham on the shoulders.

"I met her on my first trip up the river," he explains, "and I've been coming back to this restaurant ever since."

The woman chats for a minute with Graham, then gives Stacy, Dave, and me a good looking-over. She touches Stacy's hair and feels the fabric of my dress, then gestures to show that she thinks Dave has very broad shoulders. She says something to Dave. Graham translates. "My friend wants to know how much you earn per year."

Dave shrugs. "Between Jenny and myself we make a decent living."

Graham translates the exchange. "How much exactly?" When neither of us answers, he laughs. "Get used to it. You'll find that everyone in China wants to know how much you make."

The woman seats us and shouts back to the kitchen, and immediately a young girl brings out a platter of boiled calamari. Within minutes large dishes begin appearing: pork in a rich red sauce, rice noodles with shredded beef, spicy green beans, tofu with diced chicken. She brings us two warm bottles of Tsing Tao beer, which she pours into four glasses.

"Jenny tells me you do business in China," Dave says.

"Used to," Graham replies. "Crane safety. In the eighties, with Deng Xiaoping's reforms, the whole country went wild with construction. New shops and apartment buildings started going up all over the place. Loads of money to be made by foreigners and Chinese businesses alike. My company's job was to make sure the cranes were safe for the workers."

"What made you get out of the business?"

"The Three Gorges Dam. The government was extolling the virtues of the dam, and people were making money hand over fist. I admit I saw dollar signs, just like everyone else. But the more I read about the project, the more uncomfortable I felt."

"Isn't the dam supposed to create power?" Dave asks. "Control flooding?"

Graham shrugs. "That's what they say. And maybe, to a small extent, it's true. But, ultimately, the cost is too great. I've been up and down this river dozens of times. I can't imagine just plugging it up. It's all very sad."

The conversation dies out. Around us, the sounds of the city: on the street, hundreds of bicycle bells jingle. Vendors shout at passersby. A group of elderly men just outside the doorway slap mahjong tiles onto a table and tick off their scores in loud, excited voices. Occasionally they burst into laughter. Beyond the red curtain that separates the dining room from the kitchen, dishes crash. Stacy eyes her beer without drinking it and I shift a fish head around on my plate. The dead eye gazes up at me. Graham seems lost in thought. Dave, meanwhile, is listening, looking around, taking in everything. He thrives on pandemonium. For Dave, the noisier it is, the clearer his focus. I can tell by the way he sets his chopsticks neatly on each side of his plate, like a fork and spoon, and rearranges the napkin on his lap, that he's about to launch into a line of questioning.

"Graham," he says. "I understand you have Lou Gehrig's disease." I give Dave a little kick under the table, but he persists. "Are you in pain?"

Far from being offended, Graham seems utterly at ease with the question. "Yes. I'm in quite a lot of pain, in fact. Not at this moment, but there's rarely a week when I'm not knocked flat by it at some point. It's not the muscle atrophy, but rather the side effects—the aches and swelling."

"God," Stacy says. "That sounds awful." She struggles with a piece of calamari, which slides through her chopsticks and lands in her lap.

"How do you deal with it?" Dave asks.

"At first I didn't. I cried like a baby, spent a lot of time in bed with the remote control and *Baywatch*. I had to keep the TV on, because when it was quiet my mind went berserk. I'd just sit there envisioning myself in the end, wheelchair-bound, taking liquids through a feeding tube. After a couple of months, I did a reality check. I decided the best thing I can do is live a little more each day. That's why I'm here—to spend my last days in the place I love."

"I read this book," Stacy says, "about a guy with Lou Gehrig's disease." Having given up on the chopsticks, she picks up a piece of calamari with her fingers and pops it in her mouth. "It was really inspirational."

"I probably read it too," Graham says. "For a while, I read everything that was published on the subject. I could recite the statistics in my sleep. Twenty percent survive five years. Ten percent make it ten years." He catches my eye. "But I'm not planning to stick around until this disease turns me into an invalid."

"A few years back I was called out on an attempted suicide," Dave says. "Forty-nine-year-old woman. She'd tried to hang herself from the light fixture in her dining room, but the rope broke and her daughter found her on the floor an hour later. Turns out she had ALS. Just didn't want to live like that."

Stacy clears her throat. Graham glances around the table and says, "Cheer up, mates," but there's nothing cheerful in his voice. After that, no one says anything for a minute. Graham lifts his bowl and drinks off the last of his soup. The waitress is immediately by his side, ladling more into his bowl.

"I'll tell you what this disease has done for me. It has taught me to recalibrate pain. When I was nineteen, I spent six months in a body cast following a motorcycle accident. Now, those six months seem like a picnic. I've reached a new threshold, a new standard by which to judge all other pain. Let me demonstrate." He says something to the waitress, who brings him a matchbook. Graham strikes the match against the side of the box, then holds it just below his open palm. The tip of the flame touches his skin, but he doesn't flinch. He holds it there until the flame reaches the end of the match; I lean forward and blow it out.

"Bravo," Dave says.

Graham holds his palm out for us to see. A small dot in the center of his broad hand is singed black. The entire wait staff has gathered around and is pointing and shouting. A pretty girl with a thin white scar that stretches from her left eye to her cheek points at Graham and shouts, "Gweilo!" The old woman says something that makes the staff and patrons laugh, then shoos everyone away from our table.

"You get my point." Graham shifts in his seat; his leg brushes mine. "That stunt I just pulled was uncomfortable, of course, but how bad can it be when you know it's going to end in a few seconds? Chronic pain is an altogether different beast. There's no getting out from under it. I look back at that nineteen-year-old boy in the body cast, and I envy him."

Dave spears a piece of pork. "I think we all envy ourselves at nineteen."

Dave, I know, sees Graham in terms of the particular case, the disease itself, in the impersonal light of reason. Dave is unencumbered by emotion. Each time he goes to work, he sees terrible things. His response to these things is professional, exact, rational. He looks at a young girl bleeding from a gunshot wound and thinks, "How can I help this girl survive?" If it is clear his patient will die, he thinks, "What can I do to make her comfortable for now, until it's over?" I wonder sometimes if he looks at me and sees a useless person. While he's saving lives, I'm telling women with platinum cards which handbag to wear with their tailored silk suits, which earrings to pair with the Hermes scarves. I wonder, sometimes, if this is why he moved out: I simply cannot compete with the ongoing drama of his job.

"And you?" Graham says, looking at Dave.

"Me?"

"What's the greatest degree of pain you've ever endured?"

"That's easy. A couple of years ago I had a cracked tooth. It became infected at the root. The dentist, Dr. De Salvo, dug around in there for more than an hour. You see, when he went to pull the thing, it shattered. He had to yank each piece out individually. And worst of all, because the infection was at the nerve, it all had to be done without any Novocain. By the time he was finished, I had passed out. When I came to, he was standing above me, apologizing. But that wasn't the worst of it. Apparently, he'd left the nerve exposed. I went home pumped up on drugs, and sometime in the middle of the night the drugs wore off. Ouch."

"He was crying like a baby," I say.

"This guy?" Stacy says. "Crying? That's hard to believe."

What I remember most from that time is the intensity of feeling I had for Dave. Seeing him in pain made me look at him, at us, in a new way. Suddenly, this man who had always been so sure of himself in every situation was vulnerable. Dave had always been the rescuer, but during those brief days, he had to depend on me. Years before, my fondness for him had evolved into love because he was there when Amanda Ruth died; he had known exactly what to say, ushering me through those first horrible days and weeks after her murder. Although I hated seeing Dave in so much pain, I secretly relished his weakness. I watched over him like a careful mother. For the first time in our marriage, I felt that he needed me, that I was the one in control of the situation.

"Well?" Graham says, nudging me with his elbow. "What was it for you? What event established your pain threshold?"

"I was fourteen," I say, trying to avoid Graham's eyes, certain that my attraction toward him must show, that my voice comes out weak when I speak to him. "This was in Alabama. I was having my riding lesson— Miss Linda was teaching me how to canter—and my horse bucked, reared up, and fell on top of me. My pelvis was broken, both my hips fractured."

Dave is looking at me like I'm a stranger who just walked in off the street. Graham leans toward me. I'm wearing a sleeveless dress, and I can feel the rough fabric of his shirt against my shoulder. "Go on," he says.

"The ride to the hospital and the emergency room is a blur. But I have a clear memory of the orderlies transferring me to a cold metal table in the X-ray room. Then I was alone with just one nurse, a skeletal woman named Ramona who smelled like she'd been smoking nonstop for the last twenty years. 'Okay, hon,' she said. 'Count to three now, and I'm gonna slide this thing here under your behind.' She tricked me. On two she jerked my hip up and slid the X-ray plate underneath. Then she pressed down on my pelvis and flipped the switch. It hurt about a hundred times more than actually falling off the horse. Ramona did twelve different X-rays, and each one seemed to last forever. So that's my threshold.

Nothing else has even compared."

"I've never heard that story before," Dave says.

"It was a long time ago." I bite into a lotus paste bun. The seedy filling is sickeningly sweet and dense.

Graham turns to Stacy. "Your turn."

"Nothing has happened to me."

"Come on. At some point in your life you've been in pain."

"Really," she says. "I've had an uneventful life."

"Then make something up," Dave says.

Stacy looks around the table uncertainly. All eyes are on her. "Okay. I'll tell you a story, but not a word of it is going to be true. I'm making it up as I go along."

"All the better," Graham says.

She takes a deep breath. "The worst pain I ever experienced was during childbirth. This was a couple of years ago. I'd not really been taking care of myself. I was involved with some dodgy people. Lots of drugs, even more drinking. By the time my due date came along the boyfriend wasn't in the picture."

She's picking at her fingernails, not looking at any of us. "So I'm there in the hospital, and I've been in labor for about eighteen hours, and nothing's happening, and I just want it all to be over with. I'm pretty sure I'm going to die. The nurses are telling me to calm down, to breathe, to take it easy, and my mom's in the room, holding my hand, trying to be supportive, but I'm on painkillers and she thinks I can't hear her when she says to the nurse, 'I can't believe she got herself into this mess.' And I can't believe I got myself into it either, and I'm thinking about Jimmy and his goddamn Ducati motorcycle, how we rode it all the way from Detroit to St. Louis that time and slept in crappy motel rooms that charged by the hour and shot up heroin and didn't use any birth control, because we didn't think of it, because neither of us really considered being alive long enough for it to matter.

"So finally it's time, I know it's time because the nurses are all talking in loud panicky voices, and my mom's in hysterics, but the baby's not turned in the right direction and I hear a voice say, 'We're going to have to cut it out.' So then they put this mask over my mouth and nose and my mom's face fades out, and everything is all wavy and blue, like I'm at the bottom of a swimming pool. And after that I come to and there's this baby in the room, and my mom's just looking at the baby like it's some sort of alien."

Stacy is crying, wiping her face with the back of her hand. "So I tell the nurse I want to hold the baby and my mom says, 'Sweetheart, we've discussed this,' but I say, 'No, I want to hold her,' and the nurse hands her to me, and I'm thinking how amazing it is that here's this perfect baby girl, and she doesn't look at all fucked up like I expected her to, she doesn't look like she could have come from me. 'Just let me have her for a few days,' I said. 'Please.' I was thinking about taking her home to my mom's house, and putting her in a little crib. I didn't want to keep her forever, of course, my parents and I had already discussed that, how I was too young, how I had to get my life together, all that. But I was thinking how perfect it would be to have her there with me for just a little while. 'That's not a good idea,' the nurse said. Then my mom said, 'Get it together, Stacy.'"

Stacy is sobbing uncontrollably, and she's looking at us as if we're the jury, or the nurse, or her mother, as if we have some say over how things turn out. "I never took her home. I held her for a little while and then the nurse took her, and someone wheeled me back to my room. The next day I was back at my parents' house, eating mashed potatoes and roast beef at their table, and every time I breathed it felt like the stitches would rip apart, and my dad was talking about stock options, and not once did anyone mention the baby."

Dave hands a napkin to Stacy, who wipes her eyes. As he leans over and whispers something in her ear, I know in some deep sick part of my stomach that Dave is lost to me for the rest of the trip. Like the woman he saved from the burning car on the Palisades, Stacy offers him something I can't—raw and undisguised need. Dave is moved by need in the same way other men are moved by beauty.

She glances around the table at us, tries to smile lightheartedly, and says, "Like I said, it's just a story." I smile back, pretending to believe her.

It's nearly midnight by the time we're finished with dinner. Graham hails a taxi, a tiny van with makeshift seating. He sits in a plastic lawn chair beside the driver, and Dave settles onto an old ice chest in the back. Between them is a poorly upholstered seat barely big enough for two, which Stacy and I share. The van has only one headlight. As we careen through the night, bumping and braking and shifting and screeching, the road visible through a hole the size of my shoe in the van's rusty bottom, I hold on tight to the back of the driver's seat, my heart pounding. In the back, Dave seems to be enjoying the ride, letting out a whoop every time we hit a bump. Once, when it seems we're about to topple over, Stacy grabs my arm for balance. We lock eyes. She holds on a second too long, smiles slightly, blushes and takes her hand away. Her knee brushes mine. Something familiar and sweet rushes through my veins. *She knows*, I think. *Has she been there too?*

The taxi lets us off at the dock. Graham stays behind to pay, and as Stacy begins to walk ahead, Dave says to me quietly, "She needs to talk this thing through."

"Okay," I say, which is what I always say, every time his pager goes off at 2 a.m., every time the woman from Chelsea calls. "Hi Jenny. It's me again. Sorry to call so late."

Dave hurries ahead to catch Stacy. She stops, says something to him I can't hear. The two of them step onto the floating dock that leads to the *Red Victoria*. With every step, I feel him leaving me not only in body, but in mind. By the time he reaches the ship, he will have entirely forgotten me.

Graham exchanges a few pleasant words with the driver, and then, as if it is the most natural thing in the world, he takes my hand. "Look," he says, turning around to face Nanjing. The whole city is aglitter with lights, the full moon glows red, the river rolls past, the boards of the dock creak and whine.

"It could be any city, couldn't it?"

He's right. This could be any city, any country. At night it ceases, somehow, to be China. In this light, I don't feel so far from home. Stacy and Dave have been swallowed up by the fog. Their voices carry toward us, then fade. Graham lets go of my hand and puts one arm around me.

"Is it just me?" he asks.

"What do you mean?"

"Am I fooling myself to think you might feel something too?"

"I can't answer that." The night is warm and heavy, a drop of sweat slides down my spine. My heart speeds up, my breath comes quickly. I'm afraid to say anything, afraid that when I do, I will be delivering myself to him entirely. Finally, I look up at him. "What happens next?"

"We have thirteen days. Let's make the most of it. Of course, there's the matter of your husband. He's a nice fellow."

"You mean that nice fellow who just walked away with another woman?"

"I don't want to go stepping on any toes."

"He moved out two months ago."

"In a selfish way I'm glad to hear it. Did you see it coming?"

"Not really. One night he came home late, set a bag

of take-out Chinese on the counter, and said, 'This isn't working.'"

I remember how flat Dave's voice sounded, devoid of emotion. He might as well have been telling me the newspaper hadn't come that morning, or that the Chinese restaurant had raised its prices. What made it worse was that I'd been waiting up for him, and I was wearing a new lace nightgown, trying to entice him. If he noticed the nightgown, he didn't mention it. I wonder if somehow the nightgown itself inspired him to put an end to everything that night. Maybe when he saw it, he realized I was trying to make things work; maybe that scared him.

"What did you say?"

"Nothing. I just dumped the carton of rice on the plate. We sat on the sofa and watched TV and ate without talking. Conan O'Brien was interviewing this four-year-old kid who could nibble Kraft cheese singles into the shapes of all fifty states.

"He didn't want to make this trip, but I begged him. I convinced him we should make one last-ditch effort to stay together." I feel sick at my stomach, remembering how I showed up one evening at Dave's place across the park. I was haggard from lack of sleep. I sat on the sofa for more than an hour, clutching his hand, rattling off a list of reasons I thought we should work it out. I asked him if he still loved me. He paused for two minutes. I know it was two, because I was watching the clock, the minute hand sweeping slowly over the white face. "I do," he said finally.

"Then you owe it to us to try, don't you?"

"Okay," he said. "But I can't make any promises."

I describe this scene to Graham. He listens silently. At the end of the story, I find myself laughing at the image of myself on the sofa, halfway through a box of Kleenex, begging. "Humiliating, isn't it?"

"So, this last-ditch effort to save your marriage. Is it working?"

"Every now and then Dave will do something— look at me in a certain way, or make some comment— that makes me think he still cares. But then he'll be so distant, and I'll think there's no hope for us. Maybe we're missing something that married couples are supposed to have. I'm not sure what it is, exactly."

"At least you tried. There's something to be said for that."

"Have you ever been married?"

"For about ten minutes when I was twenty-five."

"What happened?"

"I was selfish with my time, my space. And travel. I loved to travel, and I didn't want to be held back. I really enjoyed my solitude. It worked out okay, too, until recently. Then I got sick, and I started wishing I had somebody. Maybe I should have settled down with someone a long time ago. Then she'd be with me now. I wouldn't have to face this alone."

He squeezes my shoulder. I don't know how to respond, so I just put my arms around his waist and hold him. It feels strange to be holding a man who is not my husband.

"If we're not careful the ship will leave us," I say finally.

"That wouldn't be so bad. Me, you, Nanjing, some fancy foreigners' hotel."

I move away from him and walk down the dock. He follows. "I just told you my life story. Don't I even get a kiss?"

"I've been married for twelve years," I say over my shoulder. "Give me time."

When I glance back, his hands are in his pockets and he's looking at the ground, walking slowly, like a man who isn't ready to reach his destination. "That's the one thing I don't have."

***

Back in our cabin, lying in bed, Dave says, "Why didn't you ever tell me about the horse accident?"

"I never thought of it. Compared to what you see every day on the job, it's nothing." I think of stab wounds, car wrecks, domestic violence. I think of the smoldering remains of the World Trade Center, and of Dave in his ambulance, heading toward the disaster three years ago, and the sick feeling in my gut when I saw live pictures on TV of the towers collapsing, people fleeing, their faces and clothes and hair covered in a surreal pink-gray ash. At the time, pacing back and forth in our apartment, fearing for Dave's life, waiting desperately for the phone to ring, I loved him more than ever. I told God that, if He'd just bring Dave home to me, I'd patch up everything, love my husband forever, forge a new devotion. For some months afterward, the commitment held. But eventually the old malaise took hold of us, the bickering returned, and it was a struggle to stay together in that apartment, each of us trying, but failing, to hide our discontent.

"I never get horse accidents in Manhattan, you know," Dave says, laughing. "An equestrian disaster would pose a new and interesting challenge." He rolls over and kisses me on the cheek. "Good night."

"Good night."

The kiss is platonic, but it is a kiss nonetheless, the kindest gesture he has made toward me in months. I can't help feeling that we've reached an unspoken truce.

And then, unexpectedly, he sits up in bed. "You know I'm just trying to help Stacy. Don't you?"

"Yes."

"Good," he says, lying down. Moments later he is asleep. In the low light I look at him, the clean lines of his face, the gentle way his hair falls over his forehead. The boat rocks softly. It's Red Bingo night, and I can hear the faint hum of the party upstairs. I imagine Graham in his cabin, which is probably identical to ours, save for a slight difference in color scheme. I picture him in bed, turned on his side, his arm hugging a pillow. I wonder if he wears socks to bed. I wonder if he showers before turning in. Does he sleep in his underwear? Does he talk in his sleep? Then I remember him saying that he suffers from insomnia, and I rearrange the picture: he stares out the porthole at the pale orange glow of the moon. I imagine him slipping his hand beneath the sheet, finding himself, his hand moving rhythmically, alone. His mouth opens. The smallest sound escapes him.

Dave is snoring softly. The ship sways gently, a giant cradle rocking through the night.

EIGHT

In the night the river turns silver, the mountains shine down upon it, the air goes cool and wet. This is the China Amanda Ruth wanted, her moonlit landscape, her Land of the Dragon. The villages we pass become magical in darkness, carnival-like and throbbing, though in the day they seem filthy, overcrowded, rubbed raw by industry. Apartment rows crouch like creatures gone dumb with hunger, and in the air there is a stench of coal. The mist mingles with black ash and factory smoke. It takes all of my energy just to breathe.

The daytime is for Dave. With Elvis Paris as our guide, we tramp through ancient villages, allow ourselves to be dragged from one bizarre tourist trap to another. We could be any married couple, viewing bright Buddhas and crumbling temples, parks gone stiff with cement. Stacy is always at our side. One afternoon, passing through what was once a famous opium den, she tells us that she's had her own addictions, drugs and alcohol. "Sober six months," she says. "That's the real reason I'm here. My parents wanted to get me away from everyone I knew."

Dave livens up when she says this, looks her over the way he might scan an emergency case, and I know he's sizing her up for track marks, bloodshot eyes, visible signs of decline. After that, he pays her even closer attention, keeping her always in his sight, as if at any moment he might be called to pull her back from the abyss.

Every now and then Dave shares with me a private joke or remembers some moment from our past, calling up our common history. In these moments, as we walk through the crowded streets, keeping the green flag in our sight so as not to become lost from the group, I almost forget how things have become between us: that we do not make love, that we choose words with edges. For a moment I allow myself to believe that Dave might be coming around. But back in our cabin, when I try to kiss him, he allows the kiss for only a couple of seconds before closing his mouth and backing away. It is the fifth night of the cruise. Time is running out.

"So what's the schedule like tomorrow?" he says, turning his back on me to undress.

I thumb through the tour pamphlet. "Temples. World famous hanging coffins. A traditional Chinese opera."

He places his shoes side by side at the foot of the bed, folds his used socks before dropping them in the laundry bag. "I wish I were in New York." Then, seeing my disappointment, he says, "Sorry. I'm having fun. Really. It's just—you know, travel. Hard on the system."

I unbutton my blouse to reveal a new black bra, trimmed with red ribbon, which I optimistically bought for this trip. Dave glances at the bra, then looks away as if he hadn't seen it. "I guess we're up early again tomorrow." He starts laying out his clothes for morning. Suddenly ashamed of my body in front of this man who has no use for it, I go into the bathroom to change.

"What did you think of the dinner?" he says through the door. "Those dumplings weren't half-bad."

I want to scream at him, "This is the end of our marriage, and you want to talk about dumplings?" Instead I put a drop of toothpaste on the brush, press the brush to my teeth. By the time I finish getting ready for bed, Dave is already beneath the covers, eyes closed, his breath gone slow and even.

I sit on the edge of the bed, nudge his shoulder. "Dave?"

"Hmmm." He opens his eyes briefly, closes them, rolls over so that he is facing the opposite wall.

"Can we talk?"

"It's late," he moans. "Tomorrow."

"Tomorrow you'll be with Stacy."

He opens his eyes just long enough to say, "I'm beat." Within moments he is asleep again.

Watching him, I feel myself sliding into some other skin. I feel older, wiser, my mind is sharp and clear. I remove my nightgown in the dark, pull a loose dress over my shoulders and strap my sandals in the dark, feeling every place my fingers touch. Even my feet are aroused by the brush of my hands against them. Fastening the tiny buttons down the front of my dress, I feel my nipples harden. All my thoughts have turned to sex.

On the deck I find Graham. He stands against the rail, waiting for me.

"You came," he says.

"I did."

"I'm surprised you showed up."

"Why?"

"I keep thinking you'll come to your senses."

He has not so much as kissed me. But there is something so intimate in the way he stands beside me, our elbows touching lightly on the rail, or sometimes, when we are sitting, our upper arms pressed together, it is as if we have made love hundreds of times. I make unnecessary adjustments just to bring us close, brushing hair out of my face so that when I lower my arm, my hand falls a half inch nearer to his.

"Your friend," he says. "Amanda Ruth. How did she die?"

"She was strangled."

"Who did it?"

His words recall the headlines from the local paper fourteen years ago. College Girl Slain: Who Did It? splashed across the front page in large type the day Amanda Ruth was found. The next day, they ran the same headline, only this time it was larger and a subhead had been added: Police Question Chinese Father. On the third day, the same words again, larger still—as if the mystery itself made the news grow more interesting. And this time a new subhead appeared, even more sinister than the last: Lesbian Love Triangle Suspected. Sitting in my old bedroom, staring at the paper, I immediately thought of Allison, Amanda Ruth's girlfriend from Montevallo whom we'd had dinner with the day before Amanda Ruth was killed. Then it occurred to me: *triangle. A third person. Are they talking about me?*

What I don't tell Graham is that the most logical suspect was the one I wouldn't allow myself to ponder—because I could not stand to think that the killer could be someone whom Amanda Ruth trusted so completely. "Do we have to talk about this?"

"I'm sorry." He places his hands on my shoulders, rests his chin on the top of my head. He takes a deep breath, and I feel myself coming undone. Minutes pass.

"Why didn't I meet you ten years ago?" he says finally.

"It wouldn't have worked."

"How do you know?"

"Ten years ago I was twenty-two. You were forty-three. That's cradle robbery."

"You're right. Five years ago then."

"Twenty-seven and forty-eight. That's still a tough number. I would have been your mid-life crisis. Those things never work out."

"We could have been the exception."

A small boat passes, crammed with young people. The boys are wearing shiny, colorful shirts, the girls dark lipstick and very short dresses. Chinese pop music blares from the speakers. A young man raises a beer in our direction. "Gambe!" he shouts.

"Gambe!" Graham shouts back.

The boat disappears into the darkness, music and laughter trailing after. Graham is standing so close to me that I can feel his chest moving in and out as he breathes. His hands slip slowly off my shoulders, down my bare arms, until they enclose my fingers. He moves even closer, so that my body is pressed against the rail. My knees go soft. A wrecked mattress drifts by.

"I've never cheated on my husband."

Graham presses into me. He moves his hands over my hips, my stomach. The moon is deep red, the river is black, his fingers are hot on my skin. He presses his mouth against my ear. "I'm fifty-three," he says. "Why is it that I can't think of a better line than the one I'm about to use?"

"And what line is that?"

"I want to make love to you. Right here. Standing up."

I feel a slow heat building between my legs. He puts his hand on my waist and begins counting buttons downward. It seems like forever before he reaches number four, slips the button through the eye, and slides his hand inside my dress. It takes all of my energy and will to say, "Really, I'm still married."

He refastens the buttons. "Then why are you here?"

"I'm sorry."

He kisses my head. "Go to bed. I'm going to see you tomorrow. You're going to change your mind."

Even as I'm walking away from him, not looking back, I know that he is right.

NINE

Do you remember, Amanda Ruth, how I would pull you down? The river made you love me, the skin of your eyelids quivered beneath my lips. It was the heat that brought us together, shucking clothes to get to the skin, lying naked on the wooden planks that buckled from the damp. My fingers trailed the shadows newly formed beneath your breasts. The first time I tasted that electricity in you, I brought my mouth to yours and made you taste as well.

"This is you," I whispered, and you wouldn't let me go, you made me kiss you hard until we heard your parents' voices on the porch. There was something clean and warm in me that left the moment I found out that you had died. It comes back to me, that warmth, here on this river with Graham.

TEN

The *Red Victoria* sidles against the pontoon that will take us to shore, a scraping of metal on metal. Minutes later, sitting in pairs face to face, we form a deceptive foursome. From our arrangement—Stacy and Dave on one side, Graham and me on the other—anyone might guess that we are two happily married couples.

We board a bus near the docks for a ride up to Mount Lushan. Our first stop is Dongling Temple. The street outside the temple is packed with buses and Chinese tourists. Street vendors are doing a busy trade in film and postcards. The air is sweet with incense. There's a stall where you can buy small black plastic boxes manufactured by monks. If you put your ear to the box and listen, you can hear, beneath the static, the faint sounds of monks chanting.

"This temple is birthplace of the Pure Earth sect of Buddhism," Elvis Paris proclaims through a megaphone. We make our way toward the entrance. "Is almost two thousand years old." He points to big glass jars set up on either side of the temple doors. "Feel free to make offerings to the gods."

After several people, including Dave, have dutifully dropped coins into the jars, Elvis Paris laughs. "Today most Chinese people do not believe these superstitions, but maybe is good luck! Bring you very rich!" He laughs again. "Please, no photos inside the temple."

One can imagine how the shapely, brightly painted temple, in quieter times, may have been beautiful, may have inspired a sense of inner peace. Today, however, the crowds and the general atmosphere are reminiscent of Disney World. A couple of monks in bright robes hang out in doorways, looking bored and slightly annoyed, staring at the tourists. At the entrance to the temple, Graham purchases a pack of incense sticks from an old woman in rags. Inside, he lights the sticks one by one, kneels, places them on an altar at the foot of a towering golden Buddha. He stumbles as he tries to stand. I take his elbow and help him up. "You okay?"

"I trip sometimes. It's nothing."

I nod toward the incense smoldering on the stone altar. "I wouldn't have pegged you for a religious man."

"Never have been. But it can't hurt." I look up to see Dave watching us from a distance.

Within twenty minutes Elvis Paris is herding us back to the bus. Stacy and Dave end up sitting together, and Graham and I take the seat behind them. Stacy has purchased one of the black boxes. "Listen!" she says, holding the box to Dave's ear. "Close your eyes and shut everything out." Dave presses his ear to the box.

"Hear it?"

"I heard something."

Stacy slips the box into her daypack. "I think I'll become a monk. Live in the mountains and eat roots and berries." This is the first time I've seen her in a short-sleeved shirt. Her arms bear an intricate patchwork of scars. "Did you ever want to just drop everything and go? Just become someone new?"

"Many times," Dave says. He's looking out the window, and I'm wondering who he is: this man I married. Could he really give up everything, start a new life in some foreign place? I've always thought of him as the stable one, secure, but now I imagine him, alone with a new haircut, a single suitcase, and his camera, checking into a dark motel in some city I've never been to—Detroit or Philadelphia or Montreal. The night he told me he was leaving, I found myself staring at him when he wasn't looking, wondering if I'd ever known him. I noticed things that I wasn't certain I'd seen before: the scar across his nose had a tiny blue mole at its tip, the second toe on his right foot was slightly longer than the first. That night while he was sleeping, covers kicked to the foot of the bed, I took the camcorder from its case. I sat in the big leather chair by the window, pressed record, and made a movie of him sleeping. I wanted to capture every detail—the placement of his legs, the graceful arc of his hand draped over the edge of the mattress, the pattern of his breathing.

The bus makes its way in stops and starts through the jumble of street life, and then we are on the outskirts of Jiujiang. Thatched huts and low cement barracks line the road. A woman in a coat, long pants, and heels—strange in this dismal heat—leans out the door shouting our destination at the city-dwellers who stand on the roadside. If a would-be passenger hears his destination called, he simply runs alongside the bus, and the woman shouts to the driver, who slows long enough for the passenger to scramble up the steps, clinging to whatever he can find.

Gradually the barracks and thatch huts begin to thin, giving way to limestone bungalows scattered high on the hills, remnants of the British heyday in China. Chinese passengers leap fearlessly off the moving vehicle and disappear into the foliage. The air grows chilly as we ascend into mist. Banana palms march up the hillside. Released from the traffic of Jiujiang, the driver pushes the rusty bus to its limit. The road becomes a series of hairpin curves, and we swing so rapidly around them that I'm sure we're going to careen over the cliff. I am reminded of family trips to the Blue Ridge Parkway when I was a little girl—my mother begging my father to put both hands on the wheel as he sped over narrow mountain roads, gazing out at the bluish clouds far below, steering with a single finger. Twice Amanda Ruth came with us on those mountain vacations, and we'd sing church songs and play car bingo in the back seat while my mother clutched the door handle in terror and my father hummed the melodies of Kenny Rogers.

The higher we climb, the more lush the vegetation becomes. There are azaleas and peach blossoms, sycamore trees and weeping willows. If the China we have seen until now has been a hodgepodge of cement and mortar, factory furnaces and coal dust, Mount Lushan is the inspirational stuff of Chinese poetry and painting. I wish Amanda Ruth could see this. The tops of pavilions peek above thick stands of trees, and the landscape is littered with temples and pagodas that, Elvis Paris tells us, date from the Tang dynasty. The whole mountain is in bloom. Waterfalls glitter. The air smells faintly of tea.

Cameras click and camcorders hum as Elvis Paris draws our attention to various landmarks. He points to a series of peaks rising above the trees and says, "Wave to the Five Old Men," then to a hazy darkness in the distance, saying, "Who dares to enter the Cave of the Immortals?" I imagine Elvis Paris dressed in khaki shorts and army-green shirt, standing at the bow of one of those Jungle Cruise boats in Disney World, steering tourists toward Monkey Island.

Finally the bus pulls into a circular parking lot and screeches to a halt. We stumble out on shaky legs. Stacy unfolds a map and points to a spot she's marked with a red X. "The old tea grove," she says to Dave. "Want to go see it?"

"Sure." As an afterthought, he turns to me. "Do you mind?"

As soon as they're out of sight, Graham takes my hand. "Just you and me, then."

"Looks that way."

"There's a great old pavilion just beyond that cluster of banana palms," he says.

We pass a waterfall that splashes clear water onto the cobblestone path. I take off my shoes and feel the wet stones against my feet. "How are you feeling?"

"Tops."

"Isn't that a good sign? Maybe you're getting

better."

"Don't think I haven't had those fantasies myself. On the days when I'm feeling healthy, I go into denial, make up all sorts of scenarios in which the ALS goes into remission, or the doctors discover I've been misdiagnosed. But there's always the next day." He cups his hands to catch the water, then drinks from his palms. "Try it."

I hold my hands beneath the falls; the water chills my fingers. It tastes sweet and slightly green. "We could stay here," I say. "Just start over, like Stacy said. Live off the land. Build a tree house, like the Swiss Family Robinson."

We reach the pavillion, where the whole world seems to span out beneath us. Graham stretches out his arm, points, and names each landmark for me. To the east is Poyang Lake, glowing a milky green. To the west is a vast plain crisscrossed with fields of corn. To the north, the Yangtze, a massive brown ribbon spooling out endlessly.

"You know, the term Yangtze is a foreign invention," Graham says.

"What do the Chinese call it?"

"Chang Jiang."

"What does that mean?"

"The Long River. Or simply Jiang. *The* River."

From here it looks more like an ocean than a river. In comparison, any other river seems a mere nicety, a stream. I think of Demopolis River, so beloved to me in my childhood. How insignificant that meager body of water would seem to the millions of people who live on the banks of the Yangtze.

Graham moves behind me and puts his arms around my waist. I allow myself to engage briefly in the fantasy that Graham and I made this trip together, that we are going home together, that we have stood this way many times before.

"There's a legend about Lushan tea," he says. "Only virgin girls were allowed to pick it. It was the most delicate tea you can imagine. These days Lushan produces hardly any tea. They export rice instead."

We stand for a few minutes in silence. Every place my eye rests, I find a new wonder—waterfalls, caves, groves of flowering trees in full bloom—all of it appearing and disappearing seductively as the mist moves over the mountain. "It feels like we've stepped into a painting."

"Or a dream."

"How old were you the first time you came?"

"Twenty-five."

"Weren't you married then?"

"Yes. My wife was from Beijing. I met her at the university in Sydney, first love and all that. China was very different then. There was less traffic on the river. You couldn't take these big cruise ships. We had to do a lot of wheeling and dealing to be allowed on one of the Chinese steamboats."

I've seen hundreds of these boats as we've made our way upriver. They cower in size to the *Red Victoria*, and are far more crowded. Often, the water is dangerously high on the sides of the boat, so it looks as though one unexpected wave would sink it. Laundry forms a high canopy around the deck. While the passengers on our ship retreat to the air-conditioned interior, where they can nurse cool cocktails and watch through large picture windows this unfamiliar world passing by, the Chinese passengers crowd the deck, practicing tai chi, eating, smoking, singing, pressing against the rails, shouting greetings to other ships. The Chinese travelers seem almost to live on their ships, to have settled in, whereas on the *Red Victoria*, you get the feeling that many passengers already have one foot mentally on the plane back home.

"What was it that originally drew you here?" I ask.

"In a roundabout way, I suppose it was my mother. She always wanted to be back in her bed at night, so she never ventured beyond a one-hundred-mile radius around our house in Perth. As a child, I wanted desperately to go to Sydney and Melbourne, to New Zealand and London, but when we got in the car for a road trip, I knew it would never last more than three or four hours, and the longer it took to get to a place, the less time we would stay. It was as if my mother had a mental odometer. When it clicked over to a certain number, an alarm went off in her head, and, no matter if we were a mere ten miles from the eighth wonder of the modern world, she'd say, 'Better stop now.' I could always tell, though, that it was a struggle for her. I think she wanted to be adventurous. She read travel books voraciously, and could tell you bizarre details about the people of the Aleutian Islands or the history of Iceland."

Graham nuzzles his face into my hair. I feel my back sinking into his chest, amazed at how comfortable I am with him. Some instinct tells me to pull away—there are only eight days left on this cruise, eight days before I return to New York and he to Australia. I wonder if we will ever see each other again once this trip is over. I imagine the letters I will write to him, quietly erotic, their honesty fueled by distance. I imagine his letters slowing down, and then the weeks and months when none come, when I have to assume that he has died. I still have the letters Amanda Ruth wrote to me when she went away to Montevallo. In them, she declared her love without reserve, as I did in mine, although Amanda Ruth's letters became fewer and farther between as the semester wore on. In November she sent a picture postcard of the Little Pigeon River; on the back she had scribbled a note about a trip she'd taken to Tennessee with a girl named Allison. After that, her letters stopped altogether.

"Have you done much traveling?" Graham asks.

"I've been to most of the States. And I once backpacked through Europe with Dave."

"What do you think of China?"

"To be honest, if it weren't for Amanda Ruth, I never would have come. Now that I'm here, my curiosity is piqued, but I think I took the wrong approach, with the westernized food and the organized tours. It seems like the real China is out of reach." I twist around in his arms. "What about you? Why

China? Why not Alaska or Paraguay or India?"

"Most places are too accessible these days. China's still a challenge. It's still foreign. It will always have secrets I'm not privy to. The best travel is the type that requires a car, a bus, a plane, a train, a boat. I want to go far enough away that there's no possibility of getting home in a day or two."

"I'm just the opposite. I like the idea of my bed, my clothes, my pots and pans. There's something peaceful to me about New York City."

"New York seems like a strange place for a girl from Alabama."

"After Amanda Ruth died, Alabama never felt quite right. I saw a side of human nature I never want to see again."

"The murder, you mean."

"No. The stuff that followed. The locals were like sharks circling in for the kill. They wanted blood, humiliation. I was afraid to leave my house because everywhere I went, people stared and pointed."

I don't tell him just how bad it got—that pastors preached sermons in which Amanda Ruth, Allison, and I were perverts and villains. One of the papers even ran an editorial with the headline, "Protecting Our Kids from Lesbians and Gays," as if gays were hanging out on street corners, lying in wait to convert innocent children. It bordered on mass hysteria; I felt as if I'd been caught up in some strange Kafkaesque plot.

Then, a month later, there I was in New York City, stepping off the plane into the chaos of LaGuardia

Airport, and no one looked at me. No one bothered me. New York City welcomed me in a way my hometown never would; they didn't care who I'd loved or what I'd been accused of. For all they knew, I was just another New Yorker.

"I've only been home a few times since then, but rarely a day goes by that Amanda Ruth doesn't cross my mind. Is that strange?"

I think of Amanda Ruth, her desperate desire to see China, the picture books she kept hidden beneath her bed with artists' renderings of the Forbidden City, the mountains of Guilin along the Li River, the bright lights of Shanghai. Taped to the wall inside her closet, behind her summer dresses, she had a black-and-white photograph of the Three Gorges. In the photo, walls of stone reached toward a strip of sky, which seemed small compared to the cliffs themselves, and between these cliffs lay a narrow reach of river, flat and shadowed. In the foreground was a small dark blemish that we discovered only after the photograph had been hanging in Amanda Ruth's closet for months. We took a magnifying glass to the blemish and realized that it was a sampan. Beneath its U-shaped cover, through which a bit of evening light shone, we made out a miniature figure—a man, standing upright, steering with a long slender pole. Amanda Ruth and I looked at each other in startled silence. The sheer size of the Gorges, and of the river itself, was something we could not begin to comprehend. After a minute she put the magnifying glass back in the top drawer of her dresser and said,

"Well, it's obvious now. I have to go there."

I was amazed by her self-assurance. Going to China seemed as unlikely to me then as winning the lottery or becoming president of the United States. "How will you ever get there?"

She laughed. "I'll fly, doofus." I think that was the moment Amanda Ruth solidified her resolve to see China.

The mist has thickened. As Graham and I head back to the bus, we lose our way. We take a path that looks identical to the original one, but instead of ending at the parking lot, it leads directly into the mouth of a cave. Only later does it occur to me that the rational action at this moment would have been to turn around, retrace our steps, and try to find the bus, which was scheduled to depart in half an hour. But I am attracted by instinct to the cave at the end of the path, as if we have arrived here by fate. The opening is just high enough for me to walk through without difficulty. Graham follows, bending deeply to enter. Inside, the ceiling is high. The cave is damp and cool, the dirt floor packed hard and smooth. The entryway allows a soft infusion of light, by which I can make out an old coal stove in the corner. A small bucket gathers dust by the stove. Graham moves into the light, plunging the cave into darkness. I can hear him breathing. He steps close to me. His mouth on my neck, his hand in the hollow of my back. And then he is kneeling before me, his hands trembling as he lifts the hem of my summer skirt. I feel the fabric brushing against the tiny hairs on my thighs, his hands touching mine, bidding me to hold the skirt around my waist, leaving me exposed in the cool darkness of the cave. He slides my underwear down my thighs, my knees, lifts one foot to release me, presses my inner thigh with his hand, silently commanding me to open up for him. His mouth parts to take me in, and my legs go weak. I clutch his shoulders, try to pull away so that I can lie down, desperate to have something solid inside me, to feel the weight of him pressing down, but he holds my hips firmly, refusing to let go. My raw sounds echo in the closeness of the cave, and I am certain that, all down the mountain, people hear me. Only after my legs tense and I come, long and deep, my heat spilling into his mouth, does he release me.

I crouch and lean against the wall, all my energy gone.

He stands over me, only the outline of him visible in the strange light. I reach out, wanting to do something for him, but he catches my hands, holds them firmly. His strength surprises me. He leans down, pinning my arms against my sides, and kisses me, his lips still warm.

"The bus is waiting," he says.

"Stay here." I imagine a night alone with him, his long body laid out on the dirt floor, a coal fire glowing dimly in the corner of our cave. I feel primitive, undone, incapable of emerging into the light of day and reuniting with the other passengers, especially Dave, who will surely know just by looking at me exactly what has happened.

He pulls me up and for a moment we stand, his body pressed hard against me. Rather than experiencing the excitement of something new, a romance in the making, I feel as though the scene is dredged up from memory—not this particular cave at the end of this particular path—but a familiarity in our stance, something known in the smell of his skin, the heat of his hands, my own desperation. I try to trace the source of the memory, but it is lost, like a flicker of light at the far end of a darkened hall that disappears as you draw near.

At the bus, Elvis Paris throws his hands in the air and says, "We almost leave you!" but another couple has yet to return, and it is some time before we depart. Dave and Stacy are already on the bus, talking and laughing, sitting close together. Dave seems not to notice that I've been gone. I look at the back of his head, the little hairs growing at the base of his neck, and think, *I cheated on you*. It's the first time in our entire marriage that I have done this. It strikes me as both monumental and predestined. How easily I crossed the line, from what I was to what I am—faithful wife to adulterer. I feel wracked by guilt and stunned by pleasure, simultaneously. I want to laugh and cry. I'm certain I must look different, sound different. As Dave and Stacy chatter in front of us, talking with the ease of old friends or lovers, Graham slips his hand under my thigh. If Dave were to turn around, surely he would see the guilt on my face as clearly as he can see the needle marks on Stacy's arm. Would he be angry, sad, relieved?

Finally, the engine turns, the bus belches exhaust into the air, and we're speeding down the mountain. Dark smoke rises from shacks along the winding road, black dust mingling with the rain. Everything is gray. Graham takes off his cardigan and wraps it around my shoulders. He reaches up to move a strand of hair from my face. On his fingers, a faint familiar scent.

ELEVEN

In the winter when it rained, Amanda Ruth would sweep out the small iron stove in the boathouse, and I would take a box of matches from the old tin by the window. Amanda Ruth was deft at making fires. It was as if her touch contained enough heat to set the dampest mix of wood and paper burning.

I remember her fingers crinkling up the old newspaper, her hand disappearing into the darkness of the stove. The way she set the kindling in, piece by piece, crisscrossed one over the other—"four splinters of pine," she said, "any less and it won't light, any more and you'd be wasting." And how she stacked the wood, those pale triangles with their earthen smell, first picking off any insects that had been hiding in the wood pile, because she didn't want to burn them. She took a match from the box that lay open in my palm, struck it against the side of the tin—one hard, clean stroke—and the tip burst into flame. Then she held the match just under the edge of the paper. The edges of the kindling would glow bright orange, the heat slowly moving to the center of the stove, and then the wood itself would begin to smolder. "Done," she'd say, closing the door and sliding the vent open all the way. I always marveled at the way she trusted her own instincts, closing the door before we could see the fire come fully to life. But moments later it always did—I'd hear the great whoof of air as the world within the stove combusted, and through the small vent the logs glowed red. We'd sit underneath a blanket on the creaking wooden floor while slowly the room began to heat.

Sometimes we would take stones from the river and arrange them on top of the stove. After a while, we wrapped the hot stones in dishtowels, placed them beneath the blanket at the bottom of the mattress. The heat began at our feet and moved up our calves, our thighs, our bellies. Sometimes she held a wrapped stone in her palms, then placed her hands on my naked body, and I could feel her handprint like a tongue of fire, my skin beneath her touch ignited. Sometimes she slipped a hot finger inside me, and the presence of her there was like a revelation I couldn't name—all my night-mares and dreams combined in one explosive moment: her finger, my fear, the smell of creosote, the rain beating on the tin roof, the memory of the dark river outside the boathouse, the dampness of the air, the sweat that formed in the dip of her collarbone as I began to shudder.

Later, when the room was warm and the fire had died out, we'd pierce jumbo marshmallows with unfurled metal coat-hangers. She taught me how to turn the marshmallow slowly, several inches from the glowing coals. The marshmallows burned our fingers. They were crunchy and sweet, the melted middle coating our burnt tongues white. I still remember the outline of her face lit by the open stove, her small straight nose, the wild mess of her hair in the firelight.

Her father was always trying to get her to comb it, but I could imagine nothing lovelier than Amanda Ruth's hair, the softness of it in my fingers, the scent of it newly washed, still damp, strands of it clinging to her face.

It wasn't just the fire. There were so many things she could do that I could not. She would take any odd mix of vegetables from the garden, a small basketful that seemed insufficient to feed us, and turn it into a feast, the deep fragrance of which filled the house for hours. From a few pods of okra, some lettuce leaves, an ear of corn, and a carrot she created dishes alive with color.

She could turn any old rag into a costume. A fifty-cent skirt from the D.A.R. thrift store, a pair of cloth sandals from K-Mart, a swath of red velvet from Hancock Fabrics: in her hands these disparate and discarded things became an elaborate outfit—too original for our town, where the girls all wore khaki skirts and alligator belts, polo shirts and Topsiders. "Nice outfit," they'd say, tittering, but she didn't care. Riding the bus to school over the two-lane road that wound through endless Mobile subdivisions, she imagined herself a daughter of China, held high in a golden chair on the shoulders of slick strong men up a misty mountain road. While the rest of us tried to fit in, to disappear into the unruly crowd and survive as one of its members, she learned to take pride in the difference that had been pointed out to her from earliest childhood—by her mother's family, who called Amanda Ruth "mixed," by the annual school report that identified her as

"Oriental," by the redneck boys who wouldn't think of dating "that Chinese girl."

I wonder sometimes if she can hear me. In Sunday School they used to tell us that the dead would always be with us, that if we loved them well enough in life their spirits would remain close by. But it is not a presence that I feel these fourteen years since her death— just a long and silent absence. Day after day, when I am alone, I find myself talking to her, not just in my mind but aloud, the way lunatics do on the streets of New York City, as if, in the barren air beside them, they can see the face of someone they once knew. They pause and laugh and nod their heads, as if they fancy themselves one half of a lively conversation. I envy them this illusion, the sound of other voices filling up the awful silence. I talk and talk, often embarrassed by the sound of my own voice in an empty room, or on the deck of this ridiculous ship, but she does not respond. Not once has she responded. Only in my dreams does she speak to me, and in that blurry space between consciousness and sleep, I try hard to stay inside the dream, just to keep her with me. But then I wake, and I know that I have conjured her, that any words she spoke were merely words of my own invention. Again and again I wake in the cool sweet dark to find her, once again, gone.

TWELVE

In the dusky light the hills are a deep, luxurious green. The river itself is amber, thick with muck. Garbage rushes past: plastic shoes, paper cups and tin cans, beer bottles, a wicker basket, a pair of pants. Another body bobs down the river—the fourth I've seen—this one newly dead, the pretty face of a young girl emerging from a tangle of dark hair, a silver necklace glinting on her pale neck. A lone figure walks a riverside path, balancing a long pole on his shoulder. Both ends of the pole are heavy with baskets. Factory furnaces glow on distant hillsides. A pagoda shimmers in the rain, several of its tiles missing. Everywhere, these pagodas—remnants of China's deeply aesthetic past, before industry was king.

"Famous Wind Moving Pagoda of Anqing," The Voice says. "It is king of all pagodas." I feel sometimes as though The Voice is wired to my brain, as if she knows what I'm thinking.

I turn to Graham. "Why is this one king?"

"Legend has it that the autumn moon festival brings pagodas here from all over the world to pay homage. It's called Wind Moving Pagoda because it sometimes sways with the breeze."

At the moment, the air is calm and the pagoda is perfectly still.

The door from the lounge opens and slams shut.

Loud footsteps approach. A big man in a wide white hat and cowboy boots appears at the rail several yards away. Arms crossed over his chest, he surveys the riverbank. His wife sidles up to him. She wears a pink nylon jogging suit with gold trim, lots of gold bracelets and necklaces, big turquoise rings, shockingly white leather Nikes, tennis socks with little pink pompoms dangling from her ankles. The couple doesn't seem to notice us.

"What a shame," the man booms. His accent is unmistakable, the long deep drawl of Texas. "Just look at those hills over there. They could be gorgeous, no kidding, this place could be top notch. If I could have a whack at it, do you know what I'd do? I'd tear down all those factories and shacks and ragtag apartment buildings. And then I'd put up a brand spanking new resort—the works—palatial rooms, marble floors, claw foot tubs, a state-of-the art gymnasium. Hell, I might even level a mountain and add a golf course."

"Sounds like paradise," his wife says.

"And I'd hire these pretty little Chinese girls, and I'd make them wear those long silk dresses with the slits up to here, and they'd wait on you hand and foot. They'd fetch your slippers, do your laundry, give you a massage. They'd wear red lipstick, and fingernails out to here painted with white dragons. I'd charge an arm and a leg, and people would be lining up to pay for it. I'd put together a package deal—air fare to China, a cruise up the Yangtze, one week in the Oriental Palace."

His wife corrects him gently. "You can't say

Oriental anymore, hon. Let's call it the Yangtze Jewel."

"Yeah, the Yangtze Jewel. And it'd be like you're in China, only better—because you've got all the comforts of home. We'd serve steak and potatoes, hamburgers and hash browns. It'd mean jobs for all these poor folks you see washing laundry in the river and selling wrinkled little vegetables and driving rickshaws. What a mess they've made of this place."

"Indeed," his wife says. She turns to me and Graham with a slightly surprised look, as if she's just realized she and her husband aren't alone on deck. "I tell you, the air's so filthy I can't even breathe. It ought to be illegal, what they're doing to this river."

Graham frowns in their direction.

The man hitches his pants over his enormous belly and says, "Well," as if it's the last word, the end of the matter. Then, as quickly as they came, they are gone. They retreat back into the glass walls of the lounge, a too-flowery perfume and the stench of cigarette smoke trailing after.

Our ship trundles along, its big engine humming, churning up silt and debris. Sampans and junks unlucky enough to be caught in our wake bob up and down like corks on the choppy waves. I think of Demopolis River and how it used to flow through Greenbrook and out into the Gulf, rich with fish and growing things. A couple of years ago, when I went home to Mobile to see my family, I took a drive out to Greenbrook. An entire section of the town along the river had been demolished. Where Amanda Ruth's house used to stand, there was a huge shopping complex: Wal-Mart, Home Depot, Pottery Barn, Chili's, PetSmart, Payless Shoes. The river itself had been diverted. I had a lunch of green beans, macaroni and cheese, and banana pudding at a diner Amanda Ruth and I used to frequent, a diner fortunate enough not to lie in the path of destruction.

"What happened?" I asked Miss Betsy, the woman who'd run the place as long as I could remember. She had dyed black hair, enormous breasts, and crow's feet made deeper by layers of dark foundation. There was a rumor that she'd once had an affair with Lyndon B. Johnson. She was one of those women who could have been forty or sixty-five; it was impossible to tell.

She refilled my coffee and looked out the window. "Nobody here wanted the project. Most of the property along the river belonged to a man named Grady Watson, and everybody leased from him. He lived on the river his whole life, and loved it just as much as he loved his wife and kids. But when Grady died, another developer came calling, and Grady's kids saw dollar signs."

Two miles of Demopolis River now run through a man-made concrete canal that forms the back border of the shopping mall and an adjacent golf course. The developer put in a few benches and a stand of azalea bushes, so the shoppers who purchase hamburgers and frozen yogurt cones and stuffed potatoes from the food court can watch the river rippling past. The complex is called River Eden Shopping Center, and, perhaps in the spirit of this misnomer, the developer allowed three giant old oaks that stood in the way of the parking lot to remain. Now the oaks are stapled with banners and flyers, and when something happens to inflame the public spirit—a missing girl or a national disaster—the oaks are adorned with big yellow ribbons. In the last ten years, Greenbrook has gone from a quaint town of 4,000 to a poorly planned suburban mess of 35,000. Big green swaths of land that used to hold a single home or cabin are now dotted with dozens of identical houses, placed primly on clear-cut cul-de-sacs with names like Oak Branch Court and Dogwood Grove.

At night, when the River Eden Shopping Center is closed, kids go down to the edge of the canal to smoke pot and drink beer and listen to music and have sex. Their used condoms mingle with beer cans and Cracker Jack boxes. The adults in town complain that kids have no respect for Greenbrook, but it is no wonder. Living in Greenbrook once meant living on the river. To be from Greenbrook was to know a certain smell of moss-hung trees after the rain, the specific sound of frogs on summer nights, the particular feel of the mud at the bottom of *your* river, Demopolis River, which was different from the algae-slicked bottom of Dog River or the crab-scuttled silt around Petite Bois Island or the silky white sand of Gulf Shores. To be from Greenbrook, in those days, was to be from a particular place.

THIRTEEN

Each day with the break in the rain, I look up and see that the sky has gone soft—a low, plush layer of silver-white, furrowed like plowed snow. Sometimes the clouds thin, and for a moment the sun is visible, a surprising blaze of light high above the gloom of the river. More often, though, the ship is shrouded in mist, so that we cannot see more than a few yards in front of us. Drifting along the river in the fog, no land or ships in sight, it seems we could be anywhere, that China is only a distant dream.

Early in the morning on the ninth day of the cruise, The Voice comes over the loud speaker. "We have encountered small problem. Please come to Yangtze Room." By the time Dave and I arrive, the room is already crowded with panicked tourists. The guides are waving their flags, shouting orders, trying to run damage control. Jane Madonna, the entertainment director, stands at the center of the dance floor, her usually perfect hair uncombed, her uniform slightly askew. She speaks into a megaphone. "When everyone sit down we begin."

After about 15 minutes of chaos, Elvis Paris takes over. "We have small problem with boat," Elvis says. "We maybe not have dinner tonight in Wuhan." The disco ball revolves slowly above his head, showering him with triangular specks of colored light.

Gradually, after much hemming and hawing on the part of the crew, we learn that there is a problem with the engine. We have dropped anchor to keep the current from dragging us back downstream. A voice in the crowd says gruffly, "Just how long are we gonna be stuck here?"

"Maybe one day, maybe two, maybe three," Elvis says. "No worry! We play games! Please sign up for tournament." The guides pass around clipboards and pens. They move through the crowd, urging us to sign up for badminton, table tennis, backgammon, and shuffleboard. They have even organized a tournament for video strip mahjong. Dave and I found the mahjong game our first night on board. Each time you win a game, the animated woman on the video screen takes off an item of clothing. We got her down to her bra and panties before our losing streak set in.

Amid a noticeable air of discontent, the crowd slowly disperses. Dave stretches, yawns. "I'm off for a nap," he says. At the back of the room I find Graham sitting in a chair that's too small for him, resting his elbow on a metal table.

He sees me, smiles. "So. We're stranded."

"Can't say I'm disappointed."

"Why's that?"

I pull a chair up next to him, take a deck of airline cards out of my purse, shuffle, deal seven cards to each of us, place the deck face-down on the middle of the table. He gathers his cards, surveys them. "Well?"

"It buys me more time with you."

"Good answer." He concentrates on arranging his cards. "What are we playing?"

"Go Fish."

An hour later, wandering the hallways, we come upon a door with a hand-lettered sign that says *No Entry*. Graham tries the knob anyway and it opens. Chairs are stacked four deep around the room, and the bar is covered with dust. The ship is full of such rooms, which seem to have been abandoned for no reason. Sometimes it feels as if we're traveling on a ghost ship, as if the spirits of other, better cruises, of lavish parties and elegant dinners, lurk mockingly in dark corners. We slide into a vinyl booth in the corner. A dish of stale ginger candy gathers grime on the table.

"Sorry I'm not much fun to be with today," Graham says. "I wish someone would just shoot me full of morphine."

"What hurts?"

"My hands, my feet, my back, my joints."

The lights are off in the windowless room, and the big brass clock on the wall registers an eternal 2:35. As the afternoon slides past, we lose all sense of time. Graham is in so much pain that his eyes begin to water. "I hate being this way," he says. I try to comfort him, brush his hair with my fingers. I feel used up, sick with lack of sleep and my inability to help him.

"It's so hot," he says.

I fetch ice from the dispenser in the hallway, a bucket of small cubes clinking together in the plastic liner. I hold it to his forehead, his collarbone, the soft skin of his inner elbow. "I wish I could do something."

"Just talk to me."

"About what?"

"Tell me about your time in the hospital, after the accident with the horse. What do you remember?"

"They were always bringing me ice cream and Jello. The ice cream tasted grainy and sweet. The nurses smelled like the rubber of their orthopedic shoes, and the washed metal of the trays they used to carry instruments and needles. Every couple of hours a woman with orange hair came to check my catheter. When it was time to change my sheets it took four of them to roll me. They lifted me on a sheet, and I was suspended in air above the bed. *Leave It to Beaver* played on the television. A boy in a wheelchair passed back and forth in the hallway, stopping over and over again at my door. He had an enormous forehead and no jaw on the right side of his face. He wore the plastic rings that the Candy Stripers brought around in Tupperware boxes, spiders and smiley faces."

"How long were you there?"

"Two months, maybe? Three? It's all very blurry."

What I remember most from that time is strange hands hovering over me all the time, orderlies and nurses moving my body from one surface to another, the chill of the x-ray table, the hum of the machine. I thought all my bones were being pulled apart.

"Did you have visitors?"

"My family was there. And sometimes Amanda Ruth came to see me. Once she brought me a Rubik's cube, another time a Lite Brite. For her birthday she'd gotten a rock tumbling kit, so she brought me polished stones."

Graham talks of his time in hospitals, months of misdiagnosis. "The symptoms are similar to other diseases so it's a tricky one to diagnose. ALS is only determined by process of elimination. Once they had decided it might be ALS, they conducted electomyography tests, tests to determine nerve conduction velocity, blood and urine studies including high-resolution serum protein electrophoresis, thyroid and parathyroid hormone levels, 24-hour urine collection for heavy metals, spinal tap and x-rays, MRI."

"How do you remember all that?"

"I wrote it down. I studied it. I wanted to know what they were doing to me. On the Internet I found others with ALS. I started e-mailing with them." He picks a piece of lint off his sleeve. "They'd write every day, then once a week, once a month, and pretty soon not at all."

In the afternoon, his pain subsides. We don parkas and go up on deck. The rain rocks the ship. Were we to lift anchor we would be dragged downstream. The world turns gray, we can see only a few inches in front of us. Every now and then a bolt of lightning slices through the thick air.

"Look," says Graham, awed. "You can see the exact spot where it touches."

I too believe that I see this, that I can know the lightning as surely as I know a drop of rain that splatters on my outstretched hand. All my senses seem heightened. Even the heat of the lightning is known to me, the sudden death of the tree it touches, the burning odor of the bark, the taste of everything: charred root, spent electricity, rain.

Graham collects a pool of rain in his palm, holds it out to me. "Drink." I dip my tongue into the cool, still water in his palm. I am Eve, reversed. From this man I would accept water, a poisoned apple, the fruit of the tree of knowledge of good and evil.

Drink, and you shall never thirst, said Amanda Ruth's preacher at the church in Greenbrook. Sometimes she took me there. Her mother wore a yellow robe and was placed front and center in the choir. Her father sat alone with his hands folded in his lap, the only non-white in a congregation of two hundred. For the Lord's Supper, held four times a year, the deacons passed out tiny pewter cups, like thimbles, filled with grape juice, pale oyster crackers with no taste that left a residue of flour on our fingers. During the Lord's Supper I could hear the cups rattling in the trays—hundreds of tiny cups, a dozen big silver trays, the pad of the deacons' shoes on the thick red carpet. After the drinking of the blood of Christ, the deacons collected the cups, dropped them into small round slots in the trays. A man in a shiny brown suit took Mr. Lee's cup and placed it upside down; in this way it was marked for special cleaning, perhaps disposal. Mr. Lee pretended not to notice.

I lay my head against Graham's chest. I can't stop

thinking about our time in the cave. Now, on board this ship, surrounded by chrome and plastic and other passengers, subject to the whims of the crew and the maddening sound of The Voice, it is almost as if I imagined the cobblestone path, the cave, Graham's hands pressing against my thighs.

"Thirty-two," he says. "You're a child. Do you know this is the first time I've been with a younger woman?"

I can smell the fiber of his shirt, damp from these days of rain. My own clothes are permanently wrinkled, all the crispness gone out of them; they hang limply from the wooden hangers in our tiny closet. Housekeeping cleans the cabins thoroughly every morning, but still the dampness holds on, mold grows in the crevices, strange smells attach themselves to our summer fabrics.

"And do you think I'm good for you?"

He smiles. "Too early to tell."

In the evening I go to the cabin and find Dave sprawled on top of the covers, snoring. "Dave?" I say. He doesn't wake. I touch him on the shoulder. "Dave?"

"Hmm?" He opens his eyes for a moment, closes them again.

"Time for dinner."

"Do you mind eating without me? I'm beat." He rolls over and is instantly asleep again. I never cease to be amazed by his ability to sleep, to go into a deep and dreamless hibernation no matter the time of day—as if his body is programmed to store up sleep whenever possible, imbuing him with a superhuman supply of energy, enabling him to spring into immediate action whenever his services are needed.

In the dining room I join Graham and Stacy for a dinner of bean curd, salted pork, and cabbage—the first Chinese food we've had on the ship, our best meal so far. Stacy keeps tapping her water glass with a fingernail, glancing toward the door. "Where's Dave?" she asks finally.

"Asleep."

"It's way too early for bed."

"He sleeps a lot."

"Maybe he has that condition—what's it called—chronic fatigue."

"He's just resting up for the next big emergency."

She barely touches her food and is quiet during the entire meal.

"Everything okay?"

"I just thought he'd be joining us." She excuses herself before dessert.

When she's gone, Graham relaxes, reaches across the table to touch my arm. "It's not easy. Keeping up this charade, trying to act like we're just friends."

"What are we, exactly?"

He laughs. "Scoundrels, I suppose."

Matt Dillon brings us coffee and cheesecake and clean forks, clears Stacy's place. His movements are small and precise, his carriage so graceful that he seems to come from another century.

"Not that Stacy would have noticed," Graham

adds. "Looks like she has something else on her mind."

"True." I picture Stacy in the hallway, knocking on our cabin door. I imagine Dave, groggy from sleep, getting out of bed, opening the door in his underwear. Seeing her there, he looks down the hallway in both directions, pauses for a moment, considering. "Come in," he says. She does.

Should I follow her? Catch them in the act? Maybe I'm making this whole thing up. Maybe it's true what Dave says—he just wants to help her. In any case, I don't go. There are other factors to consider. The other factor is sitting right here, scraping the last bit of cheesecake off his plate.

"Hey," he says.

"Hmmm?"

"Did I lose you?"

"I'm right here."

After dinner, Graham and I return to our empty bar, where he reads me a passage from the collected letters of Vincent Van Gogh. The excerpt is from a letter Vincent wrote to his brother in 1888: *I am beginning to consider madness as a disease like any other…it came very slowly and will go slowly too, supposing it does go, of course.*

"I'd give anything to trade my ALS for an illness like that," Graham says.

"Madness? Surely not."

"Madness, alcoholism, heart disease—anything that comes with the possibility of recovery."

"But it never got better for Van Gogh."

"Even the illusion of a cure is better than the certainty that there is none," Graham argues.

"At least you have your sanity."

"ALS leaves its victims with too much sanity. Even once you're totally paralyzed, your mind keeps running along perfectly." He closes the book, stares at the cover, runs his fingers over the self-portrait of Van Gogh's haunted face. "If you had to have a degenerative illness, which one would you choose?"

"I can't answer that."

"Try."

"Why?"

Graham runs his hands through his hair, toys with the ginger candies, looks up at me. "Every healthy person in the world should have to experience the certainty of slow death for one day at least."

I imagine Graham stretched out on a bed, reduced to half his normal weight, unable to lift a hand to scratch his face, unable to turn his head, tubes running in and out of him, nurses padding around in soft shoes, talking over him in low professional voices. It's difficult to reconcile this vision with the Graham I know.

"I'm sorry," I say. "I just remembered something I need to do." I get up and walk away so he won't see me crying.

"Wait," he says, but I keep walking. The last thing he would want from me is pity.

At times like this I wish I could be more like Dave. He would know exactly what to do in this situation. He wouldn't cry. He wouldn't have to hide his emotions, because he wouldn't have any. "I see," he would say. "Tell me, what are your symptoms? Does this hurt?"

I wander the ship and find myself standing outside our cabin, ear pressed to the door, afraid of what I might hear. Nothing. I turn the knob, tiptoe into the room. In the darkness, I listen for the sound of Dave's snoring, try to make out a shape on the bed. But there is no sound, no shape. I flip on the light. The bed is made, the cabin empty. I open the closet, stare at the row of Dave's shirts, hanging neatly on wooden hangers. Blue, brown, rust, the pale yellow one I bought him last Christmas. I wonder why he brought it, try to read something into that small act—does he mean it to be a sign? Is he trying to compromise? Is he telling me that this is a gift he wears? I imagine him in his apartment at 81st and York, dressing in the evening to go out. From dozens of shirts, he chooses this one. He buttons it slowly, remembering me.

I run my fingers over the cotton, lean into the closet, trying to breathe him in—his smell, something of his presence. But his clothes don't smell like him. They smell like the river. And then I notice a small white thing dangling from the cuff of the yellow shirt—the price tag. He has never worn it.

I lie on the bed, stare up at the ceiling, waiting. For what, I'm not sure. I feel divided, unfocused. I want to stop loving Dave. Why is it so impossible to do so? And I want to give myself, completely, to Graham, whose need for me is clear. Dave looks at me and sees nothing, or perhaps he sees the past. Graham looks at me and sees what—hope? Love? His brief future? Perhaps in some way, I'm more like Dave than I've ever wanted to admit; maybe some small part of me aches to play the savior.

There's something I need to tell my husband, but I'm not sure what it is. *I'll give you half an hour*, I think. *If you're not back in half an hour...* What? What is my ultimatum? And shouldn't someone who gives an ultimatum have something to bargain with? I watch the clock. The minutes click off in red. 9:31... 9:37... 9:45... 9:59. "One more minute," I say aloud. I count the seconds, one Mississippi, two Mississippi, three Mississippi. No steps in the hallway. No rattling of the doorknob.

"Okay," I say at 10:00, rising from the bed. I smooth my dress, slip on a pair of sandals, and check the mirror, grateful for the cheap quality of the glass, the vagueness of the reflection. A little powder, a little blush. I lock the door behind me, feeling jittery, like a teenager on her way to the prom. I go out looking. It's not Dave I'm looking for.

I search the ship, all the places where Graham and I go together, but cannot find him. I begin to panic, counting down the days we have left together, breaking the days into hours, hours into minutes, imagining my life returning to normal, a blank state of being at my apartment on 85th Street. *My* apartment, no longer *ours*, the side of the closet that used to hold Dave's clothes now empty, the top two drawers of the dresser gaping like hungry mouths. I knock on Graham's door, softly at first, then harder. No answer. Minutes later I find myself pounding on the door, saying too loudly, "Graham, are you in there?" An elderly couple passing in the hall stops and stares. The woman says, "Are you okay, sweetheart?" Only then do I realize that my face is streaked with tears.

It is Graham who finds me sitting alone in the lounge half an hour later. "I've been waiting for you," I say.

The rain continues. Graham and I go to the racquetball court, thinking there will be no one there this late. We walk past the desk and are just about to enter the court when a voice calls out behind us. "Wait! You must check in!" We go to the desk, where a sleepy attendant shoves a clipboard toward us. "You must sign here before you play." His nametag says Bill Clinton.

"It's almost midnight," Graham says. "We don't want to play racquetball."

Bill Clinton looks suspiciously at Graham. "No happy happy in recreational facility. Happy happy is against regulation."

"We're not here for happy happy," Graham says. "We just want to talk."

Bill Clinton taps the clipboard with the pen. "You want to use court, you must play. Do you have identification?"

"Okay," Graham says, writing down his name and room number and sliding his driver's license across the counter.

Bill Clinton scrutinizes the license for a couple of minutes, then says, "In one second I get two racquets, then you play racquetball." He takes a packet of tobacco out of his pocket and proceeds to roll a cigarette very slowly. He smokes it while thumbing through a magazine. The magazine is full of photographs of women in pink bikinis striking coy poses. Finally, when his cigarette has burned down to a nub, he puts the magazine down, disappears into a back room, and reappears with two racquets. "You must finish game by 12:30. At 12:30 lights go off."

Once inside, we sit in the middle of the court and lay the racquets on the floor beside us. We spend a good deal of our half hour making jokes at the expense of the grouchy attendant. We laugh so hard our eyes water. I feel like I did when I was a kid and I'd go to lock-ins at Amanda Ruth's church. We'd stay up all night playing board games and drinking Coke, and by morning we'd all be sprawled on the floor of the fellowship hall, giddy with exhaustion. "Hey," a voice calls from the observation deck. "You can only stay if you play." The attendant's words are slurred, and he's unsteady on his feet.

"Sure, mate," Graham calls, slipping into his Aussie charm. He picks up his racquet, stands, and slams the ball against the wall. I return it. We continue in this manner, miraculously keeping the ball in play, until Bill Clinton leaves. We sit down again.

Graham takes the Van Gogh book out of his satchel. "Listen," he says, opening the book to a page he has marked with a scrap of newspaper: "*About my malady I can do nothing.* That's the beauty. I *can* do something."

I feel my heart lifting. "There's some new cure? Some alternative medicine?" I have an absurd vision of Graham and me together in New York City, eating green curry chicken at Rain, watching a Woody Allen movie at Lincoln Plaza.

"No. I'm finished with medicine. What I mean is that I can take care of it myself before I'm too far into this thing."

"You don't mean—"

"Imagine—to choose one's own time and place of death. To make a conscious decision to leave this earth while you're still intact, still functioning."

Panic rises in my chest. "You don't seem like the kind of person to just give up."

"It's not living when you can't walk, you can't make love. You can't write letters or use a fork or tie your own shoes."

I stand up and toss the ball in the air, raise my racquet to meet it. "Let's go another round," I say, trying to change the subject.

I reach for the ball on its return but miss. Graham tugs at my hand. "Eventually, carbon dioxide builds up in the blood. You suffocate in your sleep."

Suddenly, the lights shut off, and the court goes black as midnight. I drop my racquet on the floor and sit down beside him. "I'm so sorry," I say, knowing that he needs something from me, and I have nothing to offer him.

"Me too."

Even in this echoing room, surrounded by the smell of mold and sweat and tennis shoes, I want him. I unbutton my shirt, place his hand on my breast. He relaxes, moves closer, and then he is undressing me and I am undressing him, our hands moving quickly over buttons and zippers. He pulls me down on top of him. I keep my eyes open and wish for light, so as to clearly see him. Dave's face intervenes—his gray eyes, his broad mouth—as much as I try to chase the image of him away, he watches me, sees all.

Graham enters so slowly, moves as if I am a fragile thing he fears breaking, strokes my body with a quiet intensity. I grip his waist with my legs, feel my body opening up as he slides inside. He holds my breasts in his hands, sits up to lick my nipples, moves his hands down my sides. Expertly he turns me over so that my back is to the cool hard floor. He lifts me by the small of my back, sinks deeper into me, moans and shudders. I expect it to be somehow different this time—an experience entirely new, some sensation I've never felt—but as it is with Dave, so it is with Graham: pain and pleasure, his need stabbing to the center of me, the physical act tied inextricably to something greater that starts somewhere in the brain and slides down to the heart. I try to keep quiet, but it is impossible. My sounds are magnified in the echoing room.

We lie still. His weight bears down on me so that it's difficult to breathe. Why is it that loving a man always seems to end this way—sublime suffocation, my lungs compressed and emptied—with me feeling somehow less substantial than I did before it began?

Minutes later we separate. "Are you cold?"

Graham asks.

"A little." He lays his jacket over me. It is made of worn brown leather with satin lining. I imagine living inside this jacket, inside this room, keeping Graham alive with the sheer strength of my desire.

"How long's it been?" he asks.

"About eight months. You?"

"Two years, give or take."

"I guess it was time."

He laughs. "Long past."

We doze off to a fitful sleep. I wake with my dress raised, Graham's hand pressing my legs open. His tongue slides over me, then inside, as his hands cradle my hips. The cool wetness of his tongue, the dark width of the room, the faint damp smell of the river. "I want you to come," he says. He kisses my inner thigh, pushes a finger inside me, crooking it upward, pressing into that white-hot center. I feel my hips lifting, the pressure building in the place where his finger rests. The pressure breaks, I cry out, feel the light rushing out of me.

He lies down beside me, and I rest my head on his chest. After a while I ask, "How will I know when it happens?"

"When what happens?"

I don't answer, because I know he understands. I imagine him in some dusty motel room in Australia, a paid nurse at his side, someone who knows how to be discreet, checking in under a made-up name. A vial of medicine. A needle. The nurse's quick retreat in the middle of the night, out a back door and into a waiting taxi. Some Jack Kevorkian disciple, with a firm belief in the integrity of her mission. I imagine her blonde and slim, pretty, young, her eyes misting as she drives the needle in. Graham looking up at her, mistaking her in the final confused moments for an angel, or a devil, depending.

There's a long silence. I can feel the ship breathing, the depth of the river like a great coffin beneath us. Finally, he clears his throat, moves his head an inch nearer to mine, so that I can feel his breath on my face when he speaks. "You'll know."

At dawn, passing by the desk, we find Bill Clinton snoring, his head cradled in his arms, a full ashtray at his elbow; he makes sleeping look so easy. Several empty bottles of Baiji Beer are scattered across the desk. The room smells of mildew, old smoke, and something else, familiar and disturbing. Walking alone through the hallway toward our cabin, I realize that the familiar smell has not left, that indeed it is our own, the memory of sex clinging to my damp skin.

FOURTEEN

One summer, about a year after Dave and I were married, my parents spent a week with us in New York City. On the last day of their trip, I took them to the Empire State Building, where I was working at the time. I was the receptionist for a children's clothing company that had an office on the seventy-second floor. My parents seemed pleased upon realizing that one of the elevator men knew my name. They were even more impressed when I showed an identification card and was allowed to skip to the front of the long line of tourists waiting to go up to the observatory.

On the viewing platform at the 86th floor, my parents held onto the latticework of bars and gazed out at the city. They had never understood my love of Manhattan, had never been able to figure out why I would choose to live there. Now, I wanted them to see New York as I saw it: the vast matrix of buildings stretching out below us, their rooftops a dizzying pattern of squares and rectangles that reflected the morning sun; the gleaming silver spire of the Chrysler Building; the mammoth towers of the World Trade Center; the constant flow of yellow taxis creeping along the organized network of streets below. Most of all, I wanted them to be impressed by the fact that I navigated this city daily.

My father took a picture of me and my mother,

standing arm in arm, the brown Hudson sliding past in the background. Then I took a picture of them together, with my father standing behind my mother, his arms around her shoulders, both of them smiling. The photo, I knew, would be identical to any number of other photos I'd taken of them on family vacations over the years; the only difference would be location.

Before leaving, we each slid a penny into a big steel machine, pulled the lever, and retrieved a flat copper oval imprinted with the image of the Empire State Building. On the way down, we shared the elevator with a family from Missoula, Montana. "Where do you live?" the woman asked.

Both of my parents spoke at the same time. "Mobile, Alabama," my mother said, while my father blurted, "Austin."

"Austin's nice," the woman said. I just stood there in confusion. Both of my parents looked at me, waiting for the fact to register. The woman told a long story about how she'd once been to Austin to see a Mac Davis concert. Meanwhile, I let the news settle. My father was no longer living with my mother. A guilty grin spread across my father's face, and then he began to giggle. He looked down at the floor and tried to stop himself, but he couldn't.

"What's so funny?" the woman's husband said. "Did I miss something?"

My dad started turning red. He put his hand over his mouth and faced the corner, trying to stifle that odd, inappropriate sound. But he couldn't, no more than he could years before when we'd received the news that his sister had cancer. He just kept laughing, while my mother retreated quietly into a corner. She wouldn't meet my eyes. The woman put both arms protectively around her two young sons, who were staring at my dad like he was a real live lunatic. When the doors finally opened on the ground level, the couple from Missoula quickly ushered the boys out of the elevator.

By now my dad was laughing so hard he couldn't catch his breath. The three of us stepped out of the elevator, into a crowd of men and women in suits. Once we were outside, my mother clutched her purse to her side and pretended nothing had happened. My father's laughter subsided. His face was red. He checked his watch and put his hands in his pockets. We began walking.

"Well?" I said.

"We were going to tell you," my mother said.

"When?"

"Soon."

"So is this a divorce?"

"No," my dad said, catching his breath. "Just a brief separation."

"You're living in different states. That sounds serious."

"We're just trying it out," he said. He stopped at a vendor's cart and bought three pretzels. We ate them without speaking, then pushed through the crowd and descended into the subway station.

While my father bought subway tokens, I asked my

mother, "What about last night?" The night before, the two of them had slept on an air mattress in the living room of my apartment. I had heard them having sex, the telltale whistling of air escaping through the tiny hole in the mattress.

She twisted the pendant on her necklace, bit her lip. "An accident," she said. "A moment of weakness."

Years before, after a brief episode between my father and a woman who managed a pet store, my mother had said, "You may stay together after something like that, but you never entirely recover." Over the years, she had become more and more bitter, while my father had grown more and more silent; so when I learned of their separation, I wasn't really surprised.

As we waited for the N train, no one spoke. I did feel sad, but more than that I felt, somehow, vindicated. For the first time in my life, I believed that I understood something that my parents didn't. Marriage seemed to me then a simple thing, and I couldn't help but think of my parents as somehow flawed. I made a mental list of the mistakes they'd made, quite certain that I wouldn't make the same ones myself.

Now, walking alone through the empty hallway, feeling somewhat bruised from my night with Graham on the racquetball floor, I have an urge to call my parents and apologize for being so smug, for feeling that marriage was a challenge I could easily meet. I imagine my mother laughing and quoting a line from a country song, something about how even good love goes bad.

FIFTEEN

I vow to tell Dave everything, and wonder if it will even faze him. When I arrive, the cabin is empty, the bed unmade. I shower and dress, rehearsing my confession. In the tiny bathroom mirror I see a woman I hardly recognize—the circles under my eyes growing darker from so many nights without real sleep, my hair brittle from the ship's hard water, my skin sallow from exposure to the pollution of Chinese cities.

In the dining room, I approach Dave at the fruit bar, where he's preparing two plates. "Hungry?"

"One's for Stacy. She's not feeling well. I thought I'd do the gentlemanly thing." He is freshly showered, his thick hair still wet, his skin glowing. He looks the picture of good health. He spears two juicy pieces of watermelon. They slide off the fork onto Stacy's waiting plate. He doesn't even ask where I was last night. For all he knows, I came to bed late and got up early, and he slept through it all.

Back at the table, Stacy is waiting. She looks tired but content. "Good morning," she says to me.

"You okay?"

"A little under the weather, but Dave's taking good care of me."

Dave blushes, sets the plate in front of her. She goes through her water quickly. Then, her own glass empty, she drinks from Dave's. He gives her a look, and she sets the glass down and smiles at me. "Sorry. I'm so thirsty I could drink straight from the river."

Dave eats two pieces of toast and reads the headlines of *The China Daily*. There's a tiny bruise on his neck, just below his earlobe. His lower lip is slightly swollen.

He catches me staring. "Something wrong?"

"No." I lean over and touch the sore on his lip. "Did you hurt yourself?" There is something startlingly natural about this gesture, some mutual communion that feels right despite everything. As Dave leans into my touch, I feel a wave of tenderness welling up in me, and jealousy, and guilt.

"I have to go," Stacy says. She looks as if she's about to cry. When she stands to leave, Dave stands too, as if to follow her, then sits back down. Stacy glances back at us once before leaving the room.

"I'm sorry," Dave says, staring down at his plate. In a flash I understand. Almost overnight, infidelity has become an unspoken condition of our crumbling marriage. "This isn't what I planned."

I stir cream and sugar into my coffee. "I know."

"You have every right to be angry."

I spread raspberry jam on a hard white roll. "No. I don't."

"Of course you do."

"Not really."

"What do you mean?"

"This business with Graham."

He swallows. "So that wasn't my imagination."

"No."

He rubs his hands back and forth across the red satin tablecloth. The cloth is speckled with oil stains. "I guess this means we're even."

"I suppose."

"Then why do I feel jealous?"

"Why do I?"

He lays his hands palm up on the table, clenches them into fists, releases. "Did you sleep with him?"

I don't say anything.

"You slept with him." He blinks as if waking.

I fiddle with the salt shaker. "You're the one who left."

He presses his thumb into the tongs of his fork. I almost reach over and take the fork away, thinking of his beautiful hands, but I catch myself; it's no longer my right. "Look at your lip, your neck. She drank out of your water glass, right in front of me. Do you think I'm blind?"

He sighs, looks away. "I'm not saying I'm one hundred percent innocent. I'm not saying I haven't made mistakes." The couple at the next table turns to stare. The woman is wearing big green earrings shaped like turtles.

I struggle to keep my voice down. "It's been six months since you touched me, even longer since we made love." I take a sip of my coffee, just for something to do. It's barely warm. The cream has gone bad; tiny white specks float to the surface.

"Sounds like you've been keeping a tally of my

shortcomings." He releases his fork. The tip of his thumb has little red dents in it. Once, when we were first married, I painted his fingernails while he was sleeping. In the morning, he stared for several minutes at the strange red tips of his hands, mesmerized. He said he'd like to trade places with me, for just one day, so he could know what it was like to be a woman. What happened to that ease between us, that raw, unashamed honesty?

"When you moved out, I expected you'd at least call every now and then." I'm embarrassed by the bitterness that creeps into my voice.

His jaw clenches, activating a faint dimple just below his left cheekbone. I'd forgotten about that dimple. Strange to think that I could forget the smallest detail of a face I've been looking at for twelve years straight. "You care about this guy?"

I nod.

"He's old for you."

"How old is Stacy?"

"Twenty-five." He studies my face, objectively it seems, as if he is looking at a stranger. "How did this happen?"

"I've been trying to figure that out myself. Maybe it started with the woman in Chelsea."

"I never slept with her."

"You didn't have to."

He takes his napkin from his lap, folds it into neat halves. "There's no reason to bring her into this."

"Do you remember where we were going the day

you rescued her on the Palisades?"

"Upstate for the weekend."

"Do you remember why?"

He shrugs.

"It was our anniversary. Our tenth. We never even made it to the B&B." Surely he remembers how he rode back to the city with her in the ambulance. I for one can't forget driving the car back to the city alone. "You spent the entire next day at the hospital."

"What was I supposed to do?"

"You saved her. That was enough. You could have let the medics take it from there."

He fishes an ice cube out of his orange juice with a spoon, drops it in again. "I did what I needed to do."

"What about the week before you moved out? You came home from work on Wednesday night, and the table was set when you got there. I had candles, wine. I'd made New York strip. I was wearing the yellow dress."

The look on his face tells me he remembers none of this. "What's that got to do with anything?"

"We'd just sat down to eat when the phone rang. I asked you not to get it."

"I'm an EMT."

"That night you didn't have to. You weren't on call."

"I have responsibilities."

"It was her. You hadn't even had a bite of your steak. Not a single sip of wine. You put on your coat and walked out."

He folds his napkin into little triangles. "She needed me."

He keeps folding the napkin. I half expect the elegant shape of a swan to emerge, but it isn't origami, just a nervous habit. He folds until the napkin is a small tight square with perfect corners. "Christ, I'm her only friend. You can't begrudge her that. The woman has third-degree burns over her entire face, for God's sake. Have you seen her face? Did you know that her boyfriend left afterward? He told her he couldn't look at her. Can you imagine what that does to a person?"

"I'm just saying..."

"Aren't you being a little selfish? Look at you. You're healthy. You've got everything in order."

"You say that like it's a flaw. Like I should be punished for it."

"That's not what I mean. But that poor woman, she was suicidal."

"You have to draw the line somewhere. You can't save everyone."

"I can't just walk away." He gives up on the napkin and starts salting his eggs. He salts them and salts them, then he starts in with the pepper. "So I've never been the perfect husband."

"I never wanted perfection."

He reaches over, puts his hand on top of mine. "This thing with Graham. Are you sure you're not just doing it to hurt me?"

"What's between me and Graham has nothing to do with you."

"Okay," he says, taking his hand away. "I'd understand if you wanted to stick it to me. Maybe I deserve
it." He picks up his water glass and is about to drink
from it when both of us notice the waxy print of Stacy's
pink lipstick on the rim. He sets it down again. "It's
just—" He stares into his eggs, which glisten with tiny
grains of salt. "It's strange to think of you with someone
else."

Matt Dillon comes over. "Would you like anything
else?"

"We're okay," Dave says.

Whitney Houston's honeyed voice spills over the
loudspeaker. Matt Dillon balances a tray of coffees on
one hand and says, "I hope you are having very good
honeymoon."

"Thanks," Dave says, "but it's not our honeymoon."

"You can pretend," Matt Dillon says. He smiles and
walks away.

Dave tugs at his collar. "I've missed you."

"Really?"

He looks hurt. "Of course. Not just for the last two
months. I've missed you for a long time. You stopped
needing me."

"No, you just thought I did."

I think of long nights sitting by the window when
he worked the graveyard shift, willing him to come
home. Each time he went out I held my breath, certain
that one day, ministering to a gunshot wound in some
greasy alley, he'd feel a knife of pain through his heart,

look down, and see that he'd been stabbed. I imagined the blood seeping through his white shirt, the look of surprise on his face, his hand going to his chest, trying to stop the flow. In that moment, would he be as practical as always? Would he consider the depth of the wound, the angle of the blade, the probabilities and proclivities of his own desperate heart? Would he count the miles to the hospital, click them off on some mental odometer, or would he begin to panic, his heart beating faster, then slowing, rattling toward his death?

"What about Stacy?" I say.

"Last night, she fell off the wagon, and she came to me for help. It was all pretty innocent."

"You'll be good for her," I say. And it's true. Dave is good for everyone. Surely he sees in Stacy a person who will bring out his best traits—yet another woman he has been called upon to save, the way he once saved me.

SIXTEEN

Nancy Eliot wore jeans and a red T-shirt, and she came bearing food and news. It had been less than a year since our class graduated from Murphy High School in Mobile, but my recollection of her had already grown vague. I remembered this about her: she was president of the debate team and was always possessed of a great number of facts. She had statistics, case histories, a whole list of bibliographical references to back up any statement. Which is why she could not be disbelieved, which is why I could not dismiss her news as hearsay or prank, some ugly rumor outside the realm of truth.

It was my Christmas vacation, and Dave and I were sitting in a diner on Canal Street in Mobile. No kisses had been exchanged between us, no inklings of romance. In New York City we were friends, weekend regulars, movie companions. He had flown down to Pensacola to visit his brother, and I'd invited him to spend a few days in Mobile, promised him an authentic taste of the deep South. He'd been sleeping in the guest room of my parents' house. Two days before we had dined with Amanda Ruth and her new girlfriend, Allison, at The Mariner. Two days before I had thought that this was not *my* Amanda Ruth, the Amanda Ruth who kept our secret, who would never think of holding hands in public. "What has she done to you?" I wanted to say, meaning Allison, with her military hair and baggy jeans, her obvious ways. I was angry to learn that they'd spent the weekend at the river house. I thought of them sitting together on our pier, grilling shrimp on our grill, making love on our old mattress.

"Have you met Mr. Lee?" I asked Allison while we waited for our food. What I meant was, "Does he know?"

Amanda Ruth and Allison looked at one another, as if they shared some secret, some truth to which I was not privy. "Sort of," Allison said.

"It didn't go over too well," Amanda Ruth confessed. "A couple of weeks ago I called to let Mom and Dad know I was bringing someone home. I figured I'd break it to them when we got there, and they could deal with it. When Dad came home from work, Allison and I were standing in the kitchen with Mom. She was trying to act like it was no big deal, but I could tell she was in shock. Dad wanted to know where my boyfriend was. He'd made big plans to go deep-sea fishing with this new guy he thought I was bringing home. He'd already made reservations for the boat, and he'd even bought a fishing rod as a gift for the future son-in-law. Just imagine the look on his face when I told him there was no boyfriend, that it was Allison I wanted him to meet."

"Brave," I said. "Definitely risky."

Dave speared a hush puppy with his fork. "How did your dad react?"

"He said something about not having any of that filth under his roof, then stormed out of the house."

"I've never seen anyone so furious," Allison said.

"You know how Mom is," Amanda Ruth added. "She pretended nothing had happened. She asked if we wanted some cling peaches with Cool Whip."

Two days later, Nancy Eliot set the plates before us: a grilled cheese sandwich for Dave, a burger for me. Two tall glasses of iced tea, a thick chocolate milkshake to share.

What I remember most about this day is that everything seemed to be going fine. I hadn't yet had any time alone with Amanda Ruth, but we'd made plans to see each other before I returned to New York, after both Allison and Dave were gone. She had said that we could drive to the river, maybe barbecue some shrimp, take the boat out to Petite Bois Island.

I was having a good time in Mobile with Dave. I was excited about seeing Amanda Ruth one on one, and happy to be going back to New York, to my studies and the friends to whom Dave had introduced me—professional types who dressed tastefully and had interesting furniture. Dave took me to off-Broadway plays, restaurants that served foods I had never even considered before: Ethiopian and Greek, Indian and Malaysian. I was eighteen; he was twenty-four and seemed incredibly mature, unlike any boy I had known in high school. I found him attractive, kind, funny, and couldn't help but wonder what it would be like to kiss him.

"Anything else?" Nancy said.

"This will do it."

She took a few steps away from our table, then turned and came back. "I guess you probably heard."

"Heard what?"

Nancy placed both hands on our table and leaned over, as if to tell a secret. Her voice was low, her eyes wide. There was a spot of ketchup on the right shoulder of her T-shirt. A blue Bic pen toppled from her apron pocket onto our table. "A girl from our class was found dead this morning. Her body was left behind the skating rink. Strangled."

"Who?"

At that moment, I harbored what one might call a prurient curiosity, nothing akin to grief. I was anxious to hear the whole story—the who and when and where, the how, and, if possible, the why. The first face that came to mind was a cheerleader named Samantha Arnold with a crazy boyfriend who once beat her up at a party while his friends stood around doing nothing. She was the sort of girl to whom a tragedy of that nature might occur, the kind of girl whose sudden death would not come entirely as a surprise.

"I didn't really know her," Nancy said. "Last name Lee."

Last name Lee. This was the moment of separation, the moment when everything changed. I went through the list of names, trying to think of someone else with the last name Lee, anyone else. Panic, followed quickly by relief, the vague memory of a girl named Danielle, who sat in front of me in chemistry. She was dowdy and sweet; she rarely passed a chemistry test. Our sophomore year she gave me a little paper sack filled with Halloween candy.

"Danielle Lee." I said it, rather than asked it, having already deemed it fact. I looked to Nancy for confirmation.

"No, not Danielle. Amanda Ruth Lee. Remember her? Cute girl. Chinese or something."

Dave was up already, risen from his seat. He was sitting beside me, his arm around my shoulder, his face bent down to mine. "Bring us the check," he said.

"I'm sorry, I didn't know you were friends."

"Bring us the check, please." Then he was folding me up in his arms. He managed to pay without ever letting go, somehow slipping the wallet out of his pocket and placing a stack of dollar bills on the table. "Let's go for a drive," he said, helping me up, leading me outside into the warm December sunlight. It was late afternoon. He opened the car door and placed me in the seat—I was not in control of my own body, he had taken charge of everything. The car started up and we were moving, his hand was on my leg and he was driving, neither of us speaking, oldies playing on the radio, Smokey Robinson singing "Tracks of My Tears." Within half an hour we had reached the coast. Our windows were down, the air smelled of salt and oak and Sunday bar-be-cue, only the hint of a chill in the air, everything was clean and fresh and the sky was clear, and the ocean seemed barely to move, more white than blue in the sunlight. Dave stopped the car at the public beach, then came around to my side, opened the door, and helped me out of the seat. He held my hand and led me over the sand dunes, past the public showers and down to the water.

From the road the waves looked minimal, but close up I could see the ocean churning, could hear waves crashing on the sand. Yellow signs had been posted to alert beach-goers of a rip tide. There were no lifeguards on this desolate stretch of beach, just the signs: *Warning! Strong Undertow. Swim at your own risk.* There was the sound of the waves breaking, and foam crackling as the waves washed out, cars moving past, a motorcycle gunning down the two-lane road, and the foam dissipating, followed by another wave. In the distance a white sail. Bits of sargasso weed strewn along the sand, an amorphous jellyfish washed ashore and dying. Dave bent down in front of me and unlaced my shoes. He slipped them off my feet, removed my socks, rolled my pant legs high above my ankles.

I had a memory of her, Amanda Ruth, kneeling before me in the gymnasium, unknotting my shoelaces. The ends of my laces were frayed, they had become tangled in the eyeholes. Her hair glowed beneath the fluorescent lights. On the other side the boys were playing Kill the Boy in the Blue Shirt. The boy in the blue shirt was Roland and they had killed him, he lay groaning on the floor and I felt her breath on my knees, her fingertips brushing my ankles.

Dave slipped off his own shoes and we were walking, and this was not breathing, this was not moving, I was not walking down the beach knowing this thing; this knowledge was not real. The sun beat down. It was snowing in New York City when we left, but here in Alabama it was too warm; Amanda Ruth always wished for cold weather at Christmas time. "I'll come visit you during the winter break," she had said, that last evening together at the boathouse. "Maybe we'll get snow. I want to see the tree at Rockefeller Center."

Dave bent and retrieved two live pair of angel wings that had just washed in with the tide. He held my palm open and placed the wings there, along with a handful of sand. Their shells were yellow and pink and blue, and the tiny animals, which had no perspective beyond this small handful of sand, continued to burrow, digging straight through the wet sand to my hand. I could feel the tickling pressure of their rubbery tentacles against my skin. I placed the lump of sand in the water, rinsed my hands.

"Baby," he called me for the first time. The only word I heard, the word that held me down, that kept me intact. What I remember most is the sense of loosening, a separating of particles that began in the chest, a feeling of coming entirely apart. But Dave was there, broad and tall and solid, he pulled me in to him and held me up, his body and his voice surrounded me. "Baby," he said again.

If it were not for his calm presence, the firmness of his arms around me, I would not have been able to stand there on the beach, to move my legs, to speak or eat or propel myself forward through the afternoon.

"Talk to me," I said. Dave understood immediately that I desired to be transported to the world of facts, of science and certainty, a domain he knew well. He needed only decide what fact to hand over to me, by what method he would bring me back to him. We walked several minutes in silence. "There," he said at last, bending to pick up a large spiral shell. He held it to my ear. The sea rumbled into my head. "Let's talk about sound," he said.

"Okay." There, we had a subject, something definite. My only goal was to listen.

"Sound enters the ear through the auricle, where it is concentrated and delivered into the external auditory meatus. It causes a vibration of the tympanic membrane, the drum." In one ear, the shell, the hollow roar of the ocean. In the other, Dave's voice, clear and monotone, telling me that the ocean did not exist in this shell, that it was only amplification and vibration. In this manner he disclosed the mystery of the sea shell, transformed myth into fact, led me out of the darkness, back to him.

We stayed at the beach until dark—walking, standing, sitting in the shadows made by moonlight and sand dune. As we drove toward home he said, "Would you like to go to the river?"

"Okay." I heard my voice in the closed space of the car. The windows were up, the air conditioner on. It was only us there, moving forward along the dark road. Beside the road were houses on stilts, the dunes, the dark of the beach.

The short drive to the river seemed to take hours. When we got to Amanda Ruth's house, he said, "Do you want to be alone?"

"Yes."

He sat in the car while I walked through the yard and down to the pier, out to the boathouse. I spent over an hour in the barbecue room, on the old mattress where Amanda Ruth and I slept the week before she left for Montevallo. At some point, I fell asleep. I dreamt of her. When I woke up I turned in the bed, expecting to find her there. I knew that I was dreaming, and believed that Nancy's words too were a dream, and that my walk with Dave on the beach had been a dream, and that now I would wake beside her, and she would emerge from sleep slightly fussy, confused, the way she always did. But when I rolled over, I rolled over onto nothing, just a damp pillow with no case, a musty blanket. I opened my eyes and looked out the window. The river moved slowly past, all black and warm in the moonlight. In the near-dark I made out the shapes of things. Amanda Ruth's sunglasses lay on the metal box beside the stove. Her flip-flops were slung haphazardly beside the door, as if she had just stepped out of them. I walked out onto the pier, searching. Nothing. I was alone. I began to panic. I went back inside, still hoping, still believing in the possibility of the dream, that Amanda Ruth had not been killed, that she was in the boat, waiting, knowing that I would find her in the dark, that I would come to her in my half-sleep, touch my mouth to her collarbone, her hair.

In the blue room the water was low. The boat knocked about. I felt happy for a moment, convincing myself that the sound of the boat in the water was really the sound of Amanda Ruth, that she was below deck, knocking her knuckles against the fiberglass walls, calling me. I stepped into the boat, avoiding the two fishing poles that lay on the slippery floor, their reels slightly uncoiled, the lines gone slack. I went down into the cabin, which was moldy and damp, and found the light switch with my fingers. There were the two long cushions that met at the bow and widened into a V, where we used to lie, our heads together, talking. There was the tiny stove, the closet with the low, flimsy toilet, the doorway where you had to stoop low so as not to bump your head. She wasn't there. I went up on deck, felt my way to the salt-stiffened chair, rested my head on the steering wheel.

Moonlight crept through cracks in the wooden walls. The water below the boat was black; the place smelled of night and old rain, of some dark thing sleeping. I thought of long summer days, when the canvas tarp was raised and sunlight flooded the room, and the water took on the blue brilliance of lapis stone. Amanda Ruth would sit on the edge of the boat, fall backward into the water, and moments later come up laughing, silver droplets clinging to her eyelashes. She wore a yellow bathing suit, with straps made of tiny blue beads. There was nothing so blue as that room, nothing so real as Amanda Ruth.

I walked barefoot up the pier, through the yard, and out to the road where Dave waited for me. He was awake, listening to the radio. The key dangled in the ignition. "Ready?" he asked, as if he had only been waiting a few minutes, as if we had just arrived.

It was in the hours and days following Amanda Ruth's death that something happened between Dave and me. One night we drove out to Gulf Shores, spread an old sheet on the sand, and drank beer long into the night. There were no stars out, just the flicker of headlights behind us on the highway, muted music drifting down the beach from the Pink Pony Pub. We sat close enough to the ocean to feel the spray from crashing waves. The air carried fish and salt and warmth, that heady Gulf Shores scent. At some point Dave leaned over and kissed me. That night I discovered his body with a passion I'd never before felt for a man. The need went beyond words, beyond lust. His touch comforted me. For the next few days he stayed at my parents' house, and they pretended not to notice that he'd moved from the guest room into my own. Only when we were making love was I able to separate myself from the horrible knowledge of Amanda Ruth's death. When he was inside me, his hands moving over my back, my legs clenched around his waist, his mouth against my ear, only then did the death exist in another place, some other world that I could push away.

One year later he asked me to marry him. There was nothing to say but yes. It is possible to love a person for being sturdy and reliable in a single, impossible moment, for responding with perfect timing and absolute precision to your unspoken needs.

SEVENTEEN

Late in the evening, the repairs miraculously completed, we feel the grumble of machine life below us,
the engine kicking to life. There is a great groaning, a
terrible ruckus, and we begin to move. Buoy lights blink
on the river. I can't stop staring at Graham—the tumble
of gray hair over his collar, the tight sinew of his neck,
the way he bites his lower lip when he is deep in
thought. In these moments it is difficult to believe that
he is a man already resigned to his own death.

It is dawn when we reach Wuhan, a day and a half
behind schedule. The city stinks of coal, even in the
downpour. The dock is crowded with boats. Along the
banks hundreds have gathered to stack sandbags for the
flood. Shirtless men labor in the glow of flashlights, the
headlights of parked cars.

The passengers, meanwhile, are unhappy. A
meeting is called in The Room of the Ancient Poets.
The walls are decorated with huge Chinese characters,
descending from ceiling to floor. Elvis Paris informs the
green group that the ship is going on, since it has
another tour group to pick up in Chonquing and take
downstream. We may remain onboard, or, for a small
additional fee, we may take rooms in town and "enjoy
the Alternate Vacation Plan, which is described in your
brochure." I have read my brochure thoroughly but
have found no such plan. According to Elvis, the alter-

native vacation involves a plane to Xian to see the Terra Cotta Warriors, followed by a train to "the charming city of Guilin, ancient inspiration of artists and poets," and a three-hour cruise down the Li River, "which is even more beautiful than the Yangtze."

"I have to make it to the Three Gorges," I tell Dave, thinking of the red tin stashed in the safe in our cabin.

"Of course. We've come this far."

I find Graham on the edge of the crowd. "What's your plan?"

"I'm staying," he says.

Stacy appears, wanting to know if we're staying or going. Dave tells her we're in for the long haul. Stacy looks relieved. "So am I."

Those of us who choose to stay are told that we "embark upon the remainder of the cruise at your own risk. Red Victoria Cruise Line cannot be held responsible for unforeseen dangers encountered due to the unexpected flooding." This disclaimer is broadcast over the intercom at regular intervals during the morning. "You will spend the day touring exciting Wuhan," The Voice says. "Those who would like alternate vacation plan, please report to the spectacular Hotel Double Happiness to join the group at 1500 hours. If you choose to go all the way to Chongqing, please report to ship by 1700 hours."

"So," Stacy says. "What's there to do in Wuhan?"

"We should go see the baiji," Graham says.

"The what?"

"It's a type of dolphin that's inhabited the Yangtze

for millions of years," Graham explains. "There are only fifty left. I believe one of them is still in captivity at the Institute of Hydrobiology in Wuhan. We'll have to find someone to take us." Graham warns us that the trip may be futile, as it is possible that QiQi, the captive dolphin, is no longer living. He saw QiQi three years ago, at which time he had a friend at the Institute, a respected scientist who was researching the threat the dam would pose to animal life. As a result of her outspoken opposition to the dam, the friend was stripped of her title and sent to do manual labor in the countryside.

We approach Elvis Paris with our request. He shakes his head. "The dolphin preserve is off-limits to foreigners."

"Is there a way to buy a ticket?" Graham asks.

Elvis shifts from foot to foot, thinks for a minute, and says, "How much can you pay for this ticket?"

"Four hundred yuan for the four of us."

"I think is not enough. Is very difficult to see the baiji. Maybe Institute is closed, I have to do special procedure."

Graham ups his offer to two hundred yuan each. Elvis contemplates this for a minute. "I think maybe I can arrange," he says finally, accepting a wad of bills from Graham and folding it into a fake leather wallet. He takes out a cell phone and makes a call, then accompanies us out to the dock, where he hails a red taxi. "I go with you," he says, climbing into the front seat.

During the heart-stopping ride through the jam-packed streets of Wuhan, Graham explains that the Chinese have several different names for the baiji: galloping white horse, river panda, king of the Yangtze, river goddess. This last title was taken from the Song Dynasty myth of how the baiji came to be. Graham says he first heard the story from a fisherman in Anhui province twenty years ago, when the baiji could still be seen swimming alongside sampans.

According to legend, a beautiful young maiden was captured and taken from her family. As she was being ferried across the river to be sold into slavery, the boatman tried to rape her. To preserve her honor, she leapt into the river, but the boatman jumped after her. God took pity on the maiden and turned her into a dolphin. In punishment, the boatman was turned into a finless porpoise, known today by fishermen as the river pig.

No one here shows much respect for lanes, and our driver is no exception. He speeds on, paying no mind to cars or cyclists. Finally, the taxi screeches up to a pair of ugly concrete buildings beside a lake. We are met by a friendly man in a white oxford shirt and gray trousers who introduces himself as Dr. Wu. "Do you have permits?" he asks.

Elvis Paris shows him a well-worn document with an official-looking red seal. I have no idea where he got this document; he didn't have time to arrange for any special permits this morning. Perhaps this piece of yellow parchment with its elaborate seal is like a skeleton key that opens many doors. Dr. Wu looks skeptical, but nevertheless accepts the document as proof that we have official permission to be here. He doesn't ask for tickets, and Elvis Paris doesn't offer him any portion of the eight hundred yuan.

"I am very glad you came," Dr. Wu says in impeccable English. "There is not much interest in the dolphin today. Everyone thinks about electricity and the economy, not dolphins."

Elvis Paris smiles. "Millions of people depend on the river," he says. "Only fifty baiji. Who is more important?"

Dr. Wu laughs nervously, then falls silent. He takes us into a building that houses a small circular pool, ten feet deep. "He is the only baiji in captivity," Dr. Wu says. "We have tried to breed him, but it is very difficult to find a mate. The female we brought here two years ago died."

QiQi is about seven feet long, with an almost comical needle nose and hauntingly human, childlike eyes. He circles the tank, twisting and rolling, showing off. He comes close enough for me to touch him, then flips over on his back and waves a white fin at us. He rolls again and lets out a long whistle.

Dr. Wu says that QiQi, who was rescued after being caught on a fisherman's rolling hooks, is fortunate to be alive. The marks from the hooks are still visible, hundreds of small scars down QiQi's back.

Dave leans over and peers into the tank. We've never had a pet, because he believes animals shouldn't be cooped up in a New York apartment. I can tell he's moved by the sight of the captive dolphin. "How long will he live?" he asks.

Dr. Wu shakes his head. "The baiji is a social creature. To be alone like this is not good for him. As a boy, I saw many dolphins on the river. My father was a fisherman. Fishermen in those days had great admiration for the dolphin. Once, my father accidentally caught a baiji in his net. At that time we were very hungry, but my father released the baiji anyway. Soon after that, Mao declared that the fishermen could not show special allegiance to the dolphin. Mao did not like that the baiji was called 'the river goddess' and 'king of the Yangtze.' He said that there were no goddesses and no kings, and to admire the baiji was counter-revolutionary."

Elvis Paris smiles, revealing a row of small gleaming teeth. "This was long time ago. Is not important now."

"The dolphin isn't the only creature that faces extinction because of the dam," Dr. Wu says. "There is also the cloud leopard, the finless porpoise, the Siberian crane." QiQi slides past, his silver-white belly upturned, and Dr. Wu reaches down and passes his fingers over the dolphin's scarred skin. Twenty years ago, he explains, there were thousands of baiji. But the dolphin has had too many enemies: boats, pollution, starvation. Over millions of years, the baiji adjusted to the darkness of the river, and they are almost completely blind. They navigate the river by sound. "But now there are too many boats," Dr. Wu says, "too much noise."

"Okay, very good, we go now," says Elvis Paris. But Dr. Wu has one more thing to show us. He takes us to another room where less fortunate baiji are on display, those who were killed by the rolling hooks. Their silver-gray skins are ripped and ragged, and their eyes stare out blankly. I snap a picture, and immediately Elvis Paris says, "No pictures here! You may take photo of QiQi, but this dead baiji is no good. Please, your film."

"Are you serious?"

Graham takes me aside. "You should give him the film. He can make problems for Dr. Wu."

I slide the film out of the camera and hand it to Elvis Paris. He drops it in the garbage can and leads us outside, into the gray afternoon.

In the night, on deck, beneath an awning that keeps me dry from the fine continuous rain, I dream of the baiji. In this dream I see the dolphin swimming back and forth in the river, but then it is not a river but a swimming pool, and finally, not a swimming pool but a bathtub. Then we are on the river again, and the dolphin is swimming alongside our ship. The dolphin is slick and white, slender, its skin extremely taut, its eyes deeply sad. The boat roars through the water, cars rumble over a bridge. Onshore, cranes howl and pick-axes ring. The dolphin, confused by the noise, twists and turns. I say to the captain of our ship, to the passing sampans, to the couple from Texas, "Look! It's the bajii! There are only 50 left in the world!" But no one comes to see. In the distance a temple rises from the hillside, and The Voice on the loudspeaker says, "World famous hanging temple of China." Everyone rushes to the back of the ship to take pictures against the backdrop of the temple. When I look down again, the dolphin is gone. There is a terrible noise, what sounds like a human cry. The river churns up red.

EIGHTEEN

About half of the passengers have stayed in Wuhan, along with a disproportionately large number of the crew. We become then a ship of survivors, the ones willingly left behind. There is excitement on board. The crew becomes more leisurely. All through the night they can be found drinking to excess with the passengers, gambling, playing charades. The ties of the stewards have been loosened. The second captain has taken over, the first opting for a few days of rest in Wuhan. Elvis Paris is in his glory; he calls us the mutineers.

The next day the rain comes down hard. "This way," Graham says.

"Where are we going?"

"So many questions."

Minutes later, I find myself in his cabin. He clears a few things from the chair, which is upholstered in stiff pink fabric. I sit, unsure what to do with my hands, my legs. I cross my feet, uncross them, look around the room. A print of London Bridge at nightfall hangs above the bed. The lamp on the table bears a British military insignia. The dressing table is covered with brown pharmaceutical bottles, their labels inscribed with unpronounceable names. There is a jar of individually wrapped syringes, another of cotton swabs. The room smells medicinal and stale.

We sit for a minute or two in silence before he says,

"How did Amanda Ruth die?"

"I told you. It was murder."

"Yes, but how?"

I am surprised by this preoccupation with details, his desire to know the intimate facts. I turn and glance out the porthole. The whole world is obscured by rain. I want to see the world outside this ship, outside this suffocating room, but there is more light inside than outside, and all I see is my own tired face and the blurred reflection of Graham's navy blue shirt, which is hanging on the doorknob.

"She was strangled."

"By whom?"

A long silence. The rain comes down, the ship sways, and everything is gray. I turn to face him. "It's difficult to talk about."

"Where did they find her?"

"Behind the skating rink, across the street from her parents' church."

When we were in junior high we went to the skating rink every weekend. I close my eyes and for a moment I can hear the clunk of wheels against the floor, rubber stoppers scudding, someone falling, a skinny referee in tight pants leading the limbo. I remember the purple pom-poms Amanda Ruth's mother gave her for her twelfth birthday, which she tied to the laces of her roller skates. The skates had glitter in the wheels. I can see her there, gliding over the smooth surface as she jiggles her hips and sings along to the song booming from the speakers, Earth Wind, and Fire—"a shining star for you to see what your life can truly be." She puts one slender leg in front of the other and leans in toward the center of the rink. The strobe light reflects thousands of multi-colored stars onto the floor, and she follows them, whirling around the room with a dancer's ease, her brown ponytail flying behind her.

This is how I want to remember her, but the other image always cuts in: Amanda Ruth clad in jeans and white T-shirt, lying haphazardly on the pavement, one arm flung wide, her right leg bent at an awkward angle, the yellow scarf tied tightly around her neck. In another photo, after the detective had untied the scarf, there was a slim purple bruise around her neck that seemed too insignificant to kill her. Three days after she'd been found, the detective slid the photos out of a manila envelope. "Is there anything in the picture you recognize?"

"The scarf," I said.

The detective ran his thick fingers over his beard. "Where did the scarf come from?"

"I gave it to her."

"Why? Was it her birthday?"

"No, just a gift."

"A gift for no reason?"

"Yes."

"That's odd."

"She was my friend."

"What kind of friend?"

"My best friend."

"Was there anything unusual about your relation-ship?"

"What do you mean?" I was not being uncooperative. I simply couldn't understand what he was asking. As he put one photo after another in front of me, forcing me to look, asking a series of questions that seemed to lead no closer to a definitive answer, I realized that this man considered me a suspect.

He repeated his question, more forcefully this time. "Was there anything unusual about your relationship?" The way he said *unusual* made me feel dirty. The word had the ring of seedy nightclubs and dark street corners, transactions between desperate people involving quick sex and small wads of sweaty cash.

"No."

There was a long pause. He leaned over the table and put his face so close to mine that I could feel his breath on my mouth. He smelled like cigarettes and breath mints, and like the bean burritos at Taco Bell. "Amanda Ruth's dad thinks different, doesn't he?"

I shrugged. The detective paced the room, like a backwoods cop in a made-for-TV movie. "Mr. Lee told us you had a little thing going with his daughter. Tell me something, are you a lesbian?"

By this point I was crying and shaking. He came up behind me, put one hand on either side of me on the table, so that I was surrounded by his bulk, his fast food smell. He put his face right beside mine and whispered in my ear, "Do you go with girls?"

"No!"

Immediately I regretted saying it, but I was too afraid to take it back. That denial, expressed as a single word in a gloomy interrogation room in a dusty old police station, has haunted me ever since—my ultimate betrayal of Amanda Ruth.

He kept at me for an hour. I watched the minutes tick off on the big metal clock on the wall. "You best stay in town," he said before unlocking the door. "We might want to talk to you again." He stood in front of the door with his hand on the knob, so that the only way for me to get out was to press past him. He slid his hand over my back and leaned down to whisper in my ear, "I bet I could make you like men." His breath was wet and smoky; my stomach turned. When I came out, the secretary handed me a Diet Coke. The can was so cold it hurt my fingers. I recognized her from the video store near my house. She was always in there with several kids, renting Disney pictures. Once, at the checkout, we had talked about the Star Wars movies. I could tell she'd heard everything. "It's just standard procedure, hon," she said, handing me a Kleenex. "You need a ride home?"

***

The skating rink is right across the street from First Baptist Church of Greenbrook. The church is huge and white, with a steeple so high it seems as if it is punching a hole in the sky. When I was a child the steeple terrified me, the way it reached so high above the telephone lines and traffic lights, so high above the skating rink. Everything around the church looked insignificant in comparison. On clear nights when the moon shone brightly, the steeple cast its long, pointed shadow over the parking lot. The girls going into the skating rink, in their tight jeans and soft, pastel-colored sweaters, made a game of walking straight down the middle of the shadow.

The skating rink was a rectangular building with aluminum siding, alternating yellow and blue panels. Behind it there was a dumpster that always stank of Sunday supper. After dinner on the ground, which followed church every Sunday night, people would dump their garbage there—big plates of potato salad, fried chicken remnants, the pink cloud they made for dessert, a too-sweet concoction of Cool Whip and maraschino cherries.

The police said that the person who did it had planned to put her in the dumpster, to conceal her body in the rubble, but had apparently been scared away "before disposing of the body in the intended fashion." They said that Amanda Ruth had not been killed behind the skating rink; "the perpetrator committed the crime at another premises and brought the victim to the site." This information was repeated several times in the papers, as if everyone had a right to know, as if the details of this death belonged to anyone who cared to read about it, anyone who wanted to tell Amanda Ruth's gruesome story over beers at The Watering Hole. Diane Shelby on Channel 5 wore bright pink lipstick and smiled an impeccable smile when she said, "The body was transported to the skating rink following Miss Lee's death."

Graham wants to know what was used to kill her.

"A scarf." Even now I can't believe that a flimsy piece of fabric, a pretty length of silk, could end a life.

"Who did it?"

"Do we have to talk about this?"

He sits down on the bed and stares at me for a long time. There is something desperate in his face I haven't noticed before. "What?" I say. He doesn't speak. He won't take his eyes off me. "What?" I say again.

"If you had to kill someone," he says, "could you?"

"What kind of question is that?"

"I'm just asking. Could you?"

"No."

"You can't imagine any situation in which you might be able to?"

"I've never considered it."

"What if the person asked you to do it?"

"I don't think so."

"Say they had a very good reason."

I go to him, straddle him where he is sitting on the bed. I squeeze his hips hard between my knees, take his face in my hands, and stare hard into his eyes. "Tell me," I say. "What do you want from me?"

He looks away, and his arms lay limp at his sides. I'm almost glad he doesn't respond; I'm terrified of his answer.

"Well," I say, releasing his face. "Could you?"

He lies back on the bed, stares up at the ceiling. "It would depend on the circumstances." He pauses, then says, "Yes. I suppose I could."

NINETEEN

Just after noon the following day, we dock at Shashi. Dave is nowhere to be seen. He didn't even come to the cabin last night. He has stopped keeping up appearances. Perhaps I should be angry or depressed, but I can no longer muster the proper emotions. He has already begun to recede into the past, something dream-like and faded, while Graham feels increasingly like the real and solid present. We go into town together and have a delicious lunch of vegetables, beef, and strong tea at a small restaurant near the entrance to a park.

After lunch, Graham says he wants to visit an old friend in town. "You can explore the park. I'll meet you at the entrance in three hours."

It's raining softly when he leaves me at a pavilion near a small pond flickering with koi. The columns of the pavilion are decorated with colorful tiles in intricate designs. In another pavilion on the opposite side of the pond, a man in a pinstriped suit sits meditating. I take out my journal and begin to scribble, thinking that one day I'll want to remember this. When I get home I'll try to locate Amanda Ruth's mother and share my impressions of China. I remember her face the day she gave me her daughter's ashes, the way she showed up at my door in big sunglasses and wrinkled slacks, her hair tied up in a green bandana. She looked unkempt and somehow younger, like a lost and frightened teenager.

Rain spatters the pavement. I've been sitting here for about ten minutes when an attractive young woman approaches me. She is wearing a yellow sundress and an expensive-looking pair of leather sandals, and her toenails are painted pale pink. She sits in the middle of the bench, right next to me, though there is plenty of room on the other end.

"Hello," she says. "I am Yuk Ming. You speak English?"

"Yes. My name is Jenny."

She's wearing tiny gold hoop earrings and a diamond ring. My first guess is that the ring must be costume jewelry. Most Chinese workers would never be able to afford such an extravagance. "You are American?" she asks.

"Yes."

"I meet much Americans," she says eagerly. "I try study English. My English very poor. I want one day visit New York City."

"Your pronunciation is extremely good," I tell her. It's true. Although her English is broken, each word is spoken precisely, with perfect inflection.

She points to my journal. "You write for newspaper?"

"No, it's just a diary to help me remember the trip."

"You are in China for vacation?"

"Yes, taking a cruise up the Yangtze."

"Oh! Is very beautiful. Longest river in the world!"

"Third longest," I correct her, though I immediately wish I hadn't.

"No, I am certain it is the longest."

I change the subject. "What kind of work do you do?"

"I am administrator in hospital."

"Do you enjoy it?"

"In China today all people like their work, not like America. In America everyone hates their work. Isn't this true?"

"Some people do. Mine's okay."

"How much they pay?"

"Enough."

"Here, workers treated very well," she says. "Pay is not too high, but is okay, because employer pays medical expense, housing, everything. No homeless people in China."

"Do you have children?" I ask, hoping to urge the conversation in a more personal direction.

"I have one son. He is seven years old. Very bright!" And then Yuk Ming is suddenly praising the attributes of the one-child policy. "To have one child is best. More is too many. If one child, you have time to spend with him, you can be perfect mother."

If I wanted to be inundated with propaganda, I'd be touring the city with Elvis Paris. I smile and stand to leave. "It was very nice meeting you."

"Don't go!" she says, smiling. She stands and touches my arm. "I am very interested in talking to you and sharing a cultural exchange. Please come to my home for lunch."

The abrupt change in my new acquaintance's English is startling. Maybe she's reciting these last sentences from a textbook on getting to know foreigners.

"We will have a nice walk," she says. "I will show you some pretty spots." More perfect phrases. It must be a very good textbook. I accept her invitation, excited by the opportunity to see a real Chinese home, not the tourist attractions that Elvis Paris is so intent on dragging us to.

"I just have to make one telephone call," she says, pulling a slender red cell phone out of her purse. She turns it on, dials, waits for a voice on the other end, and then says something quickly in Mandarin. She slips the phone into her purse. "Let's go. You can share my umbrella." Rain patters the leaves of trees lining the street. As we walk, Yuk Ming hums softly. The floral pattern of her umbrella is reflected in the wetness of the street. Our own reflections bob side by side—mine slightly taller, hers slightly thinner. "What music do you like?" she asks.

"Louis Armstrong. Nina Simone. Ella Fitzgerald. I don't admit it to many people, but I also have an addiction to eighties bands like Culture Club and Simple Minds. Have you heard of them?"

"No, but I like some American singers—Elvis Presley and Michael Jackson." She begins humming "Are You Lonesome Tonight?"

"Perfect," I say.

"Oh!" She seems pleased. "I do not know the words, though." I sing them for her, badly off key, and

DREAM OF THE BLUE ROOM

she laughs. We turn left and through a narrow alley. A dozen shirtless young men work atop a pile of rubble, breaking bricks with pickaxes, while a group of elderly women pick through the charred remains of a gutted building. They all stop to stare as we walk past. Then, in the midst of all this destruction, a brand-new building appears, a ten-story high-rise covered, like so many of the new buildings in China, with gleaming white tile that looks like it won't survive the year. I imagine it is a new Chinese invention, the disposable building: use once and then discard, no cleaning necessary.

"Here we are," Yuk Ming says, folding her umbrella and shaking the excess water onto the building's tiny patio. She punches a series of numbers on a keypad, and the door clicks open.

We take an immaculate elevator to the tenth floor and walk down a long hallway. When we're about a foot from her apartment, the door opens, as if choreographed, and a handsome young man in pressed khakis and a checked button-down appears. Yuk Ming introduces him as her husband, Wang. "We are very pleased to have your company," he says, shaking my hand.

Everything in the apartment smells new: paint, carpet, furniture. Yuk Ming proudly gives me the tour. The apartment has two ample bedrooms; one has a queen-sized bed with a black satin coverlet and a small chest of drawers. A framed picture of badly painted flowers hangs on the wall beside a small window. "And this is my son's room," she says, sweeping her hand in the direction of the second bedroom. In another life, she could have been Vanna White. The miniature mattress in the corner is covered in Mickey Mouse sheets; something about Mickey Mouse looks not quite right, although I can't put my finger on it. And then I realize that his ears, instead of the signature black, are crimson.

"Here is our comfortable and efficient study," Yuk Ming says, opening a sliding glass door to a third and smaller room. The desk is of the same shiny black material as the chest of drawers in the bedroom, and on top of the desk is a brand-new computer. Like Mickey Mouse, there's something not quite right about the computer. It takes me a moment to realize that it isn't plugged in. There are no cords, no printer, not even a keyboard, just a huge monitor and a CD-ROM tower. On the wall are three photos in identical black plastic frames: one of Mao Zedong, one of Jiang Xemin, and another of a small boy standing in front of a fountain, arms straight at his sides, looking surprised and slightly frightened. "My son!" Yuk Ming says. "He is in school right now."

"He's very handsome." I lean in closer and see that the photograph of the boy is actually a postcard.

Yuk Ming grabs my shoulder and pulls me back. "Why don't we have a seat in the den and get to know one another!" I feel as though I've stepped onto the set of an American television show, circa 1970. I half expect Yuk Ming to whip up a tuna casserole and show me her Tupperware collection.

The sofa, which is upholstered in black velour, looks as though it has never been used. The entire apartment, in fact, is strangely devoid of life. It bears no resemblance to the dozens of Chinese-owned flats I saw in New York's Chinatown while apartment-hunting with a friend. Those apartments possessed the comforting air of having been lived in. They were filled with the fragrance of food, with potted plants in varying degrees of health, crowded with chairs and couches and beds and tables that had clearly been put to good use. There is something decidedly un-Chinese about this apartment, as if Yuk Ming and her husband are trying to present to me a sanitized version of Chinese life, minus the dirt and hardship, the jumble of friends and relatives, the noises and odors and small disasters of daily life. This is Communism Chic, the New China, the goods they want me to deliver to the folks back home.

"Well," Yuk Ming says, flashing a Marcia Brady smile, teeth so white she could be the poster girl for Sparkling Baiji Toothpaste, "this is a typical modern Chinese apartment."

"Very nice," I say.

"Now we will have lunch in our comfortable dining room," Yuk Ming says. She leads me through the kitchen into a small room, also closed off by a sliding glass door. On the table is an impressive spread: dishes of pork, fish, chicken, steamed rice, several kinds of dumplings, an array of vegetables arranged expertly on dishes with delicate floral patterns. A carved white bowl in the center of the table contains shark fin soup. Yuk Ming pours tea and adds something to my plate from each dish, before she and Wang help themselves.

"This is delicious," I say, relaxing. "Where did you get it?"

"Wang made it," Yuk Ming says.

This is impossible, as the kitchen is spotless and I'm sure, if I were to open the door of the refrigerator, I would find it empty. Over lunch they ask me about my family, my job, my husband. They want to know if I'm enjoying my journey, and I please them by saying that China is fascinating. When they ask why I decided to come here, I lie. "I've always wanted to see China."

After lunch we retire to the den. Yuk Ming brings in a bowl of translucent white lichees for dessert. After I've eaten several, she asks, "What do you think of our wonderful Three Gorges Dam?"

The question catches me by surprise; I weigh my words carefully. "Many well-known Chinese scientists and engineers are worried about this dam."

Yuk Ming and Wang look at each other and laugh nervously. Wang takes the lichee bowl into the kitchen. When he returns, he pulls a chair right in front of the sofa where I'm sitting. He leans forward, elbows on his knees, and says, "There are very few true scientists and engineers in China who feel this way. Those who speak out against the dam want to frighten the people and undermine the government. The dam is very good for China. China produces many products for your country and the rest of the world. We need electricity to make these products. And too many people die each year in the floods. The dam will save lives."

"Maybe," I say, "but what about the farmers who

rely on the floodplain for their living?"

"The government is building clean new villages for them," Yuk Ming says. As if to prove her point, she hands me a brochure that is sitting rather conveniently on a small table beside the sofa. The brochure shows photographs of children playing happily in front of modern apartment buildings. In one photograph, behind the bright clean building that the photographer obviously meant to capture, is another building, also modern, but already falling apart. Yuk Ming explains that this is Ling Bau, a model resettlement village 30 kilometers from Yichang. "The government built enough new homes for all of the families of Yichang. Every apartment has a television. It is very good for the people."

Flipping through the brochure, I am reminded of an afternoon at my studio apartment in New York City during my freshman year of college. It was four months after Amanda Ruth's murder, and I'd been struggling through the spring semester in a daze, unable to complete my assignments, often missing class, going for days at a time without seeing anyone other than Dave, who would arrive at my door with John's pizza or take-out Chinese and persuade me to eat. It was two o'clock on a Thursday afternoon and I was still in bed. Dave had been gone since the previous Saturday, down in Florida for some seminar, and in his absence I'd lost all sense of time. There was hardly any food in the apartment, the phone had been disconnected, and my textbooks sat unread in a backpack I hadn't touched in a week. The doorbell rang, but I ignored it. It rang again, and I lay on my back, staring up at the ceiling, wondering who it could be. A couple of minutes passed in silence, followed by a knock at the door. I got up and put on the only thing I could find, a blue T-shirt that skimmed the tops of my thighs. I tiptoed to the door, hoping the visitor wouldn't hear me, and peered out the peephole. There was a young man standing there—no one I recognized. He was wearing a white button-down and dark tie. His hair was blond and perfectly combed.

He knocked again. "Hello? I know you're in there."

"What do you want?"

"May I have five minutes of your time?" I was looking out the peephole, and he was staring directly into it, as if he had some psychic power that alerted him to the fact that I was watching him.

"Who are you?"

"I'm with the Church of Jesus Christ of Latter Day Saints."

"I'm busy."

"I'd just like to speak with you for five minutes, ma'am."

"How do I know you're not some psycho?"

He slid a card under the door that identified him as John Slattery, member of the Church of Jesus Christ of Latter Day Saints. After the identification card came a pamphlet entitled *Sharing the Good Word*. "I won't hurt you, ma'am. I'm here to talk to you about the love of Christ."

"Just a minute," I said. I went to the bathroom and

brushed my teeth, combed my hair, and put on lipstick. When I came back and looked out the peephole again, he was still standing there. Out of curiosity, possibly boredom, I opened the door and stepped back. He glanced down at my bare legs, blushed, and looked away. I shut the door behind him. "Would you like something to drink?" I asked. "Coffee?"

"No, thank you," he said, straightening his tie. He clutched a briefcase in one hand. He tried to occupy himself by looking around the room, but the room was small and there was nothing to see—a thrift-store dresser with the drawers hanging open, a big white paper lantern, a few crates crammed with books.

"I'm sorry. I forgot. Mormons don't drink coffee, do you? I have bottled water, Sprite. Can you drink Sprite?" I slid past him into the kitchen, just four square feet of space with a tiny refrigerator tucked under the sink.

"Tap water would be good."

He was looking at the bed. The covers were turned down, the pillow dented, and I was certain he could tell I'd been sleeping. I rinsed a cup, ran water from the tap, and handed it to him. Our fingers touched. He blushed. "Thank you."

"I don't always sleep this late," I said. "I was up past midnight, studying." I wondered if he could tell I was lying. Maybe lie detection was part of his religious training. "Have a seat." He looked around the room, as if a sofa might materialize out of thin air. "On the bed," I said. "I haven't really decorated yet."

He sat carefully on the edge of the mattress, put his water glass on the floor, and glanced again at my bare legs. "There's an IKEA bus," he said. "You catch it at Penn Station and take it out to Jersey. They sell chairs pretty cheap. Me and my friend Joseph took it once."

As I sat down beside him, the bed sank with our combined weight. His face went deep red. "They have plates too, napkins, picture frames, you name it." And then, as if he remembered what he was there for, "Do you know about Jesus Christ?"

I nodded. "I grew up in Alabama. I was raised on Jesus and football." He didn't laugh. "Sorry," I said. "I guess that's sacrilegious or something."

"It's okay. God forgives." He pulled at his collar, as if he suddenly feared being choked by it. He smelled good, like bread. I wondered if he had ever had sex before. Probably not. He opened his briefcase, pulled out The Book of Mormon, then closed the briefcase and placed it on the floor. "I'd like to share a very special book with you. This is the Word of God."

"No offense, but how do you know?"

"On September 21, 1823, the resurrected prophet Moroni appeared to Joseph Smith and instructed him on the ancient record and its destined translation into the English language." As if to prove the veracity of this statement, he held the book up in front of my face, studied my expression. I could tell he wanted me to be enticed, he wanted me to snatch that book out of his hands in a desperate show of desire for the Word of God. It occurred to me at that moment that I wanted to seduce him—not only because he was attractive, but also because I needed to know if I could. Dave and I had only been going out for four months, and we had an unspoken agreement that we could both see other people, although I hadn't been with anyone else since we returned from Alabama. I knew, though, that Dave and I were rapidly moving toward something permanent, and I think I may have been looking for one last hurrah before I committed to him for good.

I moved closer to John Slattery, so that his shirtsleeve brushed against my arm. He quickly opened the book and mumbled, "I'd like to share some verses with you."

"Have you ever been on a bed with a girl before?"

"I." He swallowed. "Well."

I took the book out of his hands and laid it on the pillow, rested my hand on his thigh. He glanced over at the book, but in order to get to it he would have had to reach across my body. He looked utterly helpless. I pressed my bare leg against his corduroy one and rubbed my hand slowly up and down his thigh. He let out a surprised sigh. I pushed him back on the bed, expecting him to resist, but he didn't. He lay back stiffly and stared up at me with his mouth shut tightly, his eyes wide. I loosened his tie, unbuttoned his shirt, following each button with a kiss on his chest. He began breathing heavily. "I can't do this," he said, but he made no effort to stop me. I unzipped his pants. "No," he said. I knelt before him and took off his shoes, then made him lift his hips so I could slide his pants off. "We're not allowed to go out alone," he said. "It's against regulation. But my partner was sick and I didn't want to miss a day, so I came anyway. I shouldn't have."

"Relax," I said. He was wearing white Hanes briefs that were so bright and stiff they must have just come out of the package that morning. I slid my hand under the waistband, cupped my hand under his balls. His mouth opened and his eyes rolled back. I pulled his underwear off, arranged him on the bed, slid my mouth over his cock. He grabbed my shoulders, dug in hard with his fingers. "God."

I looked up. "I don't think you're supposed to say that."

"Sorry."

I slowly worked my mouth over him, ran my hand up his chest, slid my fingers around his throat. He was moving his hips, moaning, saying, "I have to go now." I took off my shirt, lay on top of him, kissed him for a long time. He sucked at my tongue, kissed me so hard I was afraid he'd leave bruises on my lips. I knelt over him and touched my breasts, my legs, watching the effect this had on him, then went down again and let him come in my mouth. His come was thick, nearly tasteless. I went to the bathroom and rinsed my mouth, then came back and lay down beside him. He was crying.

"It's okay," I said. "No one will know."

"God will," he said. He was staring at the ceiling, at the miniature stickers of stars and moons the previous tenant had glued there.

"But you told me five minutes ago that God forgives. I'm sure he'll understand."

He cried for a little while longer, then rolled over and started sucking my breasts. After a while he looked up and said, "I don't know what to do."

"Just lie on top of me."

He obeyed, and I opened my legs and guided him in. He moved very carefully. I held on to his back and pulled him in deeper. He stared at me, wide-eyed, as I came, then rolled off me. "That's amazing," he said. His skin was shimmering with sweat.

"That's why it's called sex."

John Slattery studied my face as if something else might happen, like maybe he thought that was only Act One. Then he cleared his throat. "Do you do that very often?"

"Not often enough."

We lay for a few minutes in silence. He stared at my naked body, ran his hands up and down the length of me. "Is this the first time you've seen a girl?" I asked.

"Yes."

"You don't have sisters or something?"

"No. Two brothers. Hey."

"Hey what?"

"Can we do this again?"

"Sorry buddy. This is a one-time thing."

"Okay. You're right. That's probably better." After a while he looked at his watch. "I'm sorry, but please, will you turn around while I dress?"

I looked out the window at the brick wall five feet away. I could hear him zipping his pants, sliding on his shirt. When he was finished dressing, he touched me on the shoulder. I put my arms around him, feeling both pleased and guilty for what I'd done. He hugged me back, then kissed me on the cheek, a dry peck.

"Thank you," he said. "Please forgive me." At the door, he pointed to the Book of Mormon that still rested on the pillow. "And please read that book. It will change your life." He shut the door behind him and left me feeling oddly disappointed, empty. He had been too easily seduced, the armor of his religion too easily punctured. Something in me had wanted him to be heroic in his resistance. I wanted to see faith in action, firsthand evidence of a higher calling.

After he left, I thumbed through *Sharing the Good Word*. There were illustrations of blonde people praying, blonde families having picnics, blonde children smiling and playing jump-rope with the Book of Mormon floating over their heads.

Now, Yuk Ming flips through her own pamphlet, pointing out photographs of Chinese people smiling, Chinese families eating in their new kitchens, Chinese children playing on the cement grounds of their new apartment complexes. It occurs to me that the gist of propaganda is the same across the board, a universal language of determined and desperate persuasion, even if the politics are varied and the causes diverse.

"See, it is a wonderful project," Yuk Ming says. "It will bring fortune and progress to the people."

I smile and place the pamphlet on the table. "Ling Bau may be good, but it's only one settlement. Time is running out. Do you really believe the government will keep its promise?"

They are both smiling so wide their faces must hurt. The smiles, like the computer and the Mickey Mouse sheets, have an inauthentic edge. "The government always keeps its promise," Wang says. "You will see. The dam will be the eighth wonder of the modern world."

He gets up from his chair and settles into the sofa beside me. In my mind I see the evangelistic scenes of my youth, when the Van for the Lord would arrive at my door late on a Friday night, and the kids from Bay View Baptist Church would flood the house, sit me down, and make me pray with them. "The future is bright," Wang says, inching closer. His breath smells of Flying Dragon Mints. "The future is filled with the promise of the Four Modernizations: Agriculture, Defense, Science, and Technology."

"Yes," Yuk Ming says. Her voice becomes very soft as she squeezes my hand. "And of course, the five loves. Love Work, Love People, Love Neighbors, Love Science, and Love Public Property."

I'm having an Amway moment, realizing that I've been brought here under the guise of friendship when in fact these two have something to sell. I look at my watch. "Better get going."

"Of course," Yuk Ming says. "I will walk with you."

"You must come visit us again!" Wang says. "Next time, bring a camera. You will take pictures of our apartment to take back to your friends in America!"

The rain has stopped, and the air smells fresh. I'm grateful to be out of the apartment, away from Wang, walking with Yuk Ming, who is treating me as if we've known each other for a long time. She talks about American movies. "I loved *Titanic*, and also *Gone with the Wind*," she says. I tell her that one of my favorite movies of the past decade was *Crouching Tiger, Hidden Dragon*.

"Yes!" she says, excited, looping her arm through mine. "This was a very good movie. I like your American actors. Brad Pitt is very handsome, and Tom Cruise." We take a different route to return to the park, and when we arrive at the bench, Graham is already there.

"I hope you haven't been waiting long," I say.

"Just a couple of minutes," he says, staring at Yuk Ming's feet.

"This is your husband?" Yuk Ming asks.

"No, this is my friend from the ship. Graham, Yuk Ming."

"I'm very pleased to meet you," Yuk Ming says, holding out her hand.

Graham eyes her suspiciously, then turns to me. "Where have you been?"

"Yuk Ming took me to her place for lunch."

Graham says something to Yuk Ming in Mandarin. His face is red, and he is talking louder than usual. Suddenly she starts yelling at him, gesturing toward me. A crowd gathers.

"Let's go," Graham says, taking my arm.

"What's going on? What did you say to her?"

"Just walk. Believe me, this woman is not your friend."

I try to say good-bye to her, but now she's yelling at me. As we walk, Yuk Ming follows us, shouting, along with the crowd that has gathered. Gradually, they begin to drop back. Graham and I are walking, and the mob is still shouting behind us, and I'm thinking about this story my friend James recently told me about a trip he and his wife took to South America. They were on an eco-tour of the Amazon jungle, and they were walking along in their backpacks and Tevas, looking at all the flora and fauna, having a splendid time. His wife noticed a little golden monkey scampering around on the tree branches along the edge of the path, and she stopped to admire it. Suddenly, the monkey leapt from the tree onto my friend's wife, grabbed the front of her poncho and wouldn't let go. He wanted her gold hoop earrings. As the monkey tried to climb up the woman's front, her poncho got tighter and tighter, and she couldn't move her arms to defend herself. She was screaming for James to help her, but every time he tried to pull the monkey off, it bit him. Finally, he leaned back and slugged the monkey in the face. The monkey was momentarily stunned, but he still held on, his claws digging into the poncho, into James's wife. James punched him again, but the monkey kept screaming and trying to grab the earrings. So, unable to think of anything better, James took off his shoe and started pummeling the monkey's head.

"So I'm standing there in the Amazon jungle," he told me, "and I'm surrounded by all these super mellow, green-friendly tourists from places like Berkeley and Seattle, and we've been having a jolly good time communing with nature and taking snapshots, and all of the sudden things turn sour. There I am, beating the living shit out of this little vicious animal with my left shoe."

I'm feeling the same way now. One minute I'm having a pleasant if disconcerting lunch with my charming new friend, and the next I'm a capitalist pig running from an angry mob.

"What the hell just happened?"

"Where did that woman take you?"

"I told you, we just had lunch."

"Let me guess. Her apartment was fairly spacious. It had all the modern conveniences. She served very good food. Something seemed slightly off, but you couldn't put a finger on it. Overall, you got an impression of wealth and prosperity. At some point she asked you how you felt about China, and then she went on about how good the dam is for the country, and how happy the Chinese people are."

"What are you saying?"

"She's with the government."

"A spy?"

"There are many people here whose job is to make sure foreigners take away positive impressions. When she saw you writing, she probably thought you were a reporter."

"But how did you know about her?"

"When I first came to China as a businessman, I had a lot of money to spend. I met a lot of people. Naturally, I attracted attention. If I was in a room with forty people—a meeting, let's say, or a party—I could predict there would be three to four party spies. I could look around and identify within about five minutes who they were. Did you see her shoes?"

"Ordinary sandals."

"Yes, but they were leather. Haven't you noticed that most of the shoes here are made of fabric or plastic? Second, her perfect pronunciation. The government probably sent her abroad to study, which is why her English is heads above that of anyone else you've spoken to here. The third clue, of course, was her luxurious apartment. I'm guessing the food she served was excellent."

I think of the shark fin soup, a delicacy. "I feel pretty stupid."

"Don't. It's happened to me several times. It's unfortunate, too, because in general the Chinese are very hospitable."

"The lunch was pretty good, though," I laugh.

Graham has a hand in his pocket. At one point he takes it out, looks down at a small glass bottle filled with liquid.

"What's that?" I ask.

"The friend I just went to see is a pharmacist."

"Is it for pain?"

"Sort of."

I don't ask what he means by sort of. There are things I'd rather not know.

It's dark by the time we get back to the ship. Graham goes back to his cabin to rest. In the Yangtze Room, I listen to a lecture on Chinese cultural artifacts. The lecturer, a distinguished older Chinese woman who works at BeiDa University, shows us slide after slide of the Terra Cotta Warriors—life-sized, cast in clay, thousands of them standing in formation in great rectangular hollows carved into the packed earth. Slides of other artifacts follow—vases and chairs, jade jewelry and elaborate altars.

The final slide is of White Crane Ridge, an eighty-yard-long strip of sandstone in the harbor of Fuling, engraved with pictures and Chinese characters. Dr. Tong points to a pair of stone carp engraved on the stone at the waterline. She explains that the fish were carved during the Tang dynasty, sometime before the year 763. The bellies of the fish represent the low-water mark at the time they were carved. By noting where the water rose on the fish, ancient river pilots could calculate the condition of the river ahead. The fish were only visible for about five months each year, in the heart of the dry season. The characters that cover White Crane Ridge were carved over many centuries by different dynasties, each entry noting the date the stone carp reappeared. "For more than a thousand years," she continues, "the people of Fuling have looked to the carp as a sign of a good harvest to come." She flips the light switch. In the brightness, White Crane Ridge is barely a shadow on the projection screen.

A voice in the back asks, "So what happens to them when the dam is built?"

"White Crane Ridge will be submerged by the reservoir, along with many temples and artifacts."

She has barely gotten the words out of her mouth when Elvis Paris wrests the microphone from her hands. "China has many artifacts," he says. "Much culture. These few things only a very small percent of China's treasures. The people are China's true treasure. The dam will bring electricity and progress to the people!"

Several hands go up, but Elvis Paris nudges Dr. Tong offstage and says, "Lecture is over now! Please go to Shining Pagoda Lounge to enjoy cocktails and traditional Chinese dancing!" The room begins to clear. As we exit, an unfamiliar man herds Dr. Tong into a corner, and the two begin to argue.

TWENTY

In all the years I knew Mr. Lee, only once did I hear him talk about China. Amanda Ruth and I were in our first year of high school. It was late at night in their big house in Mobile, and he and Mrs. Lee were talking softly in the den, which shared a thin wall with Amanda Ruth's bedroom. That morning, Mr. Lee had received a phone call from his brother in Taiwan—a brother Amanda Ruth had never heard of—telling him that their father had died.

"All these years, I never knew your father was alive," Mrs. Lee said. "I never knew you had a brother." Amanda Ruth looked at me, realizing that her mother was as much in the dark about Mr. Lee's life and family in China as she was. Amanda Ruth had read dozens of books of Chinese history, studying the pages, memorizing dates and place names, dynasties and warring factions, as if within those dense paragraphs she might find the key to her own soul. She knew about the horrors her grandparents must have seen—Japanese occupation, the Great Leap Forward, the Cultural Revolution. She had always believed that both of her father's parents were dead.

Mrs. Lee, the daughter of Southern privilege who had defied her family and her town by marrying a man they referred to in whispered tones as "that Chinaman," the woman who had never raised her voice to her husband, who had provided a safe haven for him in the small-minded world he had entered for *her* sake—was suddenly shouting. "How could you keep these things from me?"

Mr. Lee's voice sounded tired, as if it had been dragged up from the bottom of a deep well. "You think I want to remember? Ever since I came to America, I've tried to have a life apart from all that sadness. I've tried to forget my family, especially my sister."

"A sister," Amanda Ruth whispered. She had never heard of a sister. On the other side of the wall, Mrs. Lee's voice echoed Amanda Ruth's amazement. "Where is she, this sister?"

"I never knew her," Mr. Lee said. "She's thirteen years my elder. By the time I was born she was already living in Shanghai."

"Why did she leave home so young?"

Mr. Lee's voice wavered as he told of the day in 1943 when men from the city came to his village. The men, who were well-dressed and polite, went to the school and chose about thirty girls, the youngest and prettiest. They told the parents they would take the girls to Shanghai and give them work in the silk factories. They promised good wages, a clean place to live, plenty of food.

"Chunxiao was eleven years old," he said. "A baby. She didn't want to go, but my parents insisted. It wasn't until years later that we discovered that all of the girls had been sent to camps run by Japanese soldiers."

"The comfort women!" Amanda Ruth whispered,

horrified. I didn't understand what she meant. On the other side of the wall, there was a long silence, then Mrs. Lee's voice, incredulous. "My God. Your sister was in the rape camps."

"She was younger than Amanda Ruth is now," Mr. Lee said. A strange, guttural sound came through the wall. Mr. Lee was sobbing. Amanda Ruth and I sat on her bed, our ears pressed against the wall, shocked at this deluge of words and emotion coming from her father, the man who spoke so little. "They were treated like animals, worse than animals."

We heard Mrs. Lee's slippers moving over the floor. I imagined her standing beside Mr. Lee's chair, hands on his shoulders. "It's amazing that she survived," Mrs. Lee said.

Mr. Lee went on to say that his sister's camp had been liberated by the Allies fairly early. She was sent to a hospital in Shanghai to work. The family, however, thought she was dead. Years after the war, when Mr. Lee's sister was in her thirties, she sent a letter to their parents. By then, their mother was already dead— drowned during one of the floods. Their father barely survived that letter. He contacted Mr. Lee's brother in Taiwan, who went to Shanghai and found the sister cleaning toilets in a hospital. She looked like an old woman. He begged her to come back to Taiwan, promising her a good life, but she refused. She told him that he should forget her, that after what she had endured she couldn't stand to be around other people. Over the years he wrote her dozens of letters from Taiwan, but she never responded.

"Last week, my brother received a letter saying she had finally returned to the village," Mr. Lee said. The bamboo hut where the children grew up was gone. Wandering the streets she saw faces she knew, but no one recognized her. At the County Culture Office she pored through ledgers containing the names of the deceased. In one of them she found their father's—it had been inscribed there only six months before.

That night, in the dark, ears pressed to the wall, we heard the story of Mr. Lee's life—the life before Amanda Ruth's mother, before San Francisco. When he was six, Mr. Lee and his nine-year-old brother were smuggled to Taiwan. For their passage, the brothers paid an exorbitant sum, money that had been sent to them by their mother's brother, a shop owner in Taipei. Once there, Mr. Lee and his brother wandered the streets of Taipei, which were teeming with orphaned children.

"What I remember most is the sound of shoes," Mr. Lee said. "The Taiwanese wore Japanese-style wooden shoes that were always clacking on the streets."

After two weeks of wandering they found a butcher who knew their uncle. The butcher pointed the way to their uncle's house. They arrived barefoot in tattered clothes, unwashed, hungry. Their uncle took them in and fed them, arranged for schooling, but their aunt and cousins hated the boys. They slept outside, beside the latrine, and after school they worked the streets, selling anything they could pilfer from their uncle's house: bits of string, a near-rotten egg, a pocketful of rice. Despite his long hours of work, Mr. Lee excelled in school. By the time he was sixteen, he and his brother had secretly saved enough money to buy passage for one in the steerage of a ship bound for America. His brother insisted that, with his natural intelligence, Mr. Lee would be the one most likely to make it in America. Mr. Lee promised to send for his brother as soon as he had enough money. Mr. Lee was sick for most of the voyage, vomiting up the tiny rations of rotten rice served in dirty water. When he arrived in San Francisco, he had lost thirty pounds.

"I was a skeleton," he said. "But I was in America."

In addition to working 14-hour days at a spool factory, he posted signs on the bulletin boards at the University of San Francisco and got jobs washing clothes for wealthy students. For three years he had two thoughts. One was to drag himself out of poverty and become a success. The other was to make good on his promise to his brother.

In San Francisco Mr. Lee slept little, ate even less, saved money, and, three years later, wrote to his brother to say it was time. He would send him the money for passage to America. It was six months before he heard from his brother. He made a pot of tea, sat down on a cot that served as a bed in the basement room he rented, and ripped the letter open, afraid to believe, after his brother's long silence, that he was still alive, afraid that the letter itself was only a dream.

His brother had found a wife. He had a child, a son.

He had opened a stall selling Ming vases and antique chairs, stuff smuggled out of China by relatives who had no use for antiquity. Taiwan had become popular with wealthy Brits and Americans. They came to his shop, ogled the goods, some of which were true antiques, and some of which were cheap knock-offs. They paid outrageous prices. His wife was beautiful, his son strong, his life very good. "Come back to Taiwan," he wrote. "Work for me."

"What had I been doing those past three years if not working for him?" Mr. Lee said. "All my sweat and sacrifice, the flesh peeling from my hands from the bleach I used to wash the college students' clothes, the skin beneath my eyes turning puffy from lack of sleep. I had taken almost nothing for myself, only meager rations of food, a new pair of pants and shoes and two new shirts each winter, a thin jacket. Everything else I saved for my brother to come to America. And now he had the arrogance to ask me to give up all my dreams and work for *him* in Taiwan.

"That day," Mr. Lee said, "I vowed never to return."

Long past midnight, we finally heard Mr. Lee getting up from the rocking chair, two pairs of feet sliding down the hallway to their bedroom. We heard their bed knocking rhythmically against the wall, Mr. Lee's sobs, Mrs. Lee's soft reassurances. We lay in Amanda Ruth's bed, holding on to each other. That night I dreamt of the aunt Amanda Ruth had never known, a girl of eleven lying naked on a bed, rows of Japanese soldiers entering and leaving, entering and leaving, her throat parched, her body raw, her small mouth bruised and bleeding. When I woke at dawn Amanda Ruth was already up, sitting at the white wicker dressing table in front of the big round mirror. She was looking into her own face so intently she did not even notice me get up.

"I love the slight yellow tint of his skin," she said. "I love the shape of his eyes and nose. I've always known, though, that when he looks at me that's exactly what he hates."

TWENTY-ONE

The night before we are scheduled to enter the gorges, I take the silver key from the pocket of my purse, open the closet, insert the key in the lock of the miniature safe. The door creaks open. There, inside the safe—the red tin. I place it on the table beside the porthole, run my fingers over the collage of photos I know by heart— Amanda Ruth as a baby, wrapped in her proud father's arms; Amanda Ruth in her majorette's costume with gold piping at the shoulders; Amanda Ruth sitting on the narrow bed in her dorm room at Montevallo. I am as drawn to Amanda Ruth now as I was at seventeen. I cannot help but wonder what turns my life would have taken if she had not died. Would I have eventually relegated her memory to that small part of my heart and brain that everyone reserves for their first love, their childhood infatuation? Or would the image of her haunt me even then?

Dave is in the shower. I hear the water running, cutting off, then the hum of his electric razor, the rush of the comb through his thick hair.

I look out the window, but can see only my own reflection. I'm angry with that familiar face—the tired eyes, the dimples slowly sinking into a permanent fixture, the hair that I cut too short after my thirty-first birthday and which now curls just above my collar. I am angry with myself for not promising my fidelity to

Amanda Ruth, even though I know it is a contract I could not have kept. Still, if I had promised, she would not have come home that Christmas with Allison. They wouldn't have been caught together in Amanda Ruth's bedroom.

I think of Mr. Lee stepping down the hallway of his big house in Mobile, hearing a strange silence in his daughter's room, and shoving the door open. I imagine him walking into that room with its pale green walls, its hidden photos of China, his eyes fixed in horror on his daughter and Allison. What possessed Amanda Ruth to be so reckless? It is almost as if she was flaunting her sexuality in front of her father, wanting to say "This is who I am!"

Mr. Lee was not the kind of man to engage in conversations with his daughter. In all the years I knew Amanda Ruth, only rarely did I hear Mr. Lee ask her any question that did not involve her grades at school. Perhaps it was the impossibility of discussion that motivated Amanda Ruth to act so brashly in her own home, surely knowing how great were her chances of getting caught. If she could not tell him that her heart and her body cried out for the companionship of other women, not of men, then she would show him.

I've played that scene over in my mind hundreds of times, certain that I could have prevented it. If only I could have been what Amanda Ruth wanted—a girlfriend, a partner, something permanent—she would never have been in her room that day with Allison. If only I had been able to devote myself to her, she would not be dead.

The bathroom door opens. Steam from the shower fills the room. The smell of soap, the knowledge of Dave's clean unclothed body in this tiny room, the light touch of his feet on the carpet.

"Hey," he says. "Are you crying?"

And then, behind me, Dave's familiar bulk, the strength of his hands on my shoulders, the warmth of his breath on my neck, his fingers slowly massaging my back, touching my collarbone. This moment feels so natural—the way his body fills the empty space behind me, the way he wraps his arms around me, and says, "Baby, are you okay?"

He doesn't wait for an answer. His fingers so deft on the zipper of my skirt, the hook of my bra, all that fabric, damp from the rain, sliding off me, his warm hands taking over. I turn and unknot the towel from his waist. For a long time we stand this way, kissing, our bodies tilting as the boat dips and sways. In the beginning, when we first began sleeping together, everything was fast. An accidental brush of his arm against mine, a kiss on the back of the neck, his hand come to rest suddenly on my inner thigh—any touch could set us in motion. We made love as if there was a stopwatch running that might cut us off at any second. But years of waking up together, reading the newspaper over coffee, riding side by side in the car, eating peanut butter sandwiches at the little table overlooking Columbus Avenue—the cumulative effect of the shared activity of everyday life has made us patient in lovemaking. It is some time before we end up on the bed, and then the slow familiar rhythms take over. Tonight there is an added patience; both of us know, without saying it, that this is the last time.

Sitting astride him, his hands on my breasts, my knees pressing against his rib cage, I realize how difficult it will be to reach this level of physical intimacy with someone else. For twelve years we have shared a bed, along with our most strange and lovely fantasies. We know one another's preferences better than we know our own. There is no blushing, no denial, no moment when one of us fears that the other would find our request strange or selfish. One of the blessings of being married is the right to make love like married people. What I fear most about the end of our relationship is the necessity of starting over again, learning someone else's tastes from scratch, teaching someone out there in the world how to make me feel the way Dave has always been able to make me feel. He moves his hands down to my hips, presses his fingers into my back. He is looking straight into me; we have always made love with our eyes open.

The ship rocks, the engine hums, rain slaps the small round window. Outside, a dreary darkness. Inside, the yellowish light of a solitary lamp. The whole world smells wet, used up, malcontent. For the first time in years, Dave and I come together. Dave jerks, pulls me to him, presses his face into my hair. "Baby," he says.

I think of the first time I saw him, standing at a pretzel vendor on the sidewalk in front of Hunter

College. He was wearing a brown suede coat that was slightly too big for him, and a two-day beard. He looked sleepy, but alert, surveying the street around him, as if he was willing to spring into action at the first sign of anything gone awry. When our eyes met he blushed—he would tell me later that I was looking at him so intensely it caught him off guard—but he regained his composure, paid the vendor, and slathered the pretzel with mustard before walking over to me and introducing himself.

It feels like a betrayal to be on this river, Amanda Ruth's river, with Dave, while somewhere aboard this ship is yet another man to whom I have given my affections. But no man will ever hear the voice inside my head that carries on that monologue, the voice that speaks so clearly to Amanda Ruth, asking her forgiveness.

Amanda Ruth, do you know what you have done? I cannot open my legs for a man without seeing the yellow scarf, its simple pattern of small white flowers. I cannot hold a man between my thighs without imagining a scene that never happened: my own hands on your neck, pulling the scarf tighter, tighter, until you cannot breathe.

TWENTY-TWO

I wake with Dave's arms around me, the sheets kicked off the bed, our feet entangled. So many mornings, in the early years of our marriage, I lay in bed and watched him sleep, thinking how perfect it all was, how fragile. Those mornings I feared for his safety. I thought of accidents he might have as he sped through the busy streets, imagined the ambulance crashing head-first into a taxi, tires spinning, lights flashing, Dave's seatbelt snapping, his head smashing through the windshield. I imagined all the neighborhoods he went to in the line of duty, places even the cops avoided, Bedford Stuyvesant, East New York, places where he would have only his uniform to protect him. I thought of knives and handguns, infected needles that might puncture his skin. I woke, each morning, praying that he wouldn't be taken from me. I thought of all the ways that life might snap in two, destroying the clarity and order of our world. Never in those days did I fathom that loss comes gradually, so slowly you barely notice; never did it occur to me that things can simply dissolve.

I breathe in the smell of him, that bittersweet scent of soap and sleep. I lift his arms from my body, climb quietly out of bed, shower and dress without waking him, and kiss him on the forehead before leaving our cabin.

I am standing on deck at 5:30 in the morning, the

tin cradled in my arms, when The Voice comes over the loudspeaker: "Please everyone come to deck as we begin fascinating journey through magnificent Gorges." I had planned to scatter the ashes here before the other passengers awoke, but it's too late. Within minutes people have begun emerging from their cabins, zombie-like, their faces still marked with sleep. I tuck the tin under my jacket. Graham appears beside me.

Before us, a concrete wall looms, the lock of Gezhou Dam, just a few miles downstream from the new dam site. We pass through a narrow steel gateway into a wide body of water in which ships of all sizes have gathered. The sluice closes behind us. There is the sound of a releasing, water rushing in, and the ship begins to rise. It feels as if we are on an enormous elevator. Despite the early hour, the bridge above us is crowded with onlookers—the usual assortment of crumpled workers and lackluster soldiers, along with lithe elderly people doing their morning stretches. They wave and exchange greetings with the passengers. There are already a few vendors milling about, trying to sell postcards and jade trinkets, dried eel snacks and steamed buns. Bells ring, lights flash, and another set of massive doors opens. In the space of five minutes we rise seventy feet.

I can hear the noise of construction before the dam itself comes into view. Then, perfectly timed with the appearance of the dam site through a dust-soaked drizzle, The Voice announces, "We now enter world-famous Three Gorges Dam. Exploit the Yangtze.

Energy for the People." A concrete wall lines one side of the river. Enormous cranes reach heavenward, their necks disappearing into the smoky haze.

Graham points to a narrow pass far ahead through which the dark river gushes. "The wall's going right there," he says. "It's going to be six hundred feet tall." In his voice there is both awe and embarrassment. "To think, some of those cranes use my safety devices."

What looms before us now looks like some cold war–era industrial nightmare. The hillsides, shattered by explosives, are craggy banks of eroding soil dotted with tumble-down workers' shacks and piles of dirt and granite. Graham lends me his binoculars; through them I can make out small human figures dangling precariously from bamboo scaffolding.

"That used to be a mountain," Graham says. "They sliced it in half to build the locks. A 10,000-ton ship will be able to steer into the pair of locks, ascend from river to reservoir, and emerge on the other side in a lake as placid as your bathtub."

Saws hum, drills clamor, an explosion echoes through the valley. The air is gray and grainy. Simply to breathe is a challenge. My eyes water, my throat burns. And I'm here for less than a day. The Chinese government claims that it has employed 75,000 people for the construction of this dam. I think of Chernobyl, Three Mile Island, Bhopal. The government boasts of megawatts of electricity generated, the width and depth of the lake, the number of new apartment buildings erected for evacuees. But one important element has been left out of the equation—the human costs.

I gaze out in astonishment. "How can the people let this happen?"

"What do you expect them to do?" Graham laughs. "Paint signs? Stage a sit-in?"

"Well…"

"In 1992, 180 people from the Democratic Youth Party in Kaixian County did oppose the dam. They were arrested and charged with sabotage and counterrevolutionary activity. You know, the government-sanctioned opinion about Mao is that he was seventy percent right, thirty percent wrong. But he introduced to China an atmosphere of paranoia that it has yet to get over."

"Whatever happened to the 180?"

"No one's seen them since."

A small band of passengers is crowded around Elvis Paris, who is lauding the glory of the dam. He points to a mass of rock and gravel and concrete littered with cranes and drilling rigs. "This used to be Zhongbao Island," Elvis says. "Thanks to modern engineering, useless island is now foundation for world's greatest dam."

The *Red Victoria* presses on toward the narrow pass. The river seems too much for us. Here, it is deep and very fast. I see the cranes, the concrete, the mounds of blasted granite. I hear the din of drills and chisels. But these bare facts are not enough to convince me. I cannot believe that this fast and powerful river will simply stop, paralyzed behind a manmade wall. I know nothing of physics, mathematics, the intricate workings of engineering, but I can see and feel the power of this ancient and magnificent river. Instinct tells me that it may not be so easily tamed.

Soon we're approaching Xiling Gorge. Graham translates a series of huge Chinese characters painted in white on the sheer side of a cliff: *Serve the People. Develop the Three Gorges*. Layers of green hills rise out of the water. Through the mist I can make out small houses huddled close to the water, and, behind them, steep terraced hills. Solitary figures stand atop bamboo rafts, using long poles to navigate the swirling rapids at the edge of the river. Flat-bottomed boats pass us, headed downstream with loads of golden hay. Skinny goats wander the hillsides, foraging. The air is chilly, just the vaguest shadow of the sun visible through the fog.

The Voice calls out the names of attractions along the way: Sanyou Cave, Three Knives, Shadow of Lamp, Ox Temple. Behind the temple a mountain rises. "Look close at the mountain and you will see strong young man leading ox," The Voice says. Then there is Kongling Shoal, also known as the Gate of Hell, because many boats have wrecked on its dangerous reefs.

The cliffs rise sheer and steep. In some places the bases of the mountains are so close together that I am certain we will not be able to pass, but each time it seems that we are headed for disaster, the ship turns at just the right moment, to just the right degree, and we continue upstream. I feel enclosed in some strange dream—the green mountains, the pale mist, the heavy tin tucked under my jacket.

"Look," Graham says, "the tracker paths." He points to notches cut into the rock along the cliffs and explains how trackers used to haul boats through the gorges. They formed lines on either side of the river, every one of them tied round the waist with a single length of rope, so that each man was linked to all the others. If a man fell, the line kept going. He would die on the line, being dragged behind. Tens of thousands lost their lives.

"Where are they now?"

"Replaced by powerful engines. I saw them here as late as the early eighties. A haunting sight—an army of skeletons scaling sheer cliff walls. They hardly seemed human."

I imagine stick-like men struggling up the steep mountain path, dragging huge ships behind them, tons of human and material cargo. It is easy to understand the Chinese love affair with progress. For the people along the river, progress must represent luxury, an end to human suffering.

After a few minutes of silence, Graham nudges me. "What are you thinking?"

"Nothing. You?"

"Lots of things. Mostly I'm thinking how lucky I was to find you."

"There's something I should tell you. Last night..."

"Don't," he says. "It doesn't matter." After a pause, he turns to me. "If I were to ask you for a favor, would you do it?"

"Of course."

"Even if it's unpleasant?"

"What are you talking about?"

He turns and puts his hands on my shoulders, fixes me with that disconcerting stare. "Promise me."

The sun is blinding. The river looks endless. The cliffs threaten to swallow us up. "Of course," I hear myself say. "Anything."

TWENTY-THREE

The tour brochure promised that we would pass through Wu and Qutang Gorges in the daylight, but now that half of the passengers are gone, the captain is taking our itinerary lightly. Tonight—a full moon shrouded in yellow mist, its pale light moving over the blackness of the river. Cliff faces climb vertically from the water. Below deck, the muffled sound of karaoke, Gloria Gaynor's "I Will Survive," off-beat and out of tune. Earlier, I wandered into the Double Happiness Room and found Elvis Paris teaching passengers to dance the Macarena. Dave and Stacy were there, clapping their hands and swinging their hips and looking like they belonged together.

At one point, Stacy noticed me in the doorway. In between songs, she wandered over and asked me for a cigarette.

"Sorry," I said. "I quit six years ago."

"How'd you do it?"

"Chocolate."

"Oh." She looked at me for a minute, as if she was trying to come up with the right words, then said, "I'm sorry."

"Sorry?"

"You know, about Dave. It's a shitty thing to do. I always promised myself I wouldn't be that kind of person...you know, the kind who steals someone's husband."

I wondered if it could be considered theft when the object of desire was so willing to be taken. I couldn't think of anything to say. Finally, I asked, "Why are you doing it?"

"Dave's so nice. Nobody's ever been that nice to me, except psychiatrists. He doesn't seem to want anything."

"Everybody wants something."

Just then Dave walked over. He had his hands on his hips, and his face was flushed from dancing. He looked happy and slightly embarrassed. "Please tell me you didn't take pictures."

"A whole roll," I said. "Just wait till the guys at the hospital see them."

Stacy laughed, then Dave. I followed. The laughter felt vaguely sacrilegious, like the time I broke out in giggles at my Great Aunt Isabelle's funeral. I wondered if I was the only one on the verge of tears.

Now, it is half past midnight. A cold wind whistles through the gorges.

It feels good to be alone for a moment. The wind dies. The mist turns to rain. In the dark, beneath a blood-red moon, there is magic to this place. The disaster of the dam construction is only a distant memory here. The river and these high black walls of stone seem eternal, surely not subject to the whims of man. Most places I have been, whether urban or rural, grand or mediocre, have shared a common theme—the feeling that they are, in the great scheme of things, temporary points on a topography prone to change. But these gorges are an altogether different matter. It is impossible to believe that this landscape will disappear, that before the end of this decade the Yangtze will be stilled. Even now I feel the river pressing against us, the ancient flow of it urging us back in the direction from which we came. I imagine its origin high in the Tibetan Plateau, the pure white snow of Central Asia melting to feed this dark river of mud. It is as if all those cranes and ditches, those unsightly piles of dirt, the blasted granite and hardened concrete and millions of tons of gravel, are simply props on the gigantic stage that China has erected in the name of national pride.

I hold the tin to my chest. It is too dark to make out the pictures, but I know them by heart—each tiny detail, every insignificant thing. In the one taken in Amanda Ruth's dorm room at Montevallo, the lampshade beside the bed is slightly crooked. The toe of her right boot is scuffed in the picture of the junior high marching band. I could name the exact items in each photograph, the placement of Amanda Ruth's hands, the quality of the light, the shadow of another figure intersecting the frame. But it isn't just the photos that are engraved on my brain with a permanence that is alternately comforting and disturbing. I remember her gestures so clearly— the graceful manner in which she walked, placing one foot precisely in front of the other, like an acrobat on a high wire; the absentminded way she traced the birthmark on her right thigh with a single finger; how she would brush a strand of hair from her face with the back of her hand.

It has taken me fourteen years to get here. Fourteen years of Amanda Ruth, a shadow at the back of my mind, a cold stone I carry at the center of my chest, a pain in the side, a promise. Fourteen years I've waited for some sign that it's okay to let her go. I think I have expected to hear her voice calling softly through the fog. I think I expected, one night, to turn and see the figure of her there, slender and shadowed in the moonlight, waving good-bye. "Get on with your life," she would say, laughing as she turned and stepped into the dark—her face would fade first, then her hair, an outstretched hand, the hem of her skirt, the tender back of her bare foot. Of course, no sign came. She never whispered to me from dark corners. She never faded, the way the dead are supposed to do; over the years, the image of her only grew clearer.

And now I'm left on this river, her river, with a mission. I have not heard from her, but I must let her go. She's dead and can't forgive me. I must forgive myself.

The lid of the tin is tight. I pry at it with my fingers, but it won't budge. I take a coin from my pocket and work around the edges. Finally, the lid gives. Inside, there's a second barrier—a cheap plastic bag. I try to open it, but my fingernails are of no use. I dig into it with my teeth, the way Amanda Ruth used to attack a bag of potato chips. I struggle for a moment. Suddenly, the plastic rips, and Amanda Ruth's ashes go flying in all directions.

You envision an event in your mind for years. You have certain expectations about how that moment will play out. You plan a somber ritual, a flash of enlighten-ment, perhaps, a moment weighted with meaning. Maybe you even believe there will be voices from above, clouds splitting to let the sunlight through. You tell yourself that the natural world will play along, that everything will go as planned. But big moments have a tendency for anticlimax—the kiss following "I do" is an uninspired peck, the graduation diploma bears someone else's name. Instead of a silent morning in China, dawn breaking over a glassy river, ashes flut-tering like white confetti, you find that the ashes look like pebbles and bone, a solid substance with surprising heft and texture. Pebbles plink off the ship's railing, slide down your shirt, scatter downwind in the direc-tion of the karaoke bar, where someone is belting out a Jimmy Buffet tune.

It starts as a giggle, then explodes into something uncontrollable, a hard long belly laugh. Tears run down my face. I laugh so hard my stomach hurts. Amanda Ruth would like it this way, the somber ceremony gone awry. For years a voice in my mind has spoken to her, keeping up a running monologue, a voice so familiar to me now that I do not go a day without hearing its soft cadence in my head, like prayers sent by the faithful to a God they believe is listening. I find myself speaking aloud.

"How do you like that, Amanda Ruth? I bring you all the way to China just to hear someone sing 'Wasting Away in Margaritaville'." The bag is not yet empty. I lean as far as I dare over the stern and let the ashes go flying. I shake my shirt and more ashes scatter over the railing.

I remember an afternoon at Demopolis River, when Amanda Ruth wore a sundress with small blue buttons down the front and danced to this very song. Barefoot in the deep green grass, she dipped and swayed and shook her head, and held her arms out for me to join. I watched her—the sun reflecting off that smooth brown skin, her hair shining with river water. I knew then, as surely as I knew my own name, that I loved her completely.

I gaze into the dark depths of the river, looking for some reflection of the woman I am now. Surely, my face has changed. Surely, I've been marked by what just happened. But the river is opaque, and my vision is blurred. I have done what I came to do. In a few days I will go home without her. I will visit her mother. I will go through my apartment item by item, separating the things that belong to Dave from the things that belong to me. I will find a studio in some other neighborhood—the Lower East Side, perhaps, or Murray Hill—and begin my new life alone.

TWENTY-FOUR

Near dawn, rain turns to mist. The sun appears, disappears. The ship wakes. We arrive at Yeuyang, where a day and night's worth of activities have been planned. I go to Graham's cabin. He answers the door in his bathrobe. He looks stooped, almost frail, and he is sweating. "I'm feeling very bad today," he says, standing in the doorway so that I can't enter.

"I'll stay with you."

"You should go into town. I need to rest."

"Then I'll sit by the bed, in case you need me."

"Please," he says.

"Okay. I'll go to my room. You can ring if you want something."

"No." His voice is firm, almost angry. Then, more gently, "I don't want you to see me like this. Not right now."

"Okay." I stand on my toes and try to kiss him, but I barely brush his lips with my own before he pulls away.

Since Wuhan, the ship has fallen into disarray. Yesterday's breakfast trays line the hall, an abandoned housekeeping cart blocks the entrance to the stairs, and the stairwell is littered with empty Baiji Beer bottles. On the floating dock I find Dave and Stacy, talking quietly and sipping coffee from paper cups. When I approach, Dave lets his hand fall from Stacy's shoulder.

An old bus picks us up at the docks and takes us over muddy roads until we reach the village. Storefronts stand so close to the road that we could easily reach out and shake hands with someone sitting at one of the many square tables along the street. Young girls and old women crush against the bus as it inches along, trying to sell us deep-fried dough sticks and pork dumplings. The air smells salty and sweet. My mouth waters. I press four one-yuan notes into the outstretched hand of a girl in a floral print dress, and she hands me six pot-stickers wrapped in a thin layer of paper. I share them with Dave and Stacy.

"Delicious," Stacy says.

Dave wipes grease from his lips with the back of his hand. "Anybody thirsty?"

From another woman who walks alongside the bus, shouting, we purchase three bottles of orange drink, strikingly similar to the grainy, too-sweet Tang of my youth. Dave is sitting between me and Stacy on the narrow seat. I no longer begrudge her presence. In some way, she eases the burden of my guilt, makes it easier for me to go down this road with Graham. Despite the things she's been through—the pregnancy, the addiction—there seems to be a hopefulness about her that I haven't possessed myself for many years. Before Amanda Ruth's murder, I felt every bit my age: eighteen. The world seemed like a thing to be discovered, it was easy to hope and dream. But something changed in me the moment I found out that she had died. It seemed to me that there was nothing left to discover. For many years after that, I felt that the one defining moment of my life had already happened, that other events would never hold for me any real sense of drama. Everything thereafter would be like a punch line delivered long after the joke was over. I have lived my entire adult life with a sense that the timing is all off.

We pass out of the busy town center, onto a rural country road. The bus stops. "Everybody off!" Elvis Paris shouts.

The driver opens the doors and we shuffle off the bus. Something feels wrong, vaguely sinister, and then I understand what has caught me off guard: an absence of sound, the first silence I've heard in this country. Even our tour group is hushed, as if we have walked into a trap, or some sacred place. The street, empty of vendors and bicycles, feels like a ghost town. I am reminded of Destiny, a small island off the coast of Georgia that is closed to the public and can only be reached by boat. In the seventies the island was home to a naval base and a community of 6,000, but a radioactive leak caused the entire place to be evacuated in a single afternoon. When I went there as a high school junior in 1988, it was with a boy whose father was in charge of making sure the island remained unoccupied. The post required him to live on the radioactive island, in a small wooden house on the beach. The boy and I took a motorboat from Briar Island over to Destiny and spent a couple of hours there, strolling through the deserted streets. Shop doors remained open, toys rusted in driveways, and through the windows of hundreds of

identical white houses we could see the ordinary accoutrements of life caught at a standstill. Dishes set neatly
for dinner languished under a thick layer of dust.
Houses made of Lincoln Logs stood unfinished on the
floors of children's bedrooms. Newspapers lay spread
over the arms of moth-eaten easy chairs. The boy told
me that no one had died there, that the evacuation had
gone smoothly and everyone had made it out okay, but I
couldn't help but feel the presence of 6,000 ghosts
breathing through the thin walls of those empty houses.

"Jenny?" Dave says, touching my elbow. "You
okay?"

I nod and send him a silent thanks with my eyes. It
occurs to me that maybe this is all he needs—some
slight indication that I'm losing my way, that I won't
make it without him—and that if I can give him this,
not just now but forever, he'll come back to me.

After a couple of minutes in disconcerting silence, a
muffled noise approaches from somewhere down the
narrow street—the faint sound of footsteps padding
along the road, accompanied by the steady, soft beating
of drums. The mist is so thick I can only see inches in
front of my face. The drums become louder, and the
shuffling of feet increases from a whisper to a rustle.
Several figures appear, draped in white cloth. They
move slowly, methodically, the hems of their long gar-
ments billowing as they walk. Were it not for the red
cloth shoes that emerge and retreat, emerge and retreat,
beneath the white cloaks, I might believe that these figures were not human at all, but spirits whose calling it is

to wander the chilled streets of this silent town. They continue steadily toward the tour group, which parts to let them pass. It seems we are invisible to them. Beneath the rumble of the drums another sound begins to take shape—a low disturbing hum, as if thousands of invisible flies had descended. As the column progresses I see that it is not flies, but crickets, born along in bell-shaped bamboo cages by several young girls. The girls wear red fitted dresses and once-white shoes that have been stained to the dusty orange color of the road. Some of them carry colorful paper wreaths. Each girl looks straight ahead, as if entranced, her long dark braid twitching slightly with the motion of her spine.

A camera flashes, then another, and the figures continue to march, the thrum-thrum-thrum of the drums and the nervous hum of the crickets ascending into mist. Flash, click, hum. I imagine that when the photographs are developed, the videos slid into VCRs, there will be only a cool blue shading where these figures were, and the small crowd of tourists will look like lunatics, gazing intently at nothing.

"A funeral," Elvis Paris proclaims through his megaphone, breaking the spell. "They will burn effigies to send with the deceased to the spirit world."

I wonder where the body is. Has it already been burned? Several men and women bring up the rear of the procession, holding empty tin cans. They approach us, asking for money. "Guanxi for the spirits," Elvis Paris explains. As the procession disappears up the narrow street, into the swirling fog, I see Elvis Paris negotiating with one of the tin can people. He takes a few bills from the can, then returns to us, smiling. "Next we go see tower above Dongquing Lake," he says. "Much beautiful calligraphy there."

Only then does it occur to me that no one has died; the funeral procession was arranged for the tourists. We have been fooled. I've come not to China, but to an amusement park version of the country. One result of the publicity about the Three Gorges Dam is that tourists are flocking here in unprecedented numbers to see the Gorges before their disappearance. In response to the massive influx of tourism money, many of the towns and villages along the river have become stages on which a colorful comedy is performed. But I know that the real China lives behind this façade. For every staged funeral procession in which there is no body and no burial, no grieving relatives whose duty it is to send their loved one on to the netherworld, surely there is another procession that takes place when the tourists have left and the ship has gone. Surely, beneath the pithy melody that is the tourism trade, an ancient harmony hums: births, deaths, marriages, joy, sickness, jealousy, lust—all the messy stuff of the human condition, the adulteries and dirty dishes that do not make for good home videos. I long to see the true blood and bone of China, the hidden inner life. I owe it to Amanda Ruth to slip behind the curtain, find my footing, to walk beyond the props and stage lights and find out how the set is made.

Later, following a full day of shopping and eating,

Elvis Paris rounds everyone up and raises his mega-phone. "We take bus to traditional Mongolian dance!" he says. "We sleep tonight in traditional yurt!"

The ragtag band of soggy tourists cheers. No one seems to question the authenticity of this experience. We're thousands of miles from Mongolia; there are no yurts here. But this is China Lite, and no one protests. The bus sputters, farting exhaust into the air, and everyone climbs aboard. Dave hangs back to let me get in.

"You go ahead," I say. "I want to spend the night in Yeuyang."

"Please come with us," he says. I'm touched by the sincerity of his invitation, this new tenderness toward me, but I want to be alone.

Elvis Paris overhears. "Impossible," he says, step-ping between us. "No foreigner motels in Yeuyang."

"That's okay. I couldn't sleep anyway. I'll just walk around."

"Cannot do that!"

"Why?"

For a moment he is stumped, but then it comes to him. "Too dark! You cannot see! You fall and break your arm." He examines my arm with a great deal of concern, as if it is already broken.

"Thank you, but I've already decided."

"This not good. You have problems with local authorities. Not normal for foreign woman to walk alone at night." Now, I can tell he's genuinely worried—if not about me, then about himself.

"I'll be quiet. If the authorities question me, I won't

tell them I'm with the ship."

He seems relieved, but not so relieved that he doesn't argue with me for another ten minutes. The people on the bus are getting restless, though, and Elvis sees that he's not going to change my mind. "Very strange," he says, standing in the doorway of the bus. "No American woman ever do this. No Chinese woman ever do this. You come with us. Mongolian dances very beautiful."

But the driver has had enough, and the bus pulls away, spattering mud up behind it. Dusk settles over Yeuyang. At outdoor tables, people talk and laugh and follow me with their eyes. I wander into the darkest alley I can find, away from the scrutiny of so many onlookers. The blue lights of tiny television sets flicker through the windows of bamboo huts and hutongs, centuries-old structures of stone and brick. Through the narrow doorways I can see into open courtyards. In one, a young girl is bathing by candlelight in a metal tub; her wet hair flows over the edge of the tub and touches the ground. Beside her an old woman dozes. In another courtyard a shapely woman bends over a basin, brushing her teeth. From some hidden room come familiar sounds—someone is making love.

All night long I wander. Gradually, the village drifts off to sleep. At some point I find myself on a hillside, walking between the terraced rows of a newly harvested paddy field. I take off my shoes, feeling cool mud between my toes. It reaches above my ankles, making a pleasant sucking sound as I walk. The fields look green and damp in the moonlight. I remember nights on Epson Downs Street as a child, how I would wake in someone else's yard. Looking down I would see my yellow nightgown and know that I had been sleep-walking. In the stillness of the suburban night I felt a familiar panic. The smell of chlorine from neighbors' pools tinted the humid summer air. Dogs barked. In the distance, eighteen-wheelers lumbered by on the highway. Crickets chirped, oak branches moaned, pool filters hummed, the summer night filled me with a secret longing and an unnamed fear. I raced in the direction of home, certain my bare feet left telltale prints in the neighbors' lawns. In the morning they would wake, go outside to fetch their papers, and see the shape of my foot in their otherwise impeccable grass. I was sure they would call my parents, and I would be grounded for trespassing.

At some point I am overwhelmed by a desperate need for sleep. It is new to me, this longing, this feeling of my eyes sagging shut. My body aches with tiredness. I can think of nothing but sleep. At the edge of the paddy field I come upon a small square of packed red earth. I clean my feet and ankles with grass, pull my sweater tight around me and lie down on my back. The moon overhead is nearly round, the earth still damp from rain. Cars whisper on some distant road. There is the sound of night creatures, crickets, as loud as those of my childhood, their frantic hum playing backup to the silvering rush of the river. I feel an unfamiliar sensa-tion in my brain—a shutting down, a slow and soundless closing, a relief, a deep and dreamless nothing. Sleep.

***

At dawn, emerging from the fields, I find myself in another, smaller village. The sun has just begun to come up, and the village is still damp from the night, flushed an orangey pink. Entering this place I feel as if I have been here before. The slope of the narrow street, the eaves of the houses casting shadows on the pavement, the sound of footsteps in an alley—a plastic shoe hitting someone's heel, again and again and again—this rhythm I remember, this smell of new rain and old clothes dripping on a line. From out of nowhere, then, another familiar sound, the ringing of a telephone. I pass an alley and there, beneath the joined eaves of two houses, a young woman sits behind a table. In front of her there is a red rotary dial telephone, and beside that an oil lamp, its wick glowing orange. The young woman speaks into the phone, sees me, then hangs up, shouting something out to me.

"Ni hao," I say, not knowing how else to respond. "Wo bu hui shuo zhongwen."

The young woman gets up from her chair and follows me. "100 yuan America," she shouts. "You talk America, 100 yuan!"

A curtain parts on an upstairs window, and an old woman looks down at us. Then, at another window, an old man. "No, thank you," I say, as quietly as possible so as not to attract further attention, but she has grabbed my arm and is urging me to come with her. She is surprisingly strong. "100 yuan! You call America!"

Soon lights begin to flicker on, and the windows of the houses along the narrow alley are crowded with onlookers. It seems the whole street has awakened to witness this transaction. A young man is laughing, calling from his window, "You call America!" He is naked, the dark of his pubic hair showing just above the window sill. A bare white arm reaches around his waist, a girl's face appears, and she pulls him back. The curtain falls into place. I jerk my arm away and begin running. Behind me, the young woman's entreaties, the laughter of the people in the windows, the high whining sound of an *erhu*. Moments later I am alone again in the orange-tinted street, the only sound the rush of the river, the quick bursts of my own breath.

The world has become too small. Every place is a place I have been to before. Each sound is recalled from memory. Every voice, though uttering a different language, speaks with a familiar cadence. My mind begins to unwind. Amanda Ruth, Graham, Dave—each one gone from me, each one somewhere else. I think of the bodies floating on the river, the boy's red shoe, the young woman's upturned face, the wrinkled white soles of a bloated body passing, a hand caught in a net, all that death adrift on the river. The chips and pebbles, the burnt and rough-edged bone, that I added to the river as we passed through Qutang Gorge. I think of Amanda Ruth, the photographs of her body behind the dumpster, her leg bent beneath her, her dark brown hair spread across the pavement, a spot of blood on her open palm—her own blood, or the killer's? A scarf around her neck, the yellow scarf I gave her, small white flowers on a sunny background. In the photo she is wearing the scarf, but something is wrong—this is not the way she tied it. Amanda Ruth tied it loose, a single twist at the side of her neck, the ends hanging past her shoulders.

In a dream we are running down the beach, and I'm trying to catch up, the loose ends of the yellow scarf billowing behind her. I catch one end, but the scarf slides off her neck, and Amanda Ruth speeds on ahead. Exhausted, I stop, holding the scarf in my hands. Amanda Ruth keeps running, faster, faster, a figure becoming smaller against the vastness of the beach, the white sand. I call out her name, but my voice disappears in the low rumble of the river. Alone on the beach in the dark, I am struck with terror. Moss-hung oaks groan in the wind. Shadows approach, retreat, approach again. The river rises, sweeps me up. And then I am walking at the bottom of the river, my legs straining against the current. The scarf catches on the bow of a sunken ship and holds. I tug and strain but cannot loosen it. The roar of the river in my ears, the deep muck of the river bottom, schools of tiny fish nibbling at my ankles. Is it my blood in the river, or is it Amanda Ruth's? I am trying to get home.

Invariably I wake to find that four solid walls surround me. There is no blood, no silken scarf. Always, the day moves forward.

But it is not a dream, this image in my brain—the photograph the police showed me three days after they found Amanda Ruth. Fourteen years ago I saw it, yet every detail remains with me, a darkness I can't shake. A scarf around her neck, the yellow scarf I gave her, small white flowers on a sunny background. In the photo she is wearing the scarf, but something is wrong. In the photo the scarf is twisted three times around her neck and knotted, "an impressive knot," the detective said. "Extremely difficult to untie." Her face an unnatural color, her lips still stained with the light pink lipstick she wore, the lipstick only slightly smeared. The detective said it was "an unusual strangulation. Knots are highly uncommon. In most cases, the perpetrator will simply hold the rope or wire or what-have-you around the victim's neck until the victim is deceased. In this case, it's almost as if the strangler didn't trust themselves to follow through, they tied a knot they couldn't possibly undo, even if they changed their mind."

I couldn't help but notice the detective's use of the word "they" instead of "he." Weren't crimes of this type almost always committed by men? I vomited into a trash can. "You'd be surprised," the detective said, "how many killers have a conscience."

Amanda Ruth, I try to imagine what you were thinking as you looked into his eyes. Did you see your own eyes in the face of a man you had known since childhood, since your earliest memory? Did you say his name? I see your mouth wrapped around the word:

Dad. Or, in the moment of death, maybe only formal words were sufficient. Perhaps then you called him by another name—removed—the name of the ultimate authority—*Father.* At what moment did you know what was happening? When he first began twisting the scarf around your neck, perhaps you recalled some intimate scene from your childhood, the way he used to rock you in the red chair by the window, his face serene. *My little daughter,* he called you then. He was proud as any father, showing you to anyone who would look, shocked at his good fortune at bringing this small life into the world. When the scarf wound round a second time, maybe you thought of him as *Papa,* whom you had known in your earliest years, who could refuse you nothing, who played hopscotch and jump-rope with you in the small square of yard behind the house. Then, when the scarf began to tighten, you must have remembered something else—the man who had overturned the grill in the barbecue room of the boathouse, his face gone wild with anger.

The scene plays over and over in my head, with endless variations. In one you are gasping, pulling at the scarf wound round your neck, and you are saying, "Stop!" But he doesn't. I place myself inside your mind in that moment when you realized he wasn't going to let go. Struggling for breath, you remembered one cool November night when you confronted him in the kitchen. "It's natural for a girl to love a girl," you said. "It's a disease!" he shouted, and hit you so hard a dark bruise lingered on your face for weeks. Under the big oak tree at school, during lunch, I had to ask you dozens of times, day after day, before you finally admitted how you got it.

When the scarf became so tight you couldn't even gasp, surely you looked at him and pleaded with your eyes.

I think of him hunched over you, enraged—the picture in his mind clear as any photograph—a picture of you and Allison, naked in your room, his only daughter gone to the devil. It is this picture that gives him the strength to hold you down, to tie the knot, to ignore your pleading. But then, as your breaths become short, as your eyes roll up in horror, the rage turns to fear, then pity, then panic. His fingers work feverishly on the knot. But his fingers are not fast enough, he tied the knot too strong—and this is what he wanted, wasn't it, the impossibility of return? He is crying now. "Amanda Ruth! Wait! I'm sorry," and he tears at the knot with his teeth—thus the marks the detectives found on your neck—scratches made, they said, by human incisors— someone in a panic, trying to undo the knot. Suddenly you stop struggling for breath, your eyes go blank, and he is looking for something to cut the scarf, but there is nothing. For several minutes this goes on. He is holding you in his arms, rocking you, crying. He knows this is the end, you are gone, there is no undoing the thing he has just done.

He would like to grieve, but practical concerns take over. His wife is spending a couple of days with her sister in Montgomery. Every time there is a fight, she escapes, and doesn't return until the thing has blown over. When she returns, she always acts as if nothing had happened. It's not entirely his fault, he thinks; his wife should have done more to raise the girl. She should have been more strict. She lived inside those romance novels, her church, those embarrassingly cheap bottles of gin, while discipline was left to him.

Allison is gone—he can't even remember what he said to her after he found the two of you together. He will wait until night. Very late, the streets deserted, he pulls the car behind the house and struggles to put you in. He leaves the headlights off as he drives the back roads to the skating rink, then waits on the dirt road behind the rink for half an hour before getting up the nerve to drive into the parking lot. His plan is to put you in the dumpster; maybe you won't be found for several days. You are much heavier than he imagined. He hasn't held you in so many years. He remembers you as a baby, the lovely light brown of your skin, the surprising strength of your nose. How happy he was to see that nose—just like your mother's—such a narrow American nose! He remembers putting you in the back-yard swing when you were small, how you squealed in delight as the swing rose past the fence-top, your dark brown hair flying behind you, and when the swing climbed too high and you were afraid, he caught the seat with his hand, slowed you down. He remembers the high white boots of your majorette's costume, how you pranced in front of the junior high school band on the Fourth of July, slender and proud in sequins of red, white, and blue—his American daughter, who would never suffer the pain of being Chinese. And then, another memory—your head tossed back in the boat-house—you are lying on the floor, doing unspeakable things with your best friend, a girl who has spent the night in his house too many times for him to count. He feels cheated, betrayed, disgusted. He has worked hard. He has forced himself to speak perfect English, with a slight but deliberate Southern accent. He has been a faithful husband, a devoted father, a good provider. He has done everything he was supposed to do; he has achieved success. For a moment he blames himself, thinking that perhaps he raised you too American, too independent, too full of dreams and desires.

He has just gotten you out of the car when he hears something—the distant sounds of a car approaching? No time to move you into the dumpster. One quick last look at you, one final kiss, before he gets into his car and drives home.

Two days later, he will be questioned by the police. He will give them my name, and Allison's. He will cast suspicion on both of us. Because he is married to a Callahan, they will momentarily give him the benefit of the doubt. They will bring Allison back from Montevallo for questioning, and then they will call me in as well. They will talk to Amanda Ruth's high school teachers, the pastor of her church. A few days after that, Mr. Lee will be sitting in the living room when the police arrive. He will be drinking a Coke, watching the evening news. Mrs. Lee will answer the door, then watch from the kitchen as her husband is taken away. The reporter for Channel 5 will thrust a microphone in his face as the police escort him into the station. He will be unshaven, with dark circles under his eyes, and he will be looking at the ground. A reporter for the *Greenbrook Daily* will drive up to Montevallo and talk to Amanda Ruth's friends. Lesbian Killed by Angry Father, the headline will read. The very first paragraph of the article will label Mr. Lee Chinese, despite the fact that he has spent most of his life in America, speaks perfect English, and flies the stars and stripes every Fourth of July.

From then on, no article or newscast will mention Amanda Ruth without mentioning the word lesbian. The pastor of the Lees' church will deliver a sermon that is widely quoted, in which he says, "The wrath of the Lord came down upon that family." He will refer to "the disease that is sweeping the nation," though it will have nothing to do with murder and the sixth commandment. Parents will be warned to pay close attention to their children's friends. A public service announcement will air daily on local stations. "Are your teenagers dating?" If the answer is no, parents are encouraged to find out why.

My own parents will look at me over dinner as though I am a stranger. When they take me to the airport to catch a plane back to New York City, my mother will hug me as if she never plans on seeing me again. People in the small airport will recognize me from my photo in the paper; they will point and whisper and refuse to meet my eyes.

Then, at 30,000 feet, salvation: the flight attendant will look at me blankly when she asks, in a thick Long Island accent, what I'd like to drink. She will pour me a club soda that crackles over little cones of ice, and I will feel elated by her utter indifference, knowing that when she looks at me she sees only another passenger, not a misfit or a murderer.

Stepping off the plane at La Guardia, I will see Dave standing in the terminal, waiting for me. His hair will be tousled, a single dark curl falling over his forehead. I will walk into his arms, into the sweet dark anonymity of a New York City night.

TWENTY-FIVE

On day twelve we stop at Fengdu, known throughout China as the City of Ghosts. Fengdu is famous for Mount Minshan, the portal through which souls are rumored to pass on their way to hell. But it will soon be a city of ghosts in the modern sense as well; with the completion of the dam, this place will be entirely underwater. The city has already been evacuated, its three million inhabitants moved to a new, higher city on the opposite side of the river.

Our ship docks at old Fengdu to take on non-human cargo that it will carry upstream—boards from disassembled houses, scrap metal, bicycle parts, a myriad of things that were left behind in the rush to evacuate. Graham and I stand on deck watching the porters struggle up the ramp with their goods. A small duffle bag rests by Graham's feet. "What's that for?" I ask.

"This is my last stop."

"But we're not scheduled to disembark here."

"I've already made arrangements. I want you to come with me."

The city is strangely quiet. Save for a few sampans along the riverbank and the workers bringing goods on board, it feels entirely abandoned. "There's nothing here," I say.

"Do you remember when you said you'd do anything for me?" He fixes me with a stare I can't shake.

"This is all I ask."

I take his trembling hands. "Why here?"

"Just trust me."

A man driving an overloaded rickshaw up the ramp loses his balance, the rickshaw topples, and a chair and several pans go sliding toward the water. Matt Dillon, out of uniform, scrambles to help him.

"It's going to be awkward," I say, "with Dave."

Graham smiles. "You'll come with me then?"

"You knew I would." I lean into him, feeling foolish, adventurous. We stand this way for several minutes. A ragged breath escapes him. I look up, and he turns his face away. "Are you in pain?"

"Quite the opposite." He laughs. "Just astonished by my own good luck. Go talk to Dave. Pack a few things. I'll wait here."

Dave is in the lounge with Stacy, playing cards. I pull an extra chair up to their table. Stacy tugs at her earring. "Want to play?"

"No thanks. I just need to borrow Dave for a minute."

"What's up?" he says.

"I need to talk to you." There's a long pause. Dave looks at Stacy.

"Oh," she says. "Of course. Be back in a few."

"Well?" Dave says to me.

"I'm getting off the ship."

He frowns. "Here?"

"With Graham."

"But you can't."

"Why not?"

"What about our flight home?"

"I'll catch up."

Dave stares at his cards. He flips them over, face-up, one by one. "Do you have to do this?"

"Yes."

He picks up the deck and taps it twice against the table, arranging the stack into a tight rectangle. "You're making a mistake."

"Are you saying you want to move back in?"

He forms a perfect bridge with the cards. They make a soft whirring sound as he shuffles them into place. "I'm just saying that you shouldn't do something crazy to get back at me."

I stand to leave. "Good-bye, Dave."

***

Graham leads me through the empty streets. That first night on deck, I would have laughed if anyone had told me that, less than two weeks later, I'd be following this man through the streets of an unfamiliar city. Once the ship is behind us, it is as if we have entered an abandoned movie set. Nothing moves. Nothing breathes. Doors hang open on their hinges, and curtains flutter through the windows of empty apartments. Trash litters the streets. A skeletal dog scavenges in the dirt, comes running when it sees us, wagging its tail, sniffing at our ankles. "We have a friend," Graham says. He takes a package of dried fish from his duffle bag and feeds it to the dog piece by piece.

We walk a mile or more without encountering any people. Then, through the doorway of a temple I see an old monk sleeping with a candle by his side. Incense sticks lie in bundles around his feet. The platform where the carved Buddha should be is just a flat surface scattered with pamphlets.

Finally we arrive at a hotel, the dog panting at our side. There are no cars parked in front, no bicycles. The door is open. A young girl sits at the desk, sipping tea from a large brown mug, turning the pages of a magazine. At the sound of our footsteps she looks up. "Ni hao," she says, her face showing no emotion or surprise. She says something and gestures to the dog. Graham speaks firmly to it. The dog paws the ground, stands obediently outside. Graham carries on a conversation with the girl, translating for me as they talk. Apparently this hotel, which opened twenty years ago, will close two weeks from today. The only reason it is still in operation is to house the occasional inspectors who come to make sure that the evacuation order for Fengdu has been followed. "People caught living in their old houses or working their old plots of land are arrested," Graham explains.

The girl points to a brochure tacked to the wall behind the desk. The drawing on the cover depicts a grand hotel suspended above the words, *We proudly welcome guests to Hotel Tien, world class number one hotel of China.* "New hotel is on other side," the girl explains in English, pointing toward the new settlement rising high on the opposite bank. "Everyone stay at new hotel, even President Jiang Xemin."

We show her our passports, fill out several forms in triplicate, and pay cash for the room before she reaches beneath the counter and retrieves a large metal key. It dangles on a makeshift ring fashioned from a twisted length of coat hanger. "Be very careful," she says, sliding the key across the counter. "Fifty dollar fee if you lose."

Graham gets directions to our room, thanks the girl, and picks up his duffle bag. "Follow me." We pass through the large lobby, which is empty of furnishings save for a surprisingly plush chair upholstered in bright green fabric. At the end of the lobby is a doorway with no door. The hinges remain, rusting against the flaking paint. We pass into a long unlit hallway, at the end of which is an elevator. I push the button but nothing happens, then push it again and am rewarded by a loud metallic rumbling. The elevator descends slowly, like a mechanical beast awaking from hibernation. Finally, it clamors to the ground in front of us, but the doors don't open. I push the button several times to no avail, then we walk back down the long hallway, through the lobby to the desk, where the girl is twirling her hair and talking on the phone. The dog, still standing outside, sees us and begins wagging his tail.

Graham asks the girl a question. She looks up, shrugs her shoulders, shouts at Graham for a full minute, then resumes her telephone conversation.

"This way," he says. I follow him out the front door.

A middle-aged woman stands in front of the restaurant across the street, smoking. She shouts to us good-naturedly, and Graham replies, waving.

The dog tags along at our heels. I reach down and pat his head. "What did the girl at the desk say?"

"Elevator's been broken for five years."

"Why didn't she tell us that to begin with?"

He laughs. "I asked her exactly the same question."

The stairs are all the way around on the back side of the hotel. The warped wood shifts so much beneath us I fear the stairs will collapse.

At the entrance to the third floor there is a vending machine, empty except for a single ancient package of dried ginger candies. Three chandeliers hang from the low ceiling of the corridor, but none gives off any light. There are no numbers on any of the doors. Graham leaves the remaining fish snacks on the floor by the vending machine, and the dog settles down to finish them off. We try each door, one after another. At the sixth door, our key works. When we turn on the light, a roach scuttles across the threadbare carpet. The room is clean and sparse. It has two lamps with dark yellow shades, two small beds, a dresser, a spindly wooden table, a desk, and a chair. On top of the table are two tea bags and a gleaming silver thermos filled with steaming water, but no cups. A red rotary dial phone sits on top of the dresser. A single naked bulb is suspended above one bed by a length of wire.

Graham stands at the foot of the beds. "We can pull them together."

I squeeze his hand. "Or just sleep close." I pull down the blankets on both of the beds, but it turns out that only one of them has sheets. "I win," I say, feeling almost shy all of the sudden, like a young bride on her honeymoon.

TWENTY-SIX

In Fengdu, time takes on a dreamlike quality, moving as haphazardly as the mouth of a tributary where it meets the mighty Yangtze, pushing forward and folding over on itself, shifting in inexplicable ways. The eleven days and twelve nights we pushed upstream feel now like the distant past. Yesterday, from our small hotel room perched over the city, I heard the low drone of the horn urging passengers to board. The *Red Victoria* was scheduled to depart at 4:15, but an hour later she remained sidled up to the dock, gangplank lowered. Just before sundown the hawsers screeched, the bell clamored, and the old engine rumbled to life. Minutes later the ship bearing my husband pulled away from the dock, leaving a thick trail of sludge in its wake.

This morning Graham and I walked across the street for breakfast. The restaurant consisted of a dark room with three metal tables and six chairs. The woman explained that the restaurant has been ordered to remain open in order to serve the handful of workers at the hotel, the occasional inspectors. A jelly-jar-sized Buddha hung from a gold string in the doorway. We each had a plate of flat, steaming noodles with small beads of spiced pork, and between us a pot of weak tea. The pinched green leaves floated in our porcelain cups. At one point I looked up and, noticing a bit of leaf on Graham's lip, reached over and wiped his mouth with my napkin. He caught my hand, brought it to his lips, kissed the tip of each finger. The woman watched us from the doorway, where she stood smoking in exactly the same manner she had the day before. She formed her lips into a smooth round O and sent a circle of smoke drifting skyward.

When we returned to the room we stripped to our underwear, the sticky heat overcoming any sense of modesty we might feel in one another's presence. The first undressing, the night before, had been more difficult, each of us looking away from the other as cottony fabrics slipped over shoulders and thighs. The mystery of the dark cave on Mount Lushan, the spontaneity of the racquetball court, eluded us. Last night, alone in this room, its purpose so clear and unmistakable, we became suddenly shy. He removed his socks and shoes, placed them in the closet and closed the door. He then stepped into the bathroom, and I could hear water splashing in the tub as he washed his feet. This morning, however, we woke like married people, turning to kiss one another before even brushing our teeth.

"Good morning," I said.

"Hungry?"

"Famished."

As I walked naked to the window and opened the drapes, I felt no shame for the roundness of my stomach, the imperfections of my thighs. The shyness of the night before seemed like something from a long time ago. We took our time at breakfast, drinking two pots of tea and savoring our noodles, which were spiced with fish sauce and hot pepper. The proprietor sat down and carried on a long conversation with Graham.

After breakfast we returned to our room, and he disrobed while facing me. I reached forward to touch the thin gray patch of hair on his chest, just above the sternum. He placed his hand in the small of my back and guided me to the bed, where he lay me back and arranged me in a pose that pleased him: knees bent slightly to one side, arms stretched above my head.

"If only I had the talent to paint you," he said. "A Polaroid will have to do." He took his boxy black camera from the table and shot me, the camera clicking and humming. He was amazed by the flexibility of his own fingers as he compressed the black button, the control he had over his hands.

"Strange," he said, "I feel a clarity coming on. Have you ever heard of the Chinese poet Tong Sing?"

I shook my head.

"In his old age, he succumbed to an arthritis so severe that his hands were curled like paws. Supposedly, he experienced a miraculous flexibility in the hours leading up to his death." Graham held his hands in front of him in the light, as if he were witnessing a miracle. They did not shake. He came around the side of the bed and knelt beside me. He tugged gently at my legs, opening them, then placed his mouth to my inner thigh. As his mouth moved over my skin, some long-held grief in me let go. I placed my hand on his neck and felt the toughness of his skin, the uppermost knob of his verte-brae lodged like a tiny stone beneath his skull.

***

Lying face-up on the bed, Graham lifts a leg and taps the naked bulb with his foot. The bulb moves in small circles above us, its pale glow illuminating scars and cracks along the shabbily papered walls. He follows the tail of light with his eyes, tapping his fingers on his chest.

"Tien means heaven. We're in the Hotel Heaven. Did I ever mention my paper route?" He turns to face me. "This was in Perth. I was seven. I rode a red bicycle that was much too small for me. I carried the papers in a metal basket between the handlebars."

I try to imagine Graham at age seven, that thick, coarse hair framing a much younger face. I try to imagine him youthful, without pain, the ease with which he took a newspaper from the basket, snapped his wrist, and sent it sailing onto a vacant porch. I imagine his knees jutting up above the handlebars as his feet pumped the pedals. His legs, even then, must have been long. Not until I saw him unclothed in this room did I realize that the length of his legs is disproportionate to his body, that he possesses the legs of a taller man.

***

The bathroom has a tub, but no sink. Light bulbs above a rectangular mirror flicker on and off. Warm brown water sputters from the faucet, a plain copper spigot with a circle of rust on the rim. I let the water run for a few minutes before it lightens to amber, then plug the drain and step into the shallow tub. Through the crack in the bathroom door I can see the little wooden desk, and on top of it the sheath of rice paper on which Graham had been writing before I called him to bed on the second night. I had come up behind him, leaning quietly over his shoulder, and when my shadow intersected the page he had been startled, drawing the brush clumsily across the page.

"What are you writing?" I asked.

"A note to the housekeeper. I'm telling her not to come into the room for a couple of days."

"How long are we going to stay here?"

"Not long."

He slipped the note into a large envelope. I could see that it also contained other things—a key, a letter, a wad of paper money. "What's that?"

He sealed the envelope, placed it carefully on the center of the desk. "A getaway plan," he said, smiling.

"Who's getting away? From what?"

He pulled me to him and began kissing my belly, my breasts. He turned me around, lifted my shirt, and planted kisses along the length of my spine. We made love for the third time that day. Straddling him on the chair, staring into the window of an empty apartment across the street, I felt suddenly young—as if, in time, I might forget everything that came before.

***

It is morning. Our third day in Fengdu. A light rain is falling. The bulb above the bed has sputtered out. Everything is darkened, damp.

"I need your help," he says.

I hold my breath. Not now; he can't do this now. I'd almost begun to believe that he would change his mind.

From a drawer he takes a small plastic bag—the one he got from his friend in Shashi. Inside the bag is a vial of clear medicine, a syringe. He lays these things carefully on the little wooden table beside the bed. The vial catches a dim ray of light. "It isn't fair to ask this of you. But you must understand."

"Ask what of me?" I say, but I know the answer.

He lines the items up neatly across the table's scratched surface: syringe, vial, towel, alcohol, cotton swabs. "I don't want to be alone when it happens." He looks at me. Looks into me. "Jenny," he says.

Only then do I allow myself to admit just what it is he wants of me, what he has been preparing me for these last few days. I feel my heart splitting open. I feel everything slipping—the floor, time, everything that holds my life together.

"No," I say. "That's crazy."

He sits on the edge of the bed, fingers spread over his knees. He is looking at the floor, where a tiny black spider makes its way across the carpet. Everything is blurry. The room feels very hot.

"I wouldn't ask if I didn't have to."

"It's out of the question. I can't."

"You care about me?"

"Of course."

"Then you can."

"No."

"Try to imagine not being able to walk or talk or eat. Not being able to make love. Imagine spending your last months on a respirator."

I'm sobbing now. I can't control my tears, the tone of my voice. "Why not a nurse? Someone who knows what she's doing?"

"I don't want to die with a stranger. I want to be with you."

I think of Amanda Ruth's ashes, floating down the long and ancient river, to the sea. I think of Graham's body, upturned and buoyant, sharing the river with her. "This is absurd," I say through my tears. "I came to China to leave one body behind. And now you're asking me this?"

"There are people who can do this sort of thing. You're one of them. I sensed it in you the first time we met. I sense it now. That night on deck, when you told me Amanda Ruth's story, it became clear to me."

"You're wrong."

Even as I say this, even as I shake my head in denial, I'm thinking of my first cousin Debbie, who died in a car wreck in New Jersey the year I finished college. We were never close. But after the accident, I was the one who was chosen to identify the body. Her father called from Georgia and said, "We can't think of anyone else." Standing in the cold mortuary, looking into Debbie's expressionless face, I said, "It's her." I didn't cry.

A couple of years ago, my upstairs neighbor knocked on my door and told me she had a rat trapped in her bathtub. It was a Wednesday night, and several other people in the building were home, but I was the one she came to. "Could you kill it?" she said. I got Dave's baseball bat from the closet, went upstairs, entered my neighbor's bathroom, and shut the door behind me. The rat was fat and gray; it squealed and clawed the porcelain. I lifted the bat in the air, and the rat was suddenly still, looking up at me. For a moment we locked eyes. I hit it five times on the head. There was no blood, nothing. When I left the bathroom, my neighbor, who was standing in the hallway, said, "Is it dead?" I nodded. I asked her for a garbage bag and took the rat out to the alley. Back in my apartment, washing my hands, I felt only an overwhelming emptiness.

I was not always this way. Some time after Amanda Ruth died, some strength that I did not know I possessed slowly began to surface. It did not happen right away; it took months, years even. But to me it has always felt like a borrowed strength—not an essential element of my nature, but a mere act. I have never wanted to be this person. I did not want to accept Amanda Ruth's ashes the day her mother showed up at my door, pale and shaking. I did not want to identify my cousin or kill the rat. Most of all, I do not want to usher Graham along his final journey. Yet it seems I bear some false identifying mark that indicates I am capable of carrying out the undesirable tasks. Do I give off some signal, some vague unsettling vibration? Maybe Dave and I are not as different as I have always believed.

***

The brush, dipped in deep black ink. Graham holds it above the bottle, lets the extra ink run down, blots the brush on the yellow pad. He stands by the window in the dusky light, stretches out his arm, searches for something, touches the tip of the bristles to the soft white skin of his inner elbow. A single dot, a perfect black circle inscribed on the blue fullness of a vein.

I stare at the vein, mesmerized. That blue. Like something not quite real. I have a colorized photograph of my mother when she was a child. Her hair is yellow, her naturally brown eyes a clear and frozen blue—some photographer's ideal of what a young girl should look like. And I have seen this color somewhere else. It is the blue of Amanda Ruth's bathing suit in my favorite photograph of her—she is standing at the bow of her father's boat, leaning slightly forward, arms above her head, poised to dive. It is the blue of that room, our room, at a certain time of day, just as the sun was slipping behind the long row of pines across the river. And somewhere else, I've seen it.

Graham reaches up and touches my hair, brushes a tear from my face. "What are you thinking?"

"About this block in New York where I walk sometimes. 86th Street, between Columbus and Amsterdam. There's a huge brick apartment building. On the seventh floor, there's a row of tall windows that spans the entire width of the building. From the street, all you can see is this incredibly bright blue glow. I passed by that building dozens of times, wondering what was behind the windows that could give off this strange, brilliant color. One winter afternoon about three years ago, as I stood across the street, staring up, two girls came out of the big double doors. They were sixteen, maybe seventeen. They were laughing and whispering to each other, lost to the rest of the world, as though there was no one else in New York City, just them. Their hair was wet, clinging to their cheeks and necks. They wore long dresses that stuck to their damp skin. Through the dresses, I could see the outlines of their bathing suits."

"It's a pool," Graham says. He smiles.

"Here it was, the middle of winter in New York City, snow in Central Park, everybody bundled up in scarves and mittens. Just that weekend I'd watched the lighting of the tree at Rockefeller Center. I thought of all those people high up in that building, in bathing suits and swim caps, traipsing barefoot around this huge indoor pool. I found it somehow exciting—the idea of a big warm body of water on the seventh floor of an apartment building on the Upper West Side, this room where it was perpetually summer. I wanted to go swimming in that pool. Who knows, maybe I even wanted in a small way to be friends with those two girls. So I did something that's always surprised me a little since. I crossed the street and walked up to them. 'Excuse me,' I said. They stopped talking and looked at me politely, a little impatiently. I asked them who owned the pool, if they knew how I might buy a membership. The girls giggled. The taller one said, 'That's the Upper West Side Youth Club.' The other one said, 'You have to be, like, a teenager to use that pool.' I thanked them. 'Sorry, lady,' the taller girl said. I could tell she really meant it, she felt sorry for me."

"It's a good story," Graham says.

"I still pass by that building every now and then and look up at the blue room. It's a blue you wouldn't believe, with this deep miraculous shine. Even though I can't use the pool, for some reason it's comforting to know it's there."

Graham blows the ink dry. The vein is wide and sure, a hard line inscribed on the muscled length of his arm.

"Why here?" I ask. "Why this awful hotel?"

Graham stares up at the ceiling for a moment, then looks at me, puts one finger to his lips. "Hear that?" he whispers.

"What?"

"The room isn't much, but the river..."

I close my eyes and listen. Down below, the river rushes, a continuous, comforting white noise. I've become so accustomed to that sound, I no longer notice it.

"What happens afterwards?"

He points to the sealed envelope on the desk. "I've left instructions, made arrangements. You'll leave as soon as it's done."

"Surely you don't want to be left in this room?"

He sits on the bed and pulls me down beside him. "What matters is that I'm with you."

"But what about a grave? Or at least cremation. You can't just stay here." I'm lying beside him, my head resting on his shoulder.

He laughs. "Stay here? You make it sound like I'm moving in." He kisses my eyelids. The front of his shirt is damp from my tears. A warm breeze sifts through the window, and the bulb above the bed sways.

"I could come to Australia with you, you could think about it for a few weeks, and then, if you still want to do it, I'll help you. Wouldn't it be better at home?"

He props himself on his elbow and looks down into my face. "This morning, while you were asleep, I counted. I've traveled the Yangtze sixteen times. It feels more like home to me than Perth ever did. You can understand that, can't you?"

I think about my small apartment by the park in New York City, and the path around the reservoir that I've jogged every Sunday morning for years. The water of the reservoir changes with the seasons—an opaque cold gray in winter, a glassy blue in spring, and in the summer a greenish white alive with birds and growing things. The path is less than two miles around, and I know every dip and curve of it—which spots turn muddy in the rain, where I'll have to slow to make way for the tourists, where to keep my eyes on the ground to avoid stepping in horse droppings, the exact bend at which I stop and look up to see the maple trees changing colors. There is nothing of that path that reminds me of the place I grew up, nothing in it that would seem to beckon to a girl from Alabama, but when I am there I feel as if my body has come home, and the sound of the pebbles crunching beneath my feet is comforting, familiar.

I put my arms around Graham's neck, pull him closer. "I guess I do understand. But why now?"

"I've gone through my whole life alone," he says, brushing my hair away from my face. "I decided to do this months ago. I wanted to spend my last few days on the river, with someone special, but I was afraid it wouldn't be possible. I was afraid I'd have to end it in some hospital, with strangers, cold white walls and cafeteria food and all that nonsense. Promise you won't laugh if I tell you something?"

"Of course."

"This is my third Yangzte River cruise this year. I've been looking for someone—I just didn't know who. I didn't know it was going to be you. Now you're here, and these past few days have been perfect." He breathes in, out. A light breeze rattles the window-panes. "Just think of this place a few months from now. Everything here is going back to the river soon. I'll be happy to go with it. It's just—right.

"If you want me to explain the pain I've felt for the past year, if you really want to know just how bad it is, and how much worse it gets day by day, then I'll go into all the unpleasant details."

We lie for a while in silence. The decision has already been made. I am trying to figure out how things came to this. How did the trajectory of my life bring me to this moment—on a bed in an abandoned motel in China, holding on to a dying man?

"I'm glad we met," I say. I don't know what else to tell him. That nothing I have known or believed could have prepared me for this? No words are sufficient.

The syringe, shimmering in the yellowish light. Graham's finger tapping the side of the syringe, his thumb pressing the plunger, a thin stream of liquid shooting through the needle. He gets up and goes to the window, takes another look at the river, that brown ribbon threading past. He comes to me, puts his hands on my shoulders. Can he tell that my body is a package of taut electrical wires? I imagine the wires exploding, bursting into flame. I imagine the fire licking the yellowed walls of this room, leaping from the windows, turning the hotel into a heap of ash, racing through the abandoned streets, rushing lava-hot down to the river, catching everything in its path: ships exploding like firecrackers, rickshaws splintering like matchsticks, stray dogs screaming, the tips of their matted fur aflame.

"You can do this," he says, looking into my eyes. He wraps me up in his arms, buries his face in my hair. I can feel the warmth of his breath on my scalp. "You're saving me."

I sob into his chest; the cotton of his shirt grows damper. I unbutton his shirt slowly, unzip his pants, pull him onto the bed, take him into me. That filling up, that deep slow heat, that fullness, that completion. We take our time, make it last as long as we can. An hour passes, more, that throbbing, that feeling of the world splitting open. "Get closer," he says, and though it seems we cannot get any closer than we already are, somehow we do; everything is fluid, molten matter, there is no separation. Afterwards, we stay together, sweating, tired, breathing together, one breath, two breaths, three, a matching rhythm that slows and slows. I lie on top of him until he loosens, grows smaller, slips out of me.

We get up from the bed, retrieve our clothes from the floor. I button his shirt for him, he zips my dress. The cool metal of the zipper snakes up my spine, and I think of the girls in red dresses at the staged funeral procession in Yeuyang, their long black braids switching down their backs, their stained shoes padding down the dusty road. We stand for a long time by the window. Down on the river, ships float past. In the streets, there is no one, nothing, just strange geometric shadows cast by the leaving sun. "It's time," he says. He goes over to the table, picks up the syringe, presses it into my hand. He lies down on the bed. His body seems impossibly long. His calves and feet hang over the edge of the mattress. He's wearing khaki shorts and a white linen shirt, crisp and cool-looking even in this suffocating heat. I sit on the side of the bed. I look into his face and make one more plea. "I'll go back to Australia with you. I'll nurse you. Anything."

"Please, Jenny. If you want me to beg, I will."

His lips are full and pale. I lean down to kiss him. His trembling hands touch my shoulder, my neck, my breasts, my thigh. He lays his arm across the sheet.

My eyes blur. I wipe them, concentrate, focus on the black dot. The syringe in my hand feels cold, impossibly light. I touch the gleaming tip of the needle to his skin and push. His skin is surprisingly strong. I push harder; my breath stops as I break skin. The vein bubbles slightly as I enter him. The slide of the long thin needle, the shape of it moving along the underside of his skin. I hesitate.

"Good," he says. "You're doing well."

I press the plunger. It moves so slowly, as if his very blood is resisting me. I press until my thumb hits the base of the syringe.

"Yes," he says. "Now, lie down with me."

I pull the needle out, by instinct press my finger to his arm where a spot of red blood glistens. I lie down, and he takes me in his arms. For the longest time I try to match his breaths. At first it is easy, but then his breaths become longer, and I am holding my own breath just to keep time with him. His body begins to shake, then he coughs and spits up blood. I rush to the bathroom for towels. It is uglier than I imagined. There is no such thing as a clean and easy death. "I'll go get someone," I say, crying.

"No." He takes my hand, his grip surprisingly strong, his voice so weak I can barely hear him.

Time unwinds. The world unspools. My body feels light and hollow. I lie down beside him and hold on. "I love you." By the time it occurs to me to say this, he is already far past hearing.

Now, the bathwater has gone cool around me. A

tiny bar of soap floats on the surface, leaving behind a thin white trail, losing its words in the water. When I unwrapped the small square of paper, which had gone soft and damp in the heat, I couldn't help but laugh at the inscription carved into the flesh of the soap: *Happy Wash*. In the room, nothing moves. There is a glint of glass on the carpet. On the bedside table, a cup of water, and the deep green of a parched banana leaf from which we ate a feast of cold rice and pork. A boat howls on the river. In the hallway, the cleaning woman knocks about, despite the fact that there is nothing to clean.

If I lean back in the tub and tilt my head to the left I can see his thin legs stretched out on the bed, astonishingly white and nearly hairless. The yellowing sheet drapes over his head, falling to meet his wide chest, his stomach, his pelvis, the frayed hem ending just above his knees.

TWENTY-SEVEN

In Greenbrook on Sundays Amanda Ruth and I would rise early, tiptoe to the kitchen, fill a bowl with blueberries and strawberries, sliced banana and cantaloupe. In our T-shirts and underwear we would traipse down to the pier, sit on the farthest edge, dangle our toes into the river. We would go before the sun made its appearance over the thick line of trees, so there was only a suggestion of light, the knowledge of day in the making. We ate the fruit with our hands, our fingers turned sticky and sweet, and when we were done we stripped off our shirts and slid into the river. We swam out to the center, beneath the still-visible moon, while all along the riverbank birds began to call.

On the beach near the pier the water was shallow and warm, but the farther we swam from the narrow beach the colder the water became. We did the backstroke and the butterfly; we dog-paddled and floated, weightless, on our backs. I made my body stiff and, facing downward, arms straight at my sides, head plunged underwater, propelled myself with hips and thighs in the manner of The Man From Atlantis. We did not talk but instead listened to the good sounds of our river—the dip and splash of the water in response to the movement of our bodies, the slow call of a bullfrog, the high hum of a fishing boat in the distance. When we were tired we swam back to the pier, climbed the creaking wooden ladder, then lay with our bare backs to the sun until we heard Amanda Ruth's mother calling us in.

Inside the house, we would shower and dress for church. Her parents must have assumed we stopped showering together when we passed a certain age, but at eleven and twelve and thirteen we still closed the bathroom door, flung our wet swimsuits on the floor, and stepped side by side into the narrow tub. She would stand beneath the spray, her back to me, and I would work up a lather in my palms then slide my hands across her shoulders, down the groove in her spine. She would turn to face me, and I would rub the soap in circles over her flat belly. When I was finished she would do the same for me, and we would step out of the tub, wrap ourselves in thick towels, and open the closet door in the bedroom to choose our clothes for church.

I didn't own any church dresses and so I would have to borrow one of hers, which was usually too loose across the chest and too tight in the hips. By the time we had finished blow-drying our hair and shimmying into slips and dresses and sandals, Amanda Ruth's parents would be waiting in the car. The blue Impala smelled of some flowery perfume her mother wore, a fragrance that made Amanda Ruth sneeze. I remember her father on those Sundays as silent and solemn. While her mother played with the radio dial, searching for the voice of Elvis or Buddy Holly, Mr. Lee sat with both hands on the wheel and drove, occasionally glancing in the rearview mirror or lifting a hand from the wheel to adjust his collar. When he did speak, it was to instruct us to roll up our windows or to be quiet during the service.

There was no hint of China in Mr. Lee's voice. But in Greenbrook on Sundays he was nothing if not Chinese. You could see it in the faces of the church-goers who turned to stare as he walked down the aisle with his voluptuous blonde wife and American daughter, headed for the second row in the center. Those Sundays after church we ate lunch at the Red Lobster. Amanda Ruth and I always ordered the pop-corn shrimp. The regular wait staff knew the Lees by name, but the new waitresses would often talk about Mr. Lee rather than to him. "What does he want?" they would say to Amanda Ruth's mother, looking surprised when he said, "I'll have the fried oysters and iced tea." Once, in response, a very skinny waitress with brown hair that swung down to her waist said, "Oh! Your English is perfect!"

I always wondered why Mr. Lee agreed to stay there. I never understood how he could endure another Sunday in Greenbrook, or why he would even want to try.

***

And in Fengdu? What does one do on Sunday in this ghost of a city, this place that will soon be sub-merged, this city that has houses but no people, roads but no bicycles, graven images but no one to worship them?

You can take your clothes from the dresser, your passport, your empty tin, your bottle of lotion, the Polaroid photos he made of you, place these things in the pack that you brought here before you understood the manner in which you would be leaving. You can look out the window of your motel room, at the ships coming in to port, to be loaded with things that must be taken away. It is a lengthy business to dismantle a city.

You can think of your husband aboard that other ship, sailing westward, away from you. You can go away and lock the door behind you, leaving on it in plain view the note that Graham wrote in Chinese characters. "It says that we will be staying for two more days," he explained, "that we have paid up and do not want the room cleaned. It says not to disturb us. This will give you time to get away. Please put this note on the door when you leave."

Walking down the crumbling stairwell, you hold the envelope tightly. Inside it, the instructions that Graham wrote for you: *Go down to the dock at 4 p.m. A sampan will be waiting to take you to Chongching.* The envelope also contains Chinese currency, a key, and an address. The key is to a house in Sydney. "It's your house now," he told you earlier, "if you'll have it. Everything inside is yours."

In Fengdu on Sunday you can still climb one thousand stone steps to the top of Mt. Minshan, from which you can view the abandoned city below. From the single vendor who remains here, who has been allowed to stay in case any officials venture to Mt. Minshan before it is drowned, you can purchase a type of currency known as Hell Bank Notes to burn on the graves of your ancestors, a bribe for the celestial judges. The water is rising, the people are leaving, the graven images are spending their last days in the light; nonetheless you can pretend that you are on vacation in this, the City of Ghosts.

There are things you must not do in Fengdu on Sunday, things better left undone.

You must not refuse to think in terms of degree, for degree is your only salvation. Without degree murder is murder, you have killed a man—no matter that he wanted it, that he begged for you to do so, that he used many sensible words to persuade you.

"I do not want to live in pain," he said. You were lying naked beside him when he said this. His hand rested on your breast. You lay on top of the sheets, not beneath them, because the heat was intense, despite the rain. You could hear rain on the window, and see mud forming on the cracked pane. "I chose you," he said. All of the heat of the dying city had come to bear upon you in this room. Humid heat, unbreathable, giving birth to mold along the edges of the carpet, in the crevice behind the lamp. "I can't abide the thought of slow death." A ship howled in the distance, a rickshaw rattled past. "I love you." Doorknobs shook in the hallway as the housekeeper made her pointless rounds. His hand, even then, moving across your body. His lips in the hollow of your throat, his mouth on your mouth, the slight bitterness of pain medication on his tongue. Even then, the pressure of him against your thigh, the good warmth, the slow arousal, and how to confront it, then, the specter of life stirring in the body of a man who has chosen to die, a man who has chosen you.

What can be done in Fengdu on Sunday?

You can take into account circumstances, degrees, the demands of the dead.

The chill has reached into everything. At some point it subdued the heat, though you do not know when this reversal took place, at what minute and what hour you understood that your skin had gone cold, and that you had no sweater, no blanket, no means of getting warm. You cannot say how long ago it was that you ran hot water in the tub to warm yourself, waiting for the dark brown water to lighten to amber before dropping the rubber stopper into the rusty drain. The rain does not stop. You listen for the rickshaw boy, but he is gone. The ships are gone. The housekeeper in the hallway is gone. The bathwater has gone cool around you. The soap loses its words in the water, leaving behind a thin white trail. You have neglected nothing. You have done just as you were told.

There are things you must not do in Fengdu on Sunday, this Sunday or any other.

You must not think of the blue room, and how, waking from the dream of her, you went down into the boat, stepping first over the fishing poles with their lines gone slack from disuse, and then through the low doorway into the cabin. You must not think of how you searched for her there but did not find her—not in the narrow hold where you used to lie, not in the hollow space beneath the cushions where she sometimes hid. You must not dwell on how she was not there, and how the river did not rattle the boathouse, how the boathouse did not move at all, for the river was still, it was night and the river was dark, and the moon did not shine down upon it, and she did not lie with her back to the buckling boards of the pier, or on the old familiar mattress, and your fingers did not slip together in the slick warmth of river water.

You must not peer through the crack in the door, see his thin legs stretched out on the bed, startlingly white and nearly hairless. You must not hold yourself accountable.

Rising from the bath, draping the white towel around your shoulders, going out into the room as if it were any room in any town, you must not look into the face of the man you have just murdered, though he does not quite yet look dead. Save for the stillness, he could be sleeping.

TWENTY-EIGHT

In the morning, a thick mist hangs over the city. Doors stand open, but the businesses are gone. In the apartments above the shops, bright curtains flutter through open windows. A plastic cup skitters toward me on the breeze. At the base of a sycamore tree, a rusty bicycle wheel rests on a crate of kitchen sundries. There are no voices, no jingling of bicycle bells. Here and there are relics of the old life left behind: a pot perched on a stove, burnt black; three bowls of half-eaten rice on an outdoor table; laundry hanging stiffly from a window; a set of mahjong tiles atop a cardboard box. From the arrangement of the tiles I can tell that a game was stopped midway. I am reminded of photographs of Chernobyl, of the abandoned homes on the island of Destiny. It is as if life, one minute, was in full swing. Moments later, the people stood up and walked away.

I bend to dislodge a pebble caught in my sandal. As I rise a figure comes into view—an old woman standing at a tea stall. She is dressed in loose blue pants and a blouse. Her short hair is the same silver as the baiji we saw in captivity in Nanjing. I believe at first that I have imagined her, but then the apparition calls out to me. Although I can't understand the words, the gesture is familiar. With one hand she tends her stove. With the other she beckons me over.

She points to a wooden chair in front of her stall,

and I sit down. In front of us, the river. Behind us, the empty city. To our right, terraced hills rise toward the deep green pleats of mountains towering in the mist. In the air, the sweet fragrance of paddy fields mingles with the ancient smell of the river. The old woman fills two cups with steaming tea, then sits down beside me. She begins to talk. She talks for some time, her voice rising and falling, occasionally laughing at some joke she has made. All the while she looks straight ahead.

I can't understand a word she is saying, but she goes on weaving her stories, every now and then lifting her arm to point this way or that, or to make a sweeping gesture with her hand, indicating a wide expanse. I imagine that she is telling me the story of her childhood, how, as a girl, she played in these very streets. My mind is set adrift on her stories.

In those days, there were children everywhere. We skipped stones down by the river. We wore yellow dresses. My mother ran this tea shop, which before had been run by her mother, and her mother before her. My father worked the fields. I had two older sisters and a younger brother, whom we called Little Panda, because he had dark circles beneath his eyes. In those days we woke early to climb the tall steps to the temple, where we burned incense and said our prayers. Before Little Panda came, we went there with our mother to pray for a baby boy. Can you see the temple? Maybe it is gone now. For a long time I have not heard anyone saying prayers.

In the morning we went to school. We practiced calligraphy with paintbrushes on the street. On our brushes there was only water, and when the sun emerged from behind the mountains our characters disappeared. Teacher Li said that it was a good thing to paint characters in this way. 'Everything vanishes,' he said. 'All things go away.' But I drew beautiful characters, and I was angry to see them fade. So one day I secretly dipped my wet paintbrush into coal. When Teacher Li saw my characters on the street long after the sun had dried the rest, he gave me a long lecture. He was angry at my disobedience, but it was worth it!

On that street over there I met my husband. He was a tracker. He came here from Fuling, upriver. He was the tallest man in the village, and strong like an ox. The muscles of his legs were like iron from climbing the hills and pulling the junks through the rapids. He had a deep groove around his waist from the rope that was fastened around him. I was so afraid for him. Sometimes I would walk to the end of the street and look down and see a line of trackers staggering up the hill above the river, the heavy ship laboring behind. Every day we would hear about a different tracker, or several, who had died. Each day and night I waited for him to come home. When word came to the village, "Two trackers died today," I would line up with the other young wives to hear the names. But my husband only died last year, after our children and grandchildren moved into the new settlement.

The old woman talks on and on, and I wonder how disparate are the stories I imagine for her and the stories she really tells. As I listen, the threads of the stories wind around themselves in my head, old stories unraveling as new ones take shape.

The old woman pauses, as if waiting for me to say something. Then she speaks again, and from the tone of her voice I can tell she is asking a question.

"Wo bu hui shuo zhongwen," I say. *I don't speak Chinese.*

For a long moment she is silent. She drains the last tea from her cup, then, with much effort, stands and walks over to me. She puts a hand on my shoulder, then feels my face, my hair. Although her eyes are trained on me, she seems to be gazing through me rather than at me. A look of recognition crosses her face.

"Aaah, Gweilo," she says slowly. And then, again, as if by saying it aloud she can make herself believe it: "Gweilo." *White ghost.*

That is when it occurs to me: this old woman is almost blind. She is only now discovering that I am not Chinese. For weeks she has been sitting alone in her abandoned city, tending her tea shop, waiting for another human to appear. Early in the morning she wakes, heats water to bathe in the little basin in the courtyard. She hoists the awning on her tea stall, sets the kettle on the fire, spoons loose leaves into a mug, and waits for her first customer, as she has been doing for many years. But no customer comes; everyone has moved to the new settlement high in the hills across the river.

In the past, I imagine, she had many customers. The men would come every morning. They would read the paper and tell bawdy jokes to one another before heading to work. The young women would come by to rest their feet on their way to the butcher, or before going down to the river to sell rice and figs to passing junks. Sometimes children would congregate at her tea stall after school and beg for toffee peanuts and sesame snaps. The schoolchildren had neat haircuts and carried books in brightly colored satchels.

Several years ago the government people came through and held mandatory meetings to tell the villagers about the new dam. They talked about how the dam would bring power and prosperity, how it would save many lives. They promised the villagers beautiful new apartments with gleaming white tile facades, in a new city high above the old one. "Why do we need new apartments?" the old woman remembers saying. "I was born in this house. Many generations of my family have lived in this house." She could not imagine life without her courtyard, without the familiar voices of children and grandchildren and nieces and nephews.

"Your house is too old," one of the young men said gently. "You have to go down the street to use the toilet. You have to heat your bathwater on the stove. Your new apartment will be a better place to enjoy your old age."

"My house is old but it is sturdy," she said. "I will stay here."

The government man laughed at her. "This village will be underwater! Are you a fish? Do you propose to live at the bottom of the river?" Even she got a good laugh at this. She imagined herself sitting underwater at her tea stall, little sea creatures flitting past, nipping at the tea leaves. She imagined swimming side by side with the baiji. When the meeting was over she went back to her tea stall. She stayed open later than usual, because that night the village was bubbling with energy. People sat at the tables outside her stall and talked late into the night. But the old woman was not concerned. "Nonsense," a friend assured her. "A city underwater? No such thing will ever happen! Our village has been here for two thousand years."

Soon, young men from upriver came with big buckets of red paint and drew numbers on rocks high above the village. It was a lovely shade of red but the numbers meant nothing to her. In this village things were always coming and going. The Red Guard had come many years before, when she was a young woman, and on the few temples that they did not burn to the ground, they made big red signs proclaiming angry slogans.

The new red marks are different, though. Her eyesight is too poor to read them—she can only see a vague splash of bright red on buildings and hillsides—but her son explained that the red marks indicate the level to which the water will rise after the dam is built.

Some nights she dreams of the bright red numbers, she sees the river rising, first soaking the streets, then covering the floor of her tea stall. In these dreams she is always standing at her stall, and she looks down and sees that her feet are immersed in water, then her calves, her knees. The loose cotton of her pants billows as the water fills them, and then her blouse pillows out. Tea leaves rise on the water and float away. She is concerned at first for her porcelain teapot, but it is heavy and does not float away. She feels the water creeping up her chest, her neck. It is very cold. The children coming home from school are small, and the water has already risen over their heads. They walk slowly, instead of running, their little round knees pushing against the weight of the water. "Grandma Sweetcakes!" they say, holding out their hands, but their words come out garbled. Bubbles rush from their mouths. Their skin is bluish and tight. The girls' long braids float above their heads. And still the water rises. It fills her mouth, her nostrils. It is cool and coarse against her eyeballs. She had always imagined the river as a smooth presence, like silk, but no, it has a texture to it, a roughness. The river is not like other water. It is Jiang, The River.

I try to imagine what it must be like for her to be sitting here with me. For months, perhaps, she has not sold a cup of tea. And then one day, in the midst of all this loneliness, she hears footsteps. She can tell from the lightness of the steps that it is not a man, and from the quickness of the steps that it is a young woman, not an old one. Elated, she bids the traveler to rest. The traveler is very quiet, so the old woman assumes she must be tired. The old woman talks and talks, saying everything she has been saving up in her mind since the last time she saw her son. She does not have many more years, and she has plenty she wants to say.

Later, perhaps embarrassed for talking so much, she says to the girl, What is your name? Do I know you?

Have you come to retrieve things you left behind? Tell me, is the water rising yet?

Something strange happens. The girl speaks to her in an unusual voice. The words are vaguely familiar, but they have no meaning. Her tones are wrong, her words too round, as if she is blowing them through a fishnet. The woman thinks about the words, strings the sounds together. Ah, the girl is saying that she cannot speak Chinese. But this is impossible! The old woman has never met anyone who cannot speak Chinese. For years she has seen the big ships passing on the river, headed upstream to Chongqing, or downstream to Wuhan and Shanghai. She knows that these boats carry the *waiguoren*. She has heard of them, with their skin so pale, like ghosts, as if they had been laid in the sun and bleached.

"Gweilo," she says again, touching my face, my neck. She leans down and smells my hair. Perhaps she is at a loss as to what to do with this strange creature at her tea stall. Perhaps she has taken a liking to me. Perhaps she simply doesn't know what to do. She goes to her chair and sits in silence, as if she is waiting, and because she has told me so much, I begin talking to her.

I tell her about Demopolis River, how it was warm and clear on hot summer days, how it was cool and brown after a rain. I tell her about the oak trees that lined its banks, dripping pecans into the slowly moving water, and about the kids who would float on inflatable rafts, and how, late on a Saturday afternoon, Amanda Ruth and I would ride innertubes down the river, and all along its banks families would be cooking out: boiled lobster, fried catfish, shrimp kebabs. There would be picnic tables piled high with corn on the cob and potato salad, cucumbers and cantaloupes, tall clear pitchers of sweet iced tea sweating in the afternoon heat. Sometimes we'd float by at just the right moment to see Mr. Seymour split a watermelon over his knee, the black seeds would go flying, and he'd toss chunks of the watermelon out to us in the river. Sometimes we'd paddle up to the little beach behind the Stonehouse, an abandoned mansion that was named for Mr. and Mrs. Stone, who had been dead forever, and we'd walk up the tottering steps of their back porch and sit on the wooden swing, and we'd swing back and forth for hours, talking, holding hands, listening to the river, and when it was late we would take our innertubes around to the road and roll them all the way back to Amanda Ruth's, where her mother would be waiting with dinner.

I tell the old woman about Amanda Ruth's passion for China, how she borrowed Chinese language tapes from the library and covered her closet walls with maps she'd traced from the atlas, how she saved all her birthday money and babysitting wages for the trip she planned to make. I tell her how I scattered Amanda Ruth's ashes over the river.

"She's home now," I say. "Amanda Ruth finally made it home." The old woman nods and smiles, as if she understands.

After some time I look at my watch and realize that I've been sitting here for nearly an hour. A strange peace has settled over me. I have traveled hundreds of miles up what is perhaps the most important river in the world. I have visited temples and pagodas, factories and antique shops. I have seen mountains of unimaginable height, their bases shrouded in mist so that they seem to be rooted in heaven rather than in earth. I have passed through the biggest construction project on earth. But it is here at this tiny tea stall in an abandoned city that I have found the secret heart of China. This woman has seen governments come and go. It is likely that she has borne children who have given her grandchildren and great-grandchildren. Like the river, she is patient. The Yangtze may be tamed for a time, but here is the bare fact of the matter: it is still The River. Like this woman, it is patient. In the end, one cannot help but believe The River will win.

***

Walking alone through the empty streets, the sound of my shoes slapping the pavement. Down by the docks, a few lonely sampans knock about. A middle-aged man beckons, shouting a sweet adulteration of my name. In the note, Graham told me to look for the man who knew my name. He told me to go with him. Now, seeing the boatman with his weathered sampan, his shirtsleeves rolled over muscular tanned arms, I am struck by Graham's generosity. In his last days, he was thinking of me.

I remember him standing in the pavilion near

Poyang Lake, his arms wrapped around my waist. "The best travel is the kind that takes me so far away that I know I can't get home in a day or two," he said. Now, surveying the river, the small sampans captained by men whose language I do not understand, the mountains towering so high I cannot see their peaks, I know that getting home will be no easy task. I have plenty of currency, but no guidebook and no guide, no rules of order, no common language with which to find my way. And finally, I understand what Graham meant: to be away and adrift, distant and foreign and lost, alone, is to be somehow free.

I step into the sampan and point upriver. "Chongching," the man says. I nod. He gestures toward a board that stretches across the center of the boat, a few inches from the floor. I sit. He dips his bamboo pole into the river, and we begin to move away from the bank. The sun shoots out from behind a dark column of clouds. The river is a wide green sheet, beckoning and docile. The mountains tower above us, sharp cliffs of emerald and gray. Something flickers, a flash of silver rolling along in front of the sampan. And then it is standing, treading water, its nose pointing toward the sky, its belly shining in the sunlight. Stunned, I turn to the man, wanting to know if he has seen what I have seen. "Baiji," he whispers, awestruck. The dolphin dives underwater and disappears downstream.

For several minutes the man stands still, the pole resting at his side. He has not turned on the small motor, and instead allows the sampan to drift. He scans the river, waiting. To our right, the abandoned city. To our left, the buildings of the new city, their white tiles gleaming. Small waves slosh against the wooden sides of the boat.

I remember a summer afternoon in the blue room with Amanda Ruth, the two of us lying on towels on the stern of her father's boat. The boat knocked about, rising and falling as Demopolis River moved beneath us. The water cast light on the ceiling; its reflections shifted and turned. Amanda Ruth was stretched out and sleeping, the dark tangle of her hair draped over the pastel patterns of her towel. Her arm was brown and bare from shoulder to fingertip, the small hairs bleached golden, a birthmark the size of a quarter just below the elbow. The smoothness of her arm, the faint sweet smell of her skin rising in the afternoon heat, a grain of sand caught on her eyelash, a bit of broken pine straw tangled in her hair. The boat lifted and lowered, lifted and lowered. She made a sound, so quiet I almost missed it—nothing more than a sigh, a letting go of air.

Fifteen minutes later, the man is still motionless, searching. He is on his knees, peering out over the edge of the boat, his eyes inches from the surface, as if he can see through the murky water. Meanwhile, we are drifting. The sampan rocks and turns. The man's face strains with anticipation. He is waiting for the baiji to return, as if he believes this is a thing that could happen. It occurs to me that he is a man of great patience; perhaps we will wait like this for an hour, or more. I imagine my own eyes growing heavy, my body tired, as he kneels there at the bow of the boat, waiting.

I imagine us drifting through the night and into morning, into the next day, and the next, on and on through months and seasons until the river begins to rise. I imagine the surge of the river as the gigantic walls of the dam lock into place. The river rises, spills over the docks, crashes through the windows of little huts that line the bank. It rushes up the lonely streets, sweeping up pots and pans and bicycles and beds, teacups and linens and shovels and doors. The Yangtze washes through the lobby of the Hotel Tien, past the broken vending machines, the useless chandeliers. It bursts through the darkened elevator shaft, sets the small bed afloat, table, chairs, syringe, bottle, teapot. Graham.

The water comes suddenly, one strong swift current, like a storm. The town drinks the river in, sweet and wet, one long deep drowning drink.

From the hillsides then, one will see a lake spanning endless miles—a clear blue lake, and deep. Ships will glide along its surface, and it will look, to some, as if the river has always been calm, a shimmering mirror on the edge of a vast metropolis. It will look as if the life of the river is above. But there will be a memory, still, buried deep in the bones of this new city. The memory will be of another, older city, one that lies below the surface. A memory of houses and temples, of winding streets and fertile farms, of wagons and boats and people. The city will not be visible, but it will be there, underneath and barely sleeping. It will be there, like a memory of girls and husbands and lovers, a sweet unshakable knowledge. The city will not be gone, it will only be waiting.

The day grows cooler, and clouds begin to gather. Meanwhile, the man kneels and watches, but the baiji does not return. Finally he stands up, turns to me, and speaks. Although I can't understand his words, I sense that he's looking for some indication that I am tired of waiting for the phantom dolphin, some sign of impatience that tells him I think it's time to move on. He looks back and forth from me to the river, awaiting my response. "I'm in no hurry," I say, leaning back and resting my head on a bundle of clothing. Water slaps against our tiny boat. The man leans over the side of the sampan, his face close to the water, and then, shyly at first, he begins to call. It is a high-pitched, whining sound, almost a squeal. He looks back at me, laughing, beckoning me to join him. The sound is not easy to imitate, but I try. The afternoon passes in this manner, two strangers attempting with inadequate voices to raise something from the depths.

ACKNOWLEDGMENTS

Thanks to Hedgebrook for giving me time and space to write; Mr. King Yiu for the apartment in Beijing; Doug Stewart and Jay Phelan for good advice; Wiggins for the monkey story; and Bill U'Ren, Wade Williams, and Tracy Singer for influencing me in roundabout ways. Thanks to my parents, Bonnie and John Richmond, and my sisters, Monica and Misty, for many things. Thanks to the good people at MacAdam/Cage, especially Pat Walsh and David Poindexter; and to Sonny Brewer and Frank Turner Hollon for making the connection.

And of course, thanks to Kevin, whose fingerprints are on every page.